# ROAR OF LIONS

## Darkening Stars Book 3

# MARK ILES

Cover image by Magali A.Frechette:
www.stormowl17.wordpress.com

Portait picture by Mark Rutley:
www.markrutleyphotography.co.uk/

Publisher's Note:

This is a work of fiction. All names, characters, places, and events are the work of the author's imagination.

Any resemblance to real persons, places, or events is coincidental.

Solstice Publishing - www.solsticepublishing.com

# Roar of Lions

# Darkening Stars Book 3

# Mark Iles

## Dedication

To:

The Royal British Legion
Combat Stress
Help for Heroes.

*For your unyielding help and dedication to the wellbeing of Veterans.*

My special thanks to the following Beta Readers: Annette Sindall, Peter Wilhelmsen, and Jason Kurt Easter. Also to The British Science Fiction Association 'Orbiter 7' writing group members, who critiqued this book through its many stages: David Allan, Dunstan Power, Alana Farrell, Rosie Oliver, Shellie Hurst.

To Charlotte, a promise kept.

# Prelude

## A Pride of Lions

As a young child, Selena Dillon's world is torn apart when the planets ruler forces her parents to divorce. The Queen forces Selena's father to marry her, but shortly afterwards he dies in suspicious circumstances, which fuels the belief that he was murdered for refusing the Queen's demands. Overcome with grief, Selena's mother commits suicide in front of her and sets in motion a stream of events that will change the fate of humanity.

As an adult, Selena joins a band of freedom fighters, determined to rid the world of the Queen. When she and her comrades are caught trying to kill her, they're tried and found guilty for the murder of the guards and attempted regicide. Given the choice of either the death penalty or twenty–five years' service in the penal regiments, Selena chooses the latter, knowing that if she can survive then one day she'll be able to come back and try again.

Much to her surprise, Selena excels at basic training and, following an incident where she turns the tables on her instructors, she meets Commodore Van Pluy, who selects her for officer training. Passing selection with ease, Selena is promoted and posted to a small group of vessels on anti-piracy patrol, along with Kes Philips—her friend from basic training who serves as her sergeant. Her brutal reprisals against the pirates for their harsh treatment of their captives earns her a fearful reputation.

When her suspicions are raised at the pirates' successes, and their ease at evading Selena's ships, she soon discovers a mole who had been tipping the criminals off. Planting information with the pirates that their spy has been discovered and has betrayed them in turn for her freedom, Selena leaves the unfortunate woman planet-side to be murdered. Selena tracks down the pirate horde, capturing them and their government cohorts.

But something else is happening in the far reaches of the galaxy. Rumours say that the outer colonies are falling silent and it's soon discovered that they're being attacked by the alien Manta, a race hellbent on mankind's destruction. Selena and Kes are called to a meeting by Commodore Van Pluy, where he informs them that unless something can be done about the Manta, and soon, mankind is doomed. Humanity's weapons are ineffective against the alien ships and the military have had to resort to a scorched-Earth policy, destroying any human world captured by the enemy. With the Federation of Man's fleet almost destroyed, and their colonies being overrun, the human race is facing annihilation.

Van Pluy's plan is simple. He gives Selena command of the *Dutch Lady,* a ship filled with planet busters and a one-way mission, to attack and destroy the aliens' home world. But little does Selena know that she'll fall in love with her pilot Bryn Clayton, that there's a serial killer in her crew who's responsible for the death of another crew member's wife, and that this man is determined to get his revenge—no matter what the cost.

During a skirmish with the enemy, the *Magellan,* their transport to the *Dutch Lady,* is damaged and they're forced to land on Loreen, a planet of apparent little consequence. After helping to defend the military base from a joint force of rebels and colonists determined to seize the *Magellan* and make their escape, Selena calms the colonists with promises of the food and the aid they so desperately need. She sets them free, despite their crime of aiding the rebels.

The grateful colonists reveal the existence of a strange building hidden within a hill. Investigating it, Selena and her team discover a maze of interlocking underground tunnels, which they call rabbit holes, that lead first to a world they name Eden and, from there, other worlds. Many of these planets were once inhabited by the mythical ForeRunners, a race of ancient humans who were defeated by the alien Manta in a long-forgotten war.

Realising the importance of the discovery, Selena promises the colonists her utmost protection from the alien invaders, in return for citizenship for every penal soldier, past, present and future. With the agreement signed, Selena and her crew continue on their way in the *Magellan* and soon board their asteroid vessel.

Having launched their attack on the enemy planet, the *Dutch Lady* battled its way through clouds of fighters and battle stations while the Manta break through the surface of their asteroid ship. Just before impact, Selena and the others escape in a lifeboat, only to be hit by enemy fire and they crash land on a backwater world.

With Bryn mortally wounded during the landing, Selena finally comes to understand why her mother couldn't live without the man she so desperately loved. When the *Magellan* arrives to rescue the survivors Selena stays behind, planning to die at her lover's grave when the planet is destroyed. But at the last moment Selena is rescued by her teammates, Kes and Singh. They tell her that Hope, the daughter of friends on the planet Loreen, is now missing and that they need to find her.

They also tell Selena that the Manta were not destroyed in their attack. Some of the enemy survived and have now invaded Selena's home world. Realising that she must ignore her feelings and honour her obligations, Selena and the other survivors travel back to Loreen to find Hope and to help mankind in their battle against the Manta once more.

# The Cull of Lions

Believing the Manta to be destroyed, the Federation of Man fear the power the Penal Corps have gained and ambushes their fleet, killing thousands of loyal soldiers. The bitter fighting that results between the opposing forces is short-lived however, as humanity is forced to unite once again when the Manta reappear and invade Selena's home world, where they manage to build nests and begin breeding. The combined human forces attack the Manta and destroy them all barring one nest, planning their final assault the next morning.

Capulet City is attacked during the night, as a ruse to allow Manta survivors to flee into the planet's forests. F.O.M. regular forces are tasked with destroying the last nest, while Selena and her troops pursue the fleeing Manta.

The aliens have booby-trapped the nest and the regulars attacking it are killed in the resulting explosion. During their pursuit of the enemy, Selena's troops are set upon by a pack of Lenars, a race of catlike creatures who'd plagued Capulets first colonists but have long since thought to be extinct.

In a bizarre twist of fate, the Manta come to Selena's aid, and for the first time Selena finds herself facing the bug-like creatures with neither side firing in anger. The Manta are rescued by a strange amoebic vessel piloted by the Sken, allies of the Manta that no one had heard of until then. Selena finds one of the Lenar cubs, which has been abandoned and, out of pity, adopts it— naming the black-furred, six-legged creature Shadow.

With the Manta now out of the way, and the reason for the brief alliance over, the F.O.M. forces suddenly turn and attack the Penal Regiments defending Capulet in an attempt to grab the planet for themselves. When ForeRunner ships appear, and join in the battle on the F.O.M. side, Selena realises that these new foes have been behind much of the trouble that has plagued humanity. As fighting becomes desperate, a fleet of Manta and Sken vessels appear and help the Penal regiments defeat their foes.

Selena learns that in a bygone age the Manta had fought, and won, a war with the ForeRunners, who were in fact ancestors of the human race. Fearing their old enemy had returned, the Manta had lashed out at Mankind, causing the war that had devastated so many worlds. Finally realising their mistake, they and their Sken allies came to the Penal Corps' aid.

In the past, many human worlds had been abandoned and left to fend for themselves against the Manta invaders. Dismayed at their treatment, these worlds have since left the F.O.M. and joined with the Penal Corps in their newly formed Alliance of Worlds. In a historic move, both Manta and Sken also join.

When Selena discovers that the Lenars are an empathic, sentient race who can use their powers to detect ForeRunners, she instructs Lieutenant Jessica Roberts, a lieutenant in the Penal Corps, to create teams of humans and Lenars to unmask ForeRunners. In doing so she discovers one of them within her own squad.

Selena speaks to her Aunt May and is told that, as she is the Queen's step-daughter, she herself is next in line to the throne. Captured and accused of trying to kill the Queen, Selena is sent back to Loreen, demoted and given ten lashes—plus an additional five years' servitude. Enraged, Selena finally begins to plan her revenge in earnest.

# Chapter One

Clumps of dirt fell around Selena as she dug her alloy fingernails into the crumbling earth and dragged herself upwards. Breath rasping in her throat, she shoved her boots into the ground and tried to propel herself up the slope. The arid gray-brown earth coated her mouth and nose, making her choke and spit to get rid of the dusty taste in her mouth. Sweat poured down her face, making clear tracks through the grime. Cursing to herself, she pushed on.

Around her, others slipped and slid passed time and again, their breath harsh as they too strove to climb towards the peak, determination painted on their faces. There the Physical Trainer waited impatiently with a disgusted expression, next to a lonely threadbare tree.

Finally, Selena pulled herself over the ridge at the top and fell in with the few heaving, out of breath troopers who'd made it there before her. The acrid stench of sweat laced the air. Many were so exhausted they could hardly stand. Some were semi-supported by their comrades while others simply fell to their knees. The shaven-headed bulldog of a corporal's lips curled back as he looked at them with contempt and snarled:

"You're supposed to be trained soldiers, the crème-da-la-crème. The universe is supposed to be scared of you, even God himself wary while the devil salutes you. But look at you, my grandmother could do better than you lot and she's been dead for ten years. We'll wait for the stragglers to get up here and then you can shift your sorry, lardy arses back down that hill and do it all over again."

His bright blue eyes narrowed as his gaze locked onto Selena. "You have something to say, Commander?"

"No, Staff."

"Good. Think you're something special, do you?"

"No, Staff."

"That's not what I've heard. Let's see how good you really are." His eyes shone with contempt as the last few stragglers dragged themselves over the rim. Without giving them a chance to rest he bellowed, "Get yourselves back down the hill, and take these sorry excuses with you – and that means now!"

Without a word, Selena turned and leapt over the rim. They all knew that if they failed to make the grade the corporal was within his rights to recommend them to be discharged and shipped to the mines. There life was often short term.

Selena slipped and slid in the loose earth all the way to the bottom. She took a moment to catch her breath, while the others landed in clouds of dust and falling earth beside her. They waited for the start whistle and, as its shrill call cut through the crisp morning air, Selena leapt towards the slope like a woman possessed, tearing at the soil and driving herself upwards. Seeing a root jutting from the hillside, she grabbed at it, but the root came free and she slithered further down the slope. Taking advantage of her mishap, one of her peers scampered past, using one of her hands as a stepping post. Selena clenched her teeth, spat out a mouthful of soil and fought her way upwards once again, grinning insanely as the poor unfortunate ahead of her made a mistake and tumbled past her all the way to the bottom.

Using her anger and determination, she focused on the rim above and before long found herself standing in front of the corporal once again. Selena caught a glimpse of a half-sarcastic smile on his face, before it was quickly replaced by a scowl.

"So, you're first this time, Ma'am. A word to the wise, you need to remember good officers don't just lead by example. They chivvy their soldiers, and physically drag them along if need be. We don't leave troops behind. You've a lot to learn yet, Commander."

***

One of the few perks afforded Selena as an officer was her own room, which came with an ensuite shower. She stripped, dropping her clothes onto the white-tiled floor, pressed the power button and luxuriated in the two minutes' hot water afforded her. Turning it off, she pressed the dispenser and rubbed its soapy solution into her face and all over her body, to rid herself of the ingrained dirt.

An image of her mother flashed into her mind, followed by her father and Bryn—the only man she'd ever loved—all of them dead now. Selena shook her head to dispel the bitter memories and turned the shower back on again, to rinse herself. Once the water shut off, she tapped the blower. Hot air breathed over her from all sides, as she stretched and rubbed the remaining droplets from her body.

Pushing aside the shower curtain, Selena stood in front of the full-length mirror. Wiping at the steamed glass, she stared at herself. She'd lost weight again. Her body was well honed, yet her ribs showed and those once full breasts were now shrunken buns.

Picking up her garments, her nose twitched. Despite the retardants, they stank heavily of sweat and dirt. A flick of her hand sent the clothes flying across the room and into the wash bin. Striding back into her bedroom, Selena pulled fresh underwear and a uniform from a drawer and dressed rapidly, savouring the cool feeling of clean clothes. The mud and dust had fallen from the retardant material of her boots during the run back to their accommodations, yet she ran a clean cloth over them, quickly bringing them to an impressive gleam. Again, she looked at herself in the mirror. Smoothing the arms of the thin, black leather-like material of her uniform, she made a coffee from the dispenser and sat on a chair, looking out of the single window to the parade ground several floors below.

Memories of Bryn crept in; along with a vision of his grave on a faraway world. A loud knock on the door interrupted her thoughts. "What is it?"

"Commander Dillon, the Admiral wants to see you," a rough voice said through the closed, wood-effect door.

Interest piqued, Selena stood, before placing her coffee next to the pot and taking a long deep breath, before breathing out slowly. This had been a long time coming. "Tell him I'll be right there." She turned to check her outfit once more, in the body-length mirror painted onto the wall, and ran a finger through her tightly cropped hair. Satisfied, she left the room, strode out of the building and across the square parade ground, which was still damp from the light shower of rain a short time ago. Before long she stood in front of Admiral Van Pluy's office. Selena knocked, loudly.

"Come in." The now white-haired, thickset admiral looked up, as she entered and stood at attention in front of him, eyes front. "Ah, Dillon, relax and sit down." He looked across at her as she slid into one of the real wooden chairs in front of his desk. "I take it you're all healed?"

"You can't see the marks from the lashes, if that's what you mean, Sir. The cosmetic surgeons did a good job, although I asked them to leave a scar or two – you know, as mementoes. Apologies for my intrusion. I understand you wanted to see me."

"Yes, there are several things I want to talk about. First, however, is that I need you to know that we didn't have much of a choice about the punishment you were given. Queen Miranda of Capulet insisted you be punished harshly, and to be honest, quite rightly too. After all, you *did* threaten to kill her. The cam and witness evidence was irrefutable."

Her sharp blue eyes narrowed. "I've never denied it, Sir; and that promise still stands. When all of this is over, there *will* be a reckoning." She paused. "For your information, I know now that you're her brother. You were also my father's best friend, Aunt May told me all about it. She also said you all knew each other as children. "Personally, I don't believe you being the bitch's brother had anything to do with the punishment, because I know you have reason to hate her too. It must have sucked when she sent you to the regiments for trying to help her and failing, when she was forced to marry the former king. What I don't know is why you helped in my career. Was it out of friendship for my father, or just so you could keep an eye on me for your sister, in the hope that she'd forgive you and rescind your sentence?"

Van Pluy put a fat cigar in his mouth and sucked noisily until it self-ignited. He blew a long fragrant cloud of gray smoke to one side; the small aircon on his desk kicked in and battled the smoke valiantly. "I don't have to explain myself to you and I'm getting a little tired of your attitude, but for your information it was neither. When you and I met for the first time I wasn't aware of your history, nor that you were my friend, Raynor's, daughter. All I saw was a good soldier. You were selected for officer training on merit, nothing more. Dillon's a common name—how was I to know who you were?" He took another puff.

"It must have given you pause, at least for a moment."

"Not at all. I only found out about you later, when I reviewed your file. We have thousands of trainees, as you well know, and that includes a great many with your surname. As for Queen Miranda, she's the only member of my family still alive. I hadn't heard from her for a very long time, until we were sent to Capulet some years back. I didn't care if I never heard from her again. She's changed, and not for the good. Miranda's not the lovable young girl I once knew."

He sat back in his seat and returned her gaze. "Let's be frank. The crimes we've committed are irrelevant to the Penal Battalions. We're just criminals who made it through their commando course and out the other side in one lump. Now we spend our time in the service of humanity, until our sentences are completed or we die. My sister and I are no longer close. I can see from your expression that you don't believe me, so I'll tell you why."

He took another puff and blew smoke to one side. "Yes, she blamed me for failing to rescue her, and also that your parents married. She said it should have been her, and I am also aware she was responsible for your father's death. She had already forced him to divorce your mother, and to marry her when the old king 'died'. So, yes, she got your father in the end—even if it was over his dead body—and, yes, that makes me your uncle. But you'll get no favours from me.

"Miranda could have pardoned me years ago, but she wanted me to suffer. That isn't the girl I grew up with. She'd become a tyrant and is responsible for countless deaths. So, now you know where I stand, both with the Queen and you."

His coal-black eyes bored into hers. "Now that's all in the open, let's move on. The reason I called you here wasn't to discuss our personal histories, but to say there's a rather tricky problem we're sending you to deal with." He continued to meet her stare without flinching.

Selena pursed her lips. He may talk around things, but as far as she knew, had always spoken the truth. "Very well, thank you for explaining, Sir. How can I help?"

"Lieutenant Roberts tells me she's been informed that the Lenars back on Capulet are refusing to cooperate. By all accounts they're not happy about what happened to you and are refusing to work with us until you're reinstated. We need them on board, Commander, desperately. There are still a lot of ForeRunner spies out there, and the Lenar-Human search teams are the only way we have of detecting them."

Selena studied him for a moment or two, feeling her full lips tightening. Giving a slight shake of her head, she said, "You honestly expect me to go back there?"

"You're in the military; your job is to follow orders and soldier where you're sent."

Selena felt the bite of her nails digging into her palms and took several breaths to compose herself. "Well, let's face it, the Queen wasn't happy about the Lenars before this—she hates them, and I'm surprised she hasn't tried to exterminate them. I can't say that I'm looking forward to seeing the old witch again."

Van Pluy glared. "Damn it, Dillon, we need those search teams back in action, and if that means you going back there and behaving yourself, then you will! You're relieved of command of the underground Eden Complex, with immediate effect. You're going back to Capulet, along with your old team—at your current rank of Commander."

Trying to keep calm, Selena focused on the sweet-sickly fragrance of his cigar. It reminded her of Christmas when, traditionally, her father always had one to celebrate the holidays.

The fury in the admiral's eyes abated and he looked away. Standing, he walked over to his drinks cabinet. "I'm sorry if I sound harsh. Whiskey?"

She nodded, accepted the crystal glass and took a sip of the fiery amber liquid.

"Remember," Van Pluy continued, "Capulet is now a member of the Assembly of Worlds, and whether the Queen likes it or not she'll have to accept the decision for your return. Colonel Christina Delmar is in charge there and will remain so. She's a good officer. You'll report directly to her and no one else. The *Magellan* is due in tomorrow and departs the day after. You and your team will be on it. With luck, the journey will give both you and the queen time to cool down … once I've told her the news."

Selena snorted. "She doesn't know?"

"Not yet."

"I'd pay good money to see her face when she finds out."

Van Pluy's look was unfathomable. "Like I said, she hasn't a choice. Things have happened that you know nothing about. The news will hit the fan shortly, so I may as well tell you now. One of Capulet's five new cities, Ephesus, has been destroyed."

"What?" Selena's breath froze. She remembered walking through the streets, could almost hear the hubbub of the markets and enticing smells coming from many eateries. She had watched the construction of those cities and their defences, and now one of them was gone. "How?"

The admiral looked away, but for a moment she thought she saw sadness in his eyes. She must have imagined it.

"We've no idea how the ForeRunners blew it up. All that remains is a damn great hole. The defence systems were operating correctly, and were on constant alert. No inbound weapons were detected. The only thing we can assume is that someone smuggled a bomb of some kind into the city, which is why we need the Lenar-Human search teams back in action immediately. We have to find those responsible and stop them before they can destroy any of the other cities."

"How could they have bypassed our security?"

"They probably came in as colonists, or part of the work crews. And of course, with our search teams non-operational, they're almost impossible to detect. Your mission will be to get those teams working and to personally take charge of that side of things. The Queen won't like it, but, with the Lenars refusing to work without you, she'll have no choice. Either she puts up with you, or she could lose Capulet."

The very thought of being near the queen was enough to enrage Selena, yet she had to admit the admiral had a point. As long as she kept out of Selena's way, she'd keep out of hers. He was right, she had a job to do and it appeared that only she could do it. Everything else was secondary.

"I've reassigned Lieutenant Kes Philips to you, and I understand from my secretary that he's waiting outside. You'll pick up the remainder of your old team at the *Magellan,* the day after tomorrow. There's something else."

"I thought there might be, there usually is."

"When the Alliance of Worlds found out about your extra five years' sentence, there was an uproar. They're demanding this be rescinded, or there will be sanctions taken out against Capulet. The queen's livid but realizes that she has little choice in the matter, so she's left it with me."

Selena was speechless for a moment or two, while it sank in. "And?"

His coal-black eyes studied hers, and he breathed out a long stream of cigar smoke. "I've willing to commute your extra sentence, on the understanding that you volunteer for extra service, including this mission. We need you on Capulet, but you didn't deserve the extra sentence and your old one is almost up. Volunteering puts you in a whole different category; it shows dedication and everyone gets what they want."

"Except me."

He ignored her. "It'll make good publicity and hopefully inspire others to join. I know you, Selena. Things happen when you're on the scene—our goals are achieved. Let's face it, you need this and we need you; and of course, you'll be free to leave once the war is over."

"And if I don't volunteer?" she asked.

"Then the extra five years stands, and you'll be deployed there anyway."

"Kind of a catch-22 situation then, Admiral. I'm damned if I do and damned if I don't." She thought furiously. "Okay, you win. I'll volunteer."

"Thought you might. That'll be all, Commander. Dismissed."

"Thank you, Sir." Selena stood, saluted, turned on one heel and marched out of the office. Her old sergeant Kes Philips, now a lieutenant, indeed stood waiting in the corridor.

"Hey, Commander." He greeted her with a salute and a raised eyebrow. "What happened to that long blonde hair? The guys are going to be disappointed, particularly as you now look like an underweight convict."

"Well, that's what I am. But never mind me, what the hell happened to your eyes? They're completely black!"

Kes snorted. "It's the latest fad, you take the meds and wham. Harmless too, but it sure scares the shit out of the bad guys and wham. Here..." he handed over a small packet.

"What's this?"

"Tabs for your eyes. You've got to fit in, you know. Believe it or not, there's some that can change your skin colour, for a while at least. Ideal for camouflage." Kes looked at her sideways as they walked. "In case you're wondering why I'm here, Jessica told me she'd seen you heading over, so I thought I'd wait and say hi."

"Jessica. You mean Lieutenant Roberts?"

He looked a little uneasy, Selena could read him like a book. Kes had been with her since basic training and he moved with surprising grace for his swarthy build. Although she'd missed him, she knew she had done the right thing by recommending him for officer training.

"Yeah, and before you go on about my ginger hair, she happens to like it. Between you and I, we're secretly engaged to be married, and I was kind of hoping you'd be my best man, woman or whatever." He looked at her sideways, keeping pace as she strode across the parade ground towards her room.

Selena stopped and turned to face him, a genuine grin on her face. "That's brilliant news; I'm so pleased for you both!" Her smile was tinged with concern. "But you know that sort of thing isn't allowed in the Corps, so keep it quiet."

"Don't worry, we will. We intend getting wed when we've finished our sentences. If you hadn't put Jessica in charge of the search teams, and sent her here to Loreen, we might never have met. So, for what it's worth, thanks. In the meantime, the admiral tells me the team's getting back together. What's going on?"

"We're returning to Capulet, the day after tomorrow."

Kes stared, astonished. "We are? Whose brilliant idea was that? This is wrong, after what the Queen did to you the last time you were there. Sooner or later, one of you will kill the other. You know that, right?"

"Maybe. Apparently the Lenars have kicked up a fuss. They are refusing to work without our team being there. Van Pluy told me that Ephesus City has been destroyed by the ForeRunners, and they need those search teams back online ASAP to prevent it happening to any of the others."

"We just heard about it. Over a million dead, they say. That's beyond horrible."

"Well, they obviously slipped pass our defences, and unless we get those teams working it could easily happen again. By the way, tell Jessica to pack. She's coming with us. In the meantime, I'm going to say my farewells to Franks and Amanda."

Kes raised one hand, fingers high, in acknowledgement as he walked off. "We're all meeting in the Hole in the Wall 'bout eight or so. See you there."

*Oh—my—God,* Selena thought. *That could get messy.* The bar was legendary and she knew what her troops were like. Party animals, all of them.

She took a skimmer to the village, where her friends lived. The village had grown, from two lines of buildings facing each other across a dirt street, with yapping dogs and the occasional child playing outside in the mire, to what it was now. More houses had appeared. A few shops and— Selena had to look twice—a butcher's, after all this time! She hadn't seen one of those for a while. The meat she had been used to was either grown artificially by the cook staff, caught and slaughtered while in the wilds, or came prepacked.

Finding the building she wanted, she walked up the steps and knocked on the white hexagonal plate hanging haphazardly on a metal-meshed door which, despite its looks, was surprisingly strong. In the quiet of the village, the plate clanged loudly against the mesh.

"Selena!" Amanda greeted her enthusiastically, opening the door to give her a hug. "Come in. Franks, Hope, we have a guest!"

Franks and their daughter, Hope, greeted her with smiles and hugs. It didn't take much for Selena to remember that this family had been involved in an uprising the first time she and the others had arrived on this world, such a long time ago now. The *Magellan* had been damaged in a firefight with the Manta. Captain Kotes hadn't known her team's true mission and had defied Selena's orders to go straight to their objective, attacking an enemy convoy that was enroute to the embattled Bernard's Star. She could see him now, fire in his eyes shouting his denial of her orders to continue on to their destination.

It was almost as if Selena lived it again, flashbacks came and went furiously. Images of how the skirmish had ended with their ship damaged forcing them to land on Loreen—a backwater world—for repairs. There they'd discovered the base was endangered by rebels, who'd recently crash landed and stirred the locals into an uprising. Selena's group had joined in repulsing their attack on the Penal Corps Citadel. The guns barking and stuttering, beam weapons hissing, the terrible screams of agony from attackers and defenders alike; and how many rebels and locals had been captured at the end.

Afterwards Selena, Franks and Amanda had sat down and brokered a peace deal, including an agreement that Loreen became the Penal Corps home world, for the regiment's rules state they are unable to return to the worlds that birthed them on completion of service. Many troopers had taken up Loreen's offer, bringing with them employment, income and the planet a means of defence. At the time, Amanda had been eight months pregnant with Hope, the child aptly named for the promise of peace to follow.

"You're just in time for dinner," Franks greeted, breaking into her daydream as he embraced her.

"Pork gumbo, with fresh green beans and okra. One of your favourites, as I recall," Amanda continued, grinning widely. "Betcha smelled it on the way over here."

Even after the birth Amanda's remained slim, Selena noted. The only difference in her looks now was that her hair, dyed a bright-red, was now cut short.

"Sounds great," Selena said, as they all sat down to platefuls. "Beats our rations any day. Look, the reason I came here is to tell you that I've been posted, back to Capulet with my old unit—no, don't say anything. It's all been covered before, and I promise that as soon as I've finished there, I'll come back."

Amanda looked as if she was going to say something, but changed her mind and kept her eyes on her food. It was Franks who broke the silence.

"Well, at least your friends will be there to look out for you. We're glad you're coming back afterwards. Your house is finished and you could move in any time you like."

Selena raised her eyes to look at him. "One day, when my punishment is over," she said. "One day…"

\*\*\*

"Just in time, it's your round!" Singh greeted Selena, as she met up with the others just as they were about to enter the bar.

"Typical. What are you on, or need I ask?" Humour tinted her words as she sidled up to the bar and placed orders for Roget's Revenge.

"What the hell is this?" Braxis asked, staring down into his glass with a dismayed look.

Selena eyed him. He was the company buffoon— tall with broad shoulders and ears that stuck out as if they were placed there as an afterthought. Before she could reply though, Singh burst in.

"Funny you should ask that," Singh said. "This drink was invented by an ancestor of mine."

"Stop," Braxis interrupted. "I can see by the expression on Selena's face that I've walked right into something and, as it happens, I'm off to drain the lizard." Without another word, he strode off towards the old-fashioned swing doors that led to the men's toilets.

"Don't look at me like that," Selena remarked. "I never said a word."

The others wanted to know about the attack on Capulet. She'd just started to explain that she knew as much as they did, when the swing doors burst open and a marine came flying through them, with Braxis trotting after him bearing a happy and somewhat demented grin.

Kes stuck out a boot and the reeling man tripped and landed flat on his back with a slap. Several of the fellow's companions sat by the bar stood up, but taking one look at the uniform Selena and the others were wearing, most sat back down again. One of the few remaining standing charged Braxis, but Selena intercepted him. Rising quickly to her feet, she clotheslined him, hitting him in the throat with thumb-side ridge of her right hand. The man's legs shot out in front of him and he levelled out about chest high, before hitting the floor with a resounding thump, where he remained apparently unconscious. More of the marines stood, looking uncertain.

Raising one hand towards them Selena said, "Don't even think about it. There may only be five of us and a hell of a lot more of you, but we still have you outnumbered."

Her sinister smile obviously decided the matter. Two of them came and picked up their comrade. They all left the bar without another word.

"Okay, Braxis," Selena said. "What happened? Don't tell me, he attacked you and you had to defend yourself."

"Sort of."

"Come on," Selena insisted. "Spill."

"Well, I'd just been to the bathroom and was tucking the lizard away when that dumb fuck said, 'In the marines they teach us to wash our hands after going to the bathroom'."

"And?"

"All I said was, 'In the Penal Regiments they teach us not to piss on our hands'. That was it, honest. He kicked right off and tried to punch me."

Selena couldn't help but join in with the snorts of laughter from the others.

"You think that's bad," Kes said, holding his sides while tears rolled down his cheeks. "Tell her about your grippo."

Knowing that a grippo was someone who held onto a member of the military and took them out for beer, a meal, or a jolly old time in the sack, Selena listened as Braxis began his tale.

"I met this lady not so long ago and when she heard I was in your outfit, Ma'am, she invited me home to meet her parents. Said they were going to throw me a party, criminal or not. She didn't live too far away but, as per, transport was late and I had a few beers while I was waiting … well, okay, more than a few. She took one look at me and said 'You're drunk! I was going to introduce you to mum and dad but, as you're so late, we'll have to go straight to the party'."

He paused and took a swallow of his drink, eying his glass with renewed interest. "Hey, not bad is that. Bit like swallowing a hand grenade. Anyhow, you know what it's like. She introduces me to her dad and step-mum, who buy me a drink, as do her grandparents. Then comes uncles, aunts and countless friends. By two in the morning I was well out of it, so they took me home in disgust and threw me into a bedroom."

"Which was okay…" Singh began, but was interrupted by Braxis, who continued the tale.

"Which was okay but I was dying to go to the bathroom. They lived in this bungalow and when I opened the door all I could see was a corridor with other doors hanging off it. No markings, nothing. You could imagine what would happen if I'd gone into the parents' bedroom by mistake. They'd think I was trying to slip into their daughter's room and give her a good rogering. And, if I went into the girl's bedroom, she'd probably raise the roof because she was pissed off at me."

"So, what did you do?" Selena asked, eying him curiously.

"Well, I wanted a bit more than a piss like, so I didn't know what to do. I had a sudden brain wave and took off my socks and had a shit in one of them. I saw the kitchen and a door, with an old-fashioned security button-press, leading out to the garden. So, I sneaked on tip-toe into the kitchen and opened the backdoor, easy! Swinging the sock vertically in circles I lobbed it down the garden path, and then stood there chuckling to myself while taking a piss."

Despite herself, Selena was curious. "And?"

"When I turned around there was shit in a line across the floor, up the wall and across the ceiling. My bloody sock had a hole in it!"

Despite herself Selena was almost sick with laughter. "Those things are damn near indestructible, how the hell did you get a hole in one of those?"

"No idea."

"His body sweat probably," Singh muttered.

"What did you do?" Jessica asked, looking mortified. A plethora of multi-coloured tattoos peeped from under the sleeve on her right arm, as if trying to listen in on the conversation. She was small, lithe, had cropped dark hair, childlike ears and a ready smile, which combined gave her an elvish look.

"I left, sharp like. What would you have done?"

Despite prior concerns Selena found herself liking Braxis, lovable rogue that he was. She appreciated his good humour, and the way it boosted her team's spirits. Her only concern was, what the hell was he going to get up to next?

# Chapter Two

Lieutenant Kotes, Commanding Officer of the light-frigate *Magellan,* was waiting at the gangway of his ship when Selena arrived. She greeted Braxis, Singh, Jessica and Kes, who stood waiting for her, before striding up the gangway ahead of them. The entire team's eyes were now completely black and Selena liked the fact that it made them look unearthly, even demonic. Kes was right, it was scary as hell—which in her book was perfect.

Kotes was a slim man, with tight brown hair now slightly graying around the ears. To her surprise, he now bore a well-trimmed beard and moustache. He smiled warmly as he saluted Selena, before offering his hand. Greeting the others, he instructed a waiting steward to show them to their cabins, while asking Selena if she'd join him in his cabin for a moment.

"Please, take a seat," he said, as they entered. "Can I offer you a drink?"

"You certainly can. I have to say that it's good to be aboard again. The old girl doesn't change and it almost feels like home. Here, I've brought you something." Selena handed over an oblong, silver-paper wrapped box she had tucked under one arm.

"What's this?"

"Oh, a gift."

With a look of genuine surprise Kotes opened it, his delight evident. "Glenmorangie Gold? Wow, a genuine single-malt from New Scotland. I won't ask how you managed that, what with the blockades and the way things are."

Selena shrugged. "No matter what happens, smuggling goes on. The harder things are the more inventive criminals become, and I used what little influence I have left. A drop of booze never hurt anyone, in moderation. Figured I kind of owed you, what with me getting you demoted and all—not to mention what you've done for the team over the past few years. Incidentally that bottle cost me more than a month's wages, so treat it with respect."

"Thanks, you'll join me in a wee dram?" At her nod, he poured a small measure of the amber liquid into two crystal tumblers and handed her one. They both sipped, savouring the smoky taste. He appeared to deliberate for a moment or two. "Look, we both did what we thought was right back then. I was trying to save a colony when I attacked those alien ships, and I hadn't been fully briefed about the *Dutch Lady's* mission.

"What I did saved Bernard's Star and countless lives, there's no doubt about that. But you were right, it put your mission at risk and could have cost Humankind the whole damned war, so I've no hard feelings about you reporting me. You did what you had to, and so did I. Given those same circumstances, and with the limited knowledge I had, I'd do the same thing again."

She nodded and changed the subject. "Any news I should hear?"

"Nothing much, we've just returned from a sneaky trip to Earth. Did you know there's bubbled colonies there now, as well as some of the original cities in the less poisonous lands? We wanted to see what the Federation of Man are up to in the home system and often despatch sneakys there. They're building ships, Selena, as fast as they can. They could be trying to get enough numbers to stop our ships slipping in and out on raids. If they can station more mobile units at key locations in their colonies and shuffle them around, it could hinder things."

For a moment or two Kotes was silent, sipping his drink and looking embarrassed. At length, he said, "I heard about what happened to you, Selena, the whipping and all. It's abysmal, after all you've done and achieved."

"Well, life sucks but I'm okay," she replied. Undoing her top slightly she reached inside to retrieve an envelope from a hidden pocket. "Admiral Van Pluy asked me to deliver this to you personally."

Kotes took the slim, expensive-looking white-embossed envelope and eyed it warily. "Damn, these usually mean serious trouble. If it's good news, we get electronic mail."

"What's he gonna do, demote you again?" Selena replied, watching him as she took a sip of her drink. "It's no good sitting there looking at it. Open the damn thing."

"He could take my ship away..." Kotes muttered, before taking a deep breath and tearing the envelope open. He unfolded the letter it contained and read the contents.

Selena watched his jaw drop. "And?"

"I'm promoted to lieutenant commander." He read it through several times before looking at her, his eyes narrowing sharply. "You knew about this, hence your gift of the malt."

"Of course I knew. When I still had some clout, I put in a good word for you, following the success of our mission. After everything that's happened, I reckoned you deserve it. I know it's not your former rank but at least it's a step in the right direction. The admiral has only just approved it, and he thought it would be a nice touch if I gave it to you myself. You're a damn good officer, Kotes, and we all make mistakes. Let's face it, what's done is done, and things turned out all right in the end—well, sort of."

They fell silent for a bit and then Selena told him about the destruction of Ephesus, and the influence of the Lenars in getting her sent back to Capulet.

"Well," Kotes replied, "the Queen's not going to be pleased. If I was you, I'd watch my back. I'm still not sure about the Lenars either. Huge six-legged furry beasts that look like a cross between a panther and a pitbull aren't exactly my cup of tea. To be honest they scare the hell out of me. No wonder the early settlers on Capulet didn't realise they were sentient. They were probably too busy climbing up the nearest tree or wiping their arses."

Selena grimaced, as she swallowed the last of her drink. "The Lenars are fine, once you to get to know them, and Shadow's been my friend since he was a pup. Oh, and with regards to the Queen, I fully intend to watch my back, don't you worry about that." She glanced at her watch. "I don't mean to be rude but I have to go, I've an appointment with one of my troops."

They stood and shook hands, before Selena returned to her cabin. She saw that Roberts was already outside, coming to attention as she approached.

"Lieutenant," Selena said, returning her salute. They shook hands and Selena opened the door. "Come on in and take a seat."

"I received a message to report to you, Ma'am," Jessica said.

"I just wanted to personally say welcome to the team. They're a rough bunch but there's none better, particularly when you're in a fix."

"Thanks." Jessica eyed Selena, and let out her breath in a huff. "You've asked me here really to find out whether that nod I gave you on Loreen, just before your punishment, meant that I'd support you in any move against the Queen."

"And would you?" Selena replied, watching her carefully.

Jessica didn't hesitate. "Of course. Besides the fact that you're my boss and team-mate, that bitch was wrong to punish you as she did—although I can understand why she did it." She licked her lips. "While we're being open, I happen to know that you had a one-night stand with Kes. He told me about it."

*Damn*, Selena thought, before saying, "It was just a physical need at the time, and a big mistake on both our parts. Being friends is one thing, fuck buddies another. You don't need to worry, it won't happen again."

"Yeah, I know. In my opinion, Kes isn't that kind of guy. He's totally trustworthy. I wouldn't be with him if I didn't think so." Jessica paused for a moment. "He also told me about Bryn, and I can understand how you feel. No matter how much we care about our lost loves, we still have our physical needs. Kes is loyal to you, but we love each other and I have you to thank for bringing us together. I owe you Commander, and I also respect you. When the time comes let me know what you want me to do, and it's yours."

Selena stood and held out her hand. "Thanks. For what it's worth, Kes is a lucky guy and I wish you both well. Now go get some rest. We're going to have our hands full on Capulet."

\*\*\*

The wall-screen chimed as Selena threw her bags onto the bunk in her new quarters in Capulet City, the world's capital. She caught sight of the twin moons, Romeo and Juliette, peeking through the open window as they continued their never-ending journey through the night sky. She paused, taking in the way the combined moonlight highlighted the forest treetops. At a loud bleep, she turned to the screen to see who was calling. "Speak."

Instantly the image of a scrawny rat-faced, well-dressed woman that she knew far too well filled the wall screen. Selena groaned inwardly. "You certainly didn't waste any time."

"You will address me as 'Your Majesty', Selena. I heard you were back," the Queen replied, with a sardonic twist to her thin red-glossed lips. Her black bullet-like eyes that were so much like Van Pluy's, Selena now realised, bored into hers. "I see you've followed the eye fashion the battalions have adopted. It certainly doesn't enhance your looks, nor does it frighten me."

"Come to hand out more lashes for the public square have you, *your Majesty*–or should I call you S*tepmother*?"

"Come now, Commander, we have far more important things to discuss than past grievances." Her eyes glittered. "You heard about the destruction of Ephesus? That city had a population of over one million people, including troops and off-worlders. When Admiral Van Pluy informed me he was sending you back, one has to admit I was a tad miffed, but I realised that if anyone can stop this destruction from happening again, it's you. Do your job, that's all I ask."

"And what about afterwards?" Selena asked, calmly. "When all the bad guys have gone? What should I expect, a knife in the back one dark and stormy night, an assassin's bullet, poison, or perhaps imprisonment for life?"

To Selena's surprise, the Queen's lips thinned even further.

"As far as I'm concerned, Commander, I just want you to sort this issue out and get the hell off my planet. I'm sending someone by the name of Jennings to see you. He'll be there shortly. You'll find him most useful. I'm sure we'll speak again soon, but until then be careful. I'd hate for anything unpleasant to happen to you."

With that chilling ending the screen snapped off.

"Wonderful," Selena muttered. She took a moment to close her eyes and breathe deeply, focusing on the moment, the scent of flowers and the soft touch of the wind on her skin through the open window. "I hate that damn woman," she said, the thought intruding and expressing itself automatically. Best to say no more, no doubt her minions were listening to each word and watching every movement via various monitoring devices, no matter where she was.

An hour later her door chimed. A glance at the scanner showed a medium-built man, unkempt with long but receding wild gray-brown hair, the hint of a moustache and at least several days' worth of stubble. He was dressed in plain brown workman's overalls and carried a bored expression. The scanner also revealed he wasn't armed.

"Yes?" she asked, her voice carrying through the speakerphone.

"I'm Lieutenant Commander Jennings and I work for Admiral Van Pluy, as intelligence liaison. The Queen sent me and I'd rather not talk out here in the corridor, if that's all right with you. Oh, and I met this guy on the way up here." He rasped a hand through his stubble and nodded to Staff, who stepped into view besides him.

"You'd better come in." Selena opened the door and stood aside, watching as Jennings glanced around the apartment before sitting on the edge of the sofa, without breaking his bored expression.

Staff sat too, emanating displeasure and regarding Selena with a wary expression.

"Staff, I'll speak to you when this is over. Okay, Jennings, what's this about?"

Jennings looked at Staff pointedly.

"He's one of mine, you can speak in front of him."

He nodded. "Very well, call me Jenks. As you know the admiral is head of security for this sector. My team and I work directly for him, not the Queen—although it's our job to keep her in the loop. There are four of us, but I'm your point of contact. If anything happens to me one of the others will be in touch."

"You're a spook?"

"Not a word I'd use personally." His bright steely-gray eyes measured her from a hard to read but lazy looking face that now bore a frown. The droopy, thick moustache was somehow out of place with the receding hairline. Badly worn, cheap and dirty shoes peeped from underneath grubby blue trousers. His shirt lay open at the top, missing several buttons. "What we've come up with so far is that a short time prior to the explosion that destroyed the city, there was a pulse on a radio frequency which we suspect was a test signal for the bomb. That pulse was repeated at the time of the explosion, which was approximately three hours later. We monitor all frequencies as a matter of course. If another such pulse occurs, we'll know that another bomb's been tested and we haven't long to find it."

"Did you locate where it came from?" Selena asked.

"No, it only lasted for a split second, and that's too short a time to do a trace. Particularly as we weren't prepared for it."

"Well, gear-up," Selena said sharply. "The next time we hear something like that I want to know exactly where it originated, and troops ready to go and deal with it. Is that clear?"

He made a placating motion with his hands, holding them open in front of him. "It's all in hand, don't worry. If you need me, call. I've sent my contact details to your hand-held, just in case. If anything comes up my end, I'll be in touch. Now, I've somewhere to be."

"If you get in touch with Staff here later today, he'll introduce you to the rest of my team. You might need to speak to them at some time, so it's a good idea if they know who you are."

Jenks stood, gave a curt nod and left the room.

"Not much of a conversationalist," Selena muttered, glancing at Staff. He reminded her of Braxis. He had the same short, bullet-headed angry bulldog look, although his eyes held a distinct sharpness that the other lacked. "I guess you're wondering why you're here."

"Because I pissed you off?"

"No, it's because I need good men, particularly someone to keep my troops on their toes. I want you to design, and implement, a training regime for our troops here. When you're not doing that, you work directly for me."

"I have a problem with that, Ma'am," Staff said, avoiding her eyes. "It's nothing personal, but I imagine you'll be working with the Lenars?"

"What of it?"

"When we were young, my sister and I were attacked by one of the last great cats, back home on New Earth—one of the saved tiger species. She was carried off right in front of my eyes and I've had nightmares ever since, so I have to admit that I'll find it difficult to work with your 'pets'.

"Just so that you know, I've had all the PTSD treatment and still take the meds, but even so I wake up screaming most nights bathed in sweat. It's best you keep them critters away from me, cos I'm likely to lose my sense of humour and kill every last one of the fuckers."

Selena considered him. "You do that and I'll personally have you skinned alive, rolled in salt, and boiled— and don't think for a moment that I'm joking. But at least you're honest and upfront. Okay, go speak to Lieutenant Philips and set up and run the physical training establishment, and I'll do my best to keep the Lenars away from you. A word to the wise, Corporal. If you even injure one Lenar, you'll regret it. Do we understand each other?"

He nodded slowly, his eyes intent on hers. She could tell he knew she meant it, but he betrayed no emotion.

"Good. You're dismissed."

"Thank you, Ma'am." Staff stood and saluted. Turning swiftly, he left the room.

Selena sat at her desk and called up Jenks' details but, as she expected, nothing came up. Spooks were good at hiding their trails. "Singh Lacey," she said, changing tack. Immediately the wall-screen flickered into life and Singh looked back at her, somewhat surprised.

"Get the team ready, Singh, and select six others to augment us," Selena said. "We're going for a ride."

***

By the time Selena was downstairs, Singh had two skimmers waiting, and everyone else was already aboard. The sides of the sleek, black craft came up to their waists and each could carry about twenty men. In case of rain, a repeller-field snapped on overhead, keeping the water off them. Kes and Jessica were in one while Singh, Braxis and Selena crewed the second, with three of the extra troops in each vehicle. Pistol strapped to her waist, and the long curve-bladed katana slung over the right shoulder of her matt-black uniform, Selena gripped a Sunburst machine-pistol and climbed aboard the open-topped craft. None of her team said a word as the vehicles rose above the city's glittering white parapets and arched towards the forest.

Selena surveyed the others, her voice carrying to the other craft via her hand-held. "You all know why we came to Capulet. We know that sooner or later the enemy will try to destroy the other cities. Our job is to stop them, and to do that we need the Lenars. So, we're going into the forests to find them. Any questions?"

No one replied.

***

The skimmers slipped through the trees towards the late afternoon sun. By dusk, they were deep within the forests and far from Capulet City. Weaving through the close-knit trees was hard going. Some watched the branches overhead nervously, fingering their firearms and remembering their first encounter with the Lenars, while others eyed the darkness between the boles. When at last they came to a river, Selena made a decision.

"Let's leave the forest and follow the river," she said. "It's going in the direction we want and we'll be able to travel much faster."

"Why don't we climb above the trees? We'd travel faster still," Singh observed.

"Because I want to keep a low profile, you numpty, not telegraph our every position," she replied. "You never know who's watching, or what technology they have to pick us up, even though these skimmers have the latest stealth."

Singh swung his craft across the brush and kept it a few inches above the surface of the clear, swiftly flowing water. The second craft followed directly behind them. A variety of birds, including ducks and black swans which had been imported from Earth centuries ago, scattered grumpily before them. They left rills in the water with their feet until they settled down again a short distance away, muttering their discontent.

Soon they entered a narrow white-walled canyon. The steep chalk sides rose several hundred feet and birds leapt out at them from crevasses in the rock, screeching in alarm at their passing. Hours later, the causeway narrowed further still, causing the water level to rise and gain speed. They rounded a corner, to where waterfalls emptied into the churning river about them with deafening roars.

Soon they were skimming above racing white-foamed rapids, unable to hear each other through the thunderous water. Icy spray splashed over the sides of their craft, drenching them, and although they floated several inches above the water Selena still felt a gut-clenching thrill of adventure. She could tell they were all enjoying it, for no one turned on the repeller-fields to keep them dry.

Quite suddenly the canyon ended and spilled into a wide-open lake, in which water flowed far more leisurely. To Selena's delight, hundreds of water lilies carpeted the lake, their large white flowers with pink centres and golden pollen-laden stalks laced the dank scent of the water with their musky, sweet perfume.

They continued their journey, eating aboard their crafts and, as dusk fell, they passed a small, single-story cabin not far from the shore, from which warm glowing lights peeped seductively from the windows. The curtains were cast aside as they slipped past and the occupants heard their engines. A bulky shadow waved at them from the comfort of the cabin, as the last of the sun's rays were blotted by the trees.

"Didn't know they'd allowed homesteaders here," Singh said, brow furrowing but waving back before the cabin vanished into the distance. "I thought your citizens were confined to the cities."

"That used to be the case," Selena replied. "But I guess most people stayed inside because of the forest denizens, including the Lenars. We were told horrible tales of them as children, of how they used to sneak into the city before the wall was erected and snatch family members, eating them alive within earshot. Knowing the Lenars now, I don't believe half of it.

"The last time I was here the Queen hadn't given permission for anyone to settle outside, but allowing it now after what happened to those other cities makes perfect sense. At least some people will survive, if the city gets blown up."

"Be that as it may," Braxis replied, "those furry critters give me the chills. Even Kotes doesn't like them, and he's downright genial. As for Staff, he goddam hates them."

"Having settlers out here is going to make our job harder," Kes said. "We'll have to check all of them out, one by one. Do you think that queen of yours is deliberately making things more difficult for us?"

"She's no queen of mine," Selena growled. "I can tell you that for nothing."

The night air carried that special fragrance that only Capulet had, a cool mixture of exotic flowers and huge stretches of forest, tinged here by the lilies and dampness from the water. It was both beautiful and peaceful, which Selena found welcoming. Overhead, the twin moons gazed down at them as they bathed the landscape with their pale luminescence.

"Singh, find us a place to set up camp. We'll continue on in the morning."

"Yes, Ma'am."

About fifteen minutes later they pulled into a small, sandy bay. It was surrounded by a grassy plain strewn with tall weeds, hummocks of grass and areas of swamp in which assailants would struggle to pass unnoticed.

As always, sentry guns and detectors were posted and were continuously scanning the plains and forest beyond. Defendable positions had been established and finally they unpacked their sleeping bags. Guard duties were quickly determined and it wasn't long before the heart-warming scent of curry was emanating from the evening meal cooking over an open fire pit. They all found this far more communal than the self-heating ration packs they usually ate. Apart from Braxis and Jessica, who were taking their turn patrolling the perimeter, they all sat around the crackling fire, basking in its warmth and a feeling of camaraderie. As they ate they chatted quietly, occasionally taking sips from their mugs of scalding tea.

Quite suddenly a burst of firing erupted, followed by an unearthly high-pitched braying sound, filled with surprise and pain. Instantly Selena and the others dropped their mess tins and grabbed their weapons, rolling or diving into cover.

The silence was broken by the sound of Jessica cursing and Braxis laughing, his guffaws uncontrollable.

"Report, Lieutenant." Selena shouted into the darkness.

"Sorry, Ma'am. Thought I heard something. Then saw a shape coming towards me and opened fire," Jessica's voice sounded strained.

"Explain!" Selena demanded. She was starting to feel tetchy, particularly as Braxis hadn't stopped laughing. Standing, Selena glared at them as they entered camp. "Are you two on drugs or something? Braxis, shut the fuck up!"

"Sorry Ma'am, but you should have seen it," Braxis gasped. "One hell of a snap-shot that was. She turned and bam, it was dead!"

"What was dead? You better explain before I lose my patience." In the dim light Selena could still see Jessica turning a shade of purple and evading her eyes. The slim dark-haired woman's sleeves were semi-rolled up, exposing her tattoos. It was obvious to everyone there that she was embarrassed beyond words.

A gruff voice called from the darkness. "Okay, which of you clowns shot my donkey?"

Perimeter defence lights clicked on, leaving the centre of their camp in darkness while blinding those outside it. What could only be the farmer from the homestead a short distance away, stood shielding his eyes before ambling towards them. He wore stained and torn dungarees, was barefooted and had a distinctly annoyed expression.

"You goddamn idiots are gonna have to pay for shooting my Betts!"

Time slowed down for Selena. "Stop, hold it right there!" she knelt behind a paddock and, cocked her weapon, aiming it towards him. Even as she did so, beams and gunfire spat towards them from the night-cloaked land, and several small craft whizzed overhead with humming sounds. Braxis spun around, the back of his left shoulder spraying red mist and gore, his laughter turning to screams as the remains of his arm scattered in pieces into the darkness. The farmer howled in terror, covered his head with both hands and raced towards them. Metallic discs swooped out of the darkness, firing miniature beam weapons at Selena and the others, the auto-guns engaging them immediately.

"Caretakers—take them out! You," Selena bellowed at the farmer, who continued to ignore her and kept running towards them. "Freeze!"

"How the hell did they get here, and since when could those buggers fly?" Singh demanded behind her, his machine gun juddering in his arms and ejecting hot streams of spent cartridges its side.

Jessica leapt towards Braxis, tackling him to the ground. He fought against her, screaming and punching, until a solid clout from Jessica knocked him senseless. She immediately slapped a medical pack onto the gaping hole where his shoulder and arm had been. Immediately the pack began to foam, sealing the wound. Jess administered a pain-killing shot and rolled away, snatching up her weapon and returning fire in short sporadic bursts.

The stocky, fair-haired farmer bellowed, ploughing towards them. "Help! Let me –"

Selena's gun burped and cut him down mid-stride. The depleted uranium bullets tore chunks from him and blew him backwards. There was a blinding explosion before he touched the ground, and body parts scattered in all directions. The blast took out some of the fliers as they swept in for another strafing run, while gunfire from the commandos added to the explosions toll.

There was a sharp pain as something tore through Selena's left cheek, and when she automatically raised a hand to it, it came away covered in blood. She pushed a flap of skin back into the long, thin tear, trying to ignore the pain. Spitting blood, she tore an adhesive dressing from her medical pack and slapped it to the wound, hissing at the sting from the foam.

The sentry guns stopped firing and, apart from pieces of the metallic craft falling to the ground, a stunned hush fell.

Cries of "Clear!" sounded from each of the troops, as one by one they carefully inspected the site.

"How did you know?" Singh asked, standing up and thumbing the safety of his weapon.

"Those caretakers weren't firing at him, what not?" Selena mumbled, through the pain of her wound, adding, "And I got an urgent feeling from Shadow that something was wrong. The Lenars are close now, I can feel them." Giving herself a painkilling shot, Selena raised an eyebrow at Jessica, as the others policed the remains of the attackers. "You shot a donkey ... really?"

"Well, it's dark and that critter was coming at me head on. The infra-red was scrambled and I didn't have a clue what it was. And to be honest, I've never seen one before." Blushing furiously, she turned and knelt next to Braxis, checking his wound. "He'll live. With luck they might be able to regrow the shoulder and arm, so that's his sex life sorted. But we need to get him to a hospital as soon as we can. You need to go too, that's a nasty wound you have there. It'll scar but corrective surgery will sort that out."

"I'll be fine until we get back. Take one of the newbies and one of the skimmers and get Braxis back to the city. The rest of us will continue in the other one, when it's light."

They watched quietly, as the skimmer rose and shot off in the direction of Capulet.

"Kes, when we get back I want you to scare up some more troops. We need more firepower than we have now. Involve Staff, and take a look at Jessica's search teams too. Give her a hand if need be—that's our priority. As for now, you have the first watch. Shake me in a couple of hours."

"You've got it, Ma'am."

\*\*\*

By sunrise they were on their way again. Selena could feel Shadow close by, waiting for them, and she could sense that other Lenars were with him. A few hours later she ordered the skimmer to stop in a clearing about sixty metres round. There was a ring of knee-high white and brown fungus, like a pixie circle, dead in its centre. As the skimmer settled into the grass, and its hot metal began to cool down with gentle ticking noises, they saw movement in the darkness beneath the trees. Automatically they readied their weapons. But, at a sign from Selena, lowered them.

A familiar shape padded into the glade.

"Shadow," Selena said, a smile breaking through her bleak expression. Now waist-high, the short-coated, six-legged Lenar strode towards them from the darkness beneath the trees. Like them, he had black almond-shaped eyes—which blended perfectly into his short midnight-coloured fur. Thick muscles bunched and rolled beneath the dark pelt as the Lenar's pace quickened, until he stood nuzzling Selena. She knelt down and hugged him with both arms. As he did so, the other Lenars materialised out of the trees.

"It's about bloody time!" a voice cried out.

Selena's smile widened. "Cox. I hoped you'd be here."

The small, balding, and overweight scientist stepped out of the undergrowth, looking as if he'd just finished running ten miles. He patted at the sweat on his brow with a stained cloth. His lower face was lost in a deep tangle of long grayish-white hair and multi-coloured beads danced in his beard as he spoke.

"It's good to see you too, Commander." He peered at her eyes. "You've lost weight and those eyes are kinda … eerie. Oh, there's someone else here who's been working with us on what's killing the Lenars."

A huge black mass reared out of the shadows of the trees and towered above her. Like a cross between a mantis, from which they got their name, and a giant spider, the insectoid still made her pulse race and trigger finger itch. A white, livid scar ran down the right side of the Manta's face. Still raw, it slowly dribbled pus. A fist-sized ball of glowing orange light appeared and swirled above the creature's right shoulder, and that eldritch voice she'd come to know so well, finally spoke.

"Greetings Commander Dillon."

"Skar."

Even despite the peace accord between the Assembly of Worlds, the Manta and their Sken allies, Selena found herself wanting to kill the creatures on sight.

"I'm surprised to see you here." Selena eyed the multi-coloured belt forming an X across his chest, and the many unknown gadgets hanging haphazardly from it. Images of past battles flashed through her mind, where the Manta strode towards her firing their weapons, their maws gaping widely while their weapons sliced through her comrades and they tore others apart with their claws. Even though there was now peace between their races, she still had to fight back the belief that Skar and his kin would turn on them at a moment's notice.

"You asked for our help with the Lenars," Skar said, "and I gave my word that we would do what we could, so myself and a few of my kin are here to help."

"So ... how is it going?" she asked, forcing her fists to unclench as she took a deep breath and exhaled slowly.

"Quite well," Cox interjected, again using the cloth to wipe at the sweat on his brow and neck. "We've identified the cause behind the Lenars' illness, thanks to our friend Skar here. We've started trials that could, with luck, lead to both a cure for those already suffering from it and immunisation for the others. So far we've had quite promising results, and I'm hoping it won't be long before we have some excellent news."

"That's good to hear," Selena said. "but in the meantime, unless you really need these Lenars, we could do with them back in the search teams. We'll stay here with you tonight, if that's okay. We had a brush with the ForeRunners on the way here and Jessica had to go back to base with one of our wounded. She'll be back here tomorrow with another skimmer, to help transport everyone back to the city. Stragglers will be picked up on a second run. For now, our main priority is getting those teams up and running."

\*\*\*

Jessica arrived back with them early the next morning, accompanied by two troopers acting as escorts in case of attack. Forewarned that they'd be leaving first thing, Cox and the others had already packed and so it wasn't long before they were on the way back to the citadel.

After her arrival, Selena showered and changed clothes. She eyed herself in the mirror when she was finished. Yup, she'd do. The scar on her cheek was faint now, thanks to the medical foam. It looked more like a ripple in her skin than anything else.

Shadow got up from his place besides her bed, where he'd taken to sleeping, and sat on the floor next to her. His empathic abilities allowed her to know when to let him out and when to let him back in again, so that he could hunt or whatever. He was the perfect companion, one she never had to feed or chase after. Picking up her hand-held she contacted Kes. "Meet me outside on the parade ground," she said. "Bring Singh and Jessica with you, we'll need a skimmer. Oh, and Shadow's coming too. I'm going to see Aunt May, and I don't want a repeat of the last time, when the Queen's thugs ambushed me. This time I want to get there and back in one piece."

"No worries, Ma'am," Kes replied. "Is half an hour okay?"

"Yup, see you then," she said, and signed off. Jenks answered her next call in moments. "You got anything for me?" she asked, noting his stubble had progressed into a badly trimmed goatee.

"Not much. We checked out that cabin you told us about, where your group were attacked. We used battle droids due to the risk of a trap and it turned out to be a wise choice. The whole damned place went up and flattened everything around it for at least a kilometre. As you can well imagine, we lost all three droids and still have no idea if there was anybody in the building at the time of the explosion. Not much left to pick through. What are your plans?"

"The Lenars have agreed to rebuilding the search teams, as soon as we can we'll despatch some to each city. From what I can see our aerial defences look good, so once we're in place the cities should be safe at least for the time being. Keep me updated on any developments."

Jenk's lanky hair was plastered to his forehead. He'd obviously been working out, judging by the sweat trickling down his face, his damp hair and the sweat-stained tee-shirt he was wearing. Some people might even consider him attractive, she thought. Some.

"Will do, Commander. Chat soon."

Outside, Kes and the others were already aboard the skimmer, waiting. With Kes driving, they soared above the battlements and flew to Aunt May's. Within fifteen minutes, the dark craft settled slowly to the ground, the engines winding down to a low idle. For a moment or two, nobody spoke. They could only stare in disbelief.

All that remained of the cottage where Selena had grown up was a blackened ruin. The once-white picket fence lay charred, broken and scattered about the garden. The lawn itself was long and torn in places, the flowerbeds trampled—by combat boots, Selena judged, looking at the footprints. Kes averted his eyes after a few moments, while Singh put a comforting hand on Selena's shoulder.

A gentle wind brought the scent of burning and ash, a stark contrast to that of the honeysuckle, wildflowers and crops growing in the fields around them.

A tremulous voice broke the silence. "Selena, I'm sorry for your loss."

Selena turned to see Agnes, May's neighbour, standing at her own garden gate, sorrow etched on her ancient features. She wore the light-blue dress that she had on the last time Selena had seen her, and was leaning heavily on what looked like a handmade walking stick.

"Loss?" Selena gathered herself. "What happened?"

"The Queen found out that May had returned home. I didn't tell her, I swear. Somehow they already knew and came in the night, on skimmers much like yours. They must have splashed accelerants all through the cottage, because it went up so quickly. I could hear May screaming and I ran over to try and get her out, but they held me back, laughing."

"You expect me to believe that?" Selena said, turning away from witnesses to surreptitiously wipe away a tear. "You betrayed me the last time I was here, and I was captured by the Queen's men! That, despite you saying you were my aunt's friend."

"I'm sorry, I had no choice but to tell them about you. The things they did… But I didn't betray May, I swear."

"If I find out you're lying, I'll come back and gut you myself. Do you understand me?" Selena's eyes locked onto those of the old lady, and she watched as the woman she'd once considered a family friend withered.

With a shudder, the old lady drew her thin frame up as much as she could, and said defiantly, "I never forgave myself for giving you away and them capturing you, so I never told them May had returned. Ask your friendly Lenar there to check me out if you like. It'll confirm I'm not lying. May was my best friend, and what I witnessed here will haunt me to the end of my days—along with my guilt about you."

Shadow sidled up to Selena and she let her feelings slip through him, but the old woman was telling the truth. "Would you recognise those responsible if you saw them again?"

"No, I'm sorry. Like cowards, they hid their faces behind scarves, but all of them wore the uniform of the Royal Guard. The fact that they let me live tells me they wanted you to know who was responsible, not that it would be difficult to guess. Oh, and one more thing."

"Yes?" Selena asked. "Go on."

"They gave me a message for you."

In the distance, doves imported from old Earth in the first colony ships cooed softly, but the sound only served to enhance the otherwise silence and bitter smell of burning. Selena could taste the ash as it danced on the breeze. "And that was?"

"They said to tell you, 'Welcome home'."

# Chapter Three

On their return to Capulet City, Singh, Kes and Shadow followed Selena into her room. Singh flinched when she snatched up a bottle of imported scotch and threw it at the wall. The bottle shattered into a myriad pieces, casting glass and liqueur around the room.

"I was going to drink that..." Singh said.

"Fuck you, Singh! This isn't a time to be funny."

He looked hurt. "I wasn't trying to be."

Kes held his hands up and walked towards Selena, stopping to face her three paces away. "Look, they want you to react, that's why they killed your aunt. Going off the rails is only playing into their hands and May wouldn't want that, would she? I can only imagine how hard it is for you but, please, try to calm down. Remember the old saying, 'revenge is a dish best served cold'. Focus on the present, the current threat—and think clearly. It's what you're trained for, and it's also what we all need right now. Queen Miranda has overplayed her hand; she should have waited to bait you when all this is over, not now. She's been a fool, and that's not like her. I think you have her rattled."

Selena gritted her teeth, and sat on the sofa. "I'm trying, trust me."

Kes looked as if he was going to try step forward and hug her, but changed his mind. "I know it's hard, but there'll be time for a reckoning, and it's not now," he said, and paused before adding, "If you want something to distract you, go out into the city with Shadow. The walk will do you good, and God knows we need more teams out on patrol. You being out there will raise our visibility, and the peoples' trust in us."

As night fell, Selena found herself and Shadow striding through the semi-silent streets. She pulled the zipper of her matt-black outfit up to her neck and checked her trusted Sunburst weapon yet again. It fired small but shockingly powerful bullets, while underneath the shotgun magazine held a variety of rounds, all which could be quickly selected to deal with different types of situations.

Selena let her senses flow out through Shadow and into the alleyways, through which feral cats, rodents and night birds explored. The solar street lighting was often smashed or flickering, leaving many slim passages in a darkness that was broken only by the light from the moons and stars. As they walked, many people averted their eyes, others slunk into doorways and vanished from sight. Awe grew on some faces, fear on others; yet a few smiled and offered greetings, and even occasionally thanks for the regiment's presence and protection. As she walked, Selena was greeted by the occasional person she knew from her childhood, though the pain of her loss persisted. This was her home and she'd grown up here. Despite everything, she was glad to be back.

As she turned into yet another street, music drifted faintly from a shabby-looking take-away on the other side of the road. For a moment, her thoughts filled with that of a chicken shwarma, laced with garlic mayo, cucumber and fries. She was hungry but couldn't bring herself to eat at the moment. Her attention was suddenly drawn to the waves of despair and fear emanating from a young girl who looked in her mid-teens that came flooding through to her from Shadow. The girl was crammed into a small and disposable alloy box, in a shadow-filled doorway. She pulled a quilt, grubby from the dirt around her, closer around herself, seeking comfort in its softness as she tried to make herself look smaller. Frightened brown eyes looked up at them as they approached.

"Who might you be?" Selena asked softly. "And why are you out here all by yourself?"

"I'm Jas Ordain and I'm not doing anything, apart from trying to keep warm and sleep. Holy shit, what happened to your eyes?"

"It's part of our norm," Selena replied, squatting besides her, Sunburst across her knees and Shadow standing to her left. "I didn't say you were doing anything wrong," she said gently. "You seem sad. What's up, and why are you here?" She noted how Jas held her fists, clenched and semi-concealed within the sleeves of her dark-blue all-in-one.

Grime painted Jas's copper-toned face. Her clothes were soiled, torn and tatty in places. Those shoes had seen better days and above all she looked skinny. Those brown, haunted eyes watched Shadow warily.

"Well, Jas, you can put those knives away. The ones you've got concealed in your hands. I know all about them, how they can be concealed and what appears to be a punch is actually a knife attack. The punch is meant to miss, to hide the knife that will cut someone's throat as the hand goes past. I'm not going to hurt you, so put them away."

Eying Selena, Jas gave a nod and slid the weapons up her sleeves, into their sheaths, and showed her empty hands. "I'm sorry, we have to be careful out here. My parents were working in the city that got blown up. I've not heard from them since, so I guess they're dead like everyone says. I did ask their boss and others if they had any news about them, but they just ushered me away and after a while we weren't even let into the company buildings. You'd be sad too, if your parents had been killed."

"They were. I take it your parents were in Ephesus?"

"Yeah. Your parents were killed?"

Selena nodded. "Yeah, my father was murdered and my mother committed suicide."

Jas rubbed at her eyes in an attempt to hide the tears, but Selena saw them trickling down her grubby cheeks anyway, leaving clear tracks behind them.

"We were in company accommodation," Jas said. "We were allocated it when we arrived. It was lovely, a two bedroomed, fully furnished flat—much better than what we had at Yaros. You'd think the company would look after us, but they didn't. When the bills didn't get paid they threw me out, along with many others whose parents had died. They said that the company wasn't a charity."

"Hasn't anyone tried to take care of you?"

The youngster's eyes challenged Selena's. "Get a grip. Would I be here, if they had? A few of the lucky ones got taken on by local families, or other workers who had the space, but not many. The rest are out here, on the streets."

"What about food, have you eaten lately?" Selena asked, tight-lipped as she hid a half smile. This girl had spit!

"Yeah, been here ever since. We look out for each other. Finding food and shelter isn't easy and, like I said, it's not safe. Several of us have been killed, others gone missing. It's scary and we don't know who to trust. Some say it's the Manta or ForeRunners, others say it's the Lenars." Jas paused, before saying, "You're Selena Dillon, aren't you?"

Selena noticed the edge in Jas's voice, and how she tried to shrink further into the alloy box. "How do you know that?"

"Everyone does, you're famous. The girl who tried to kill the queen, got caught and punished. You saved humanity by destroying the Manta home-world."

"Or so we thought," Selena replied, "then the bugs pop right back up again. You don't sound convinced about who's being blamed for the murders. Who do you think's responsible?"

"Not any of them, that's for sure," Jas said. "The killer's human. I wasn't far away when one of the girls was murdered, and I heard her screaming and someone give a really weird laugh. I ran and reported it to the police and took them to where I thought she was. When they found her, she was dead; she'd been cut open and there was blood everywhere. It was horrible."

"I'm really sorry about your friend. What do you mean, weird?"

Jas grimaced. "It's hard to describe. Just sounded … wrong."

"Have you told anyone else about this?"

"Like who? The authorities aren't interested in what happens to us, and we've nowhere safe to go. We're just stuck here, waiting for the killer to strike again."

"Look, I think you should come home with me," Selena said, reaching down to help Jas up. Her skin was copper-toned and she was bone thin. At about five-foot-tall her afro hair was pulled behind her in a bun, by a red tatty-looking rag.

"What makes you think I trust you? For all I know you could be the killer."

"Do I look like a killer?"

"Yeah."

"Well, I'm not … well, only of those who deserve it. Like you say, you know all about me." She saw Jas still eying Shadow. "Don't worry, he won't hurt you."

"Oh, I know that. He feels comforting somehow, warm and cosy. It's strange but I know I can trust him, and also that he trusts you. If a Lenar can, then I guess I do too. Are we really going to your place? Where is it, in the citadel?"

"Yup. Then we need to figure out what to do about your friends." Selena decided to leave the discussion about "warm, cosy, and trust" for later. Right now she wanted to get this girl somewhere safe, showered and with a hot meal inside her.

***

"Are you out of your mind?" Colonel Christina Delmar demanded, slamming an open hand onto her desk. "Provide accommodation for kids? We aren't a Goddamn kindergarten!"

"Ma'am," Selena replied, biting back a retort, while ruffling Shadow's short, coarse hair. "Look, we have the facilities to help them, so why not? Besides, there's a saying, 'Where we lead others follow'. Perhaps if we do something good for these children then others will too. Someone has to look out for these kids, and there's nothing to stop us employing someone to look after them. We don't have to do it ourselves."

"The powers that be won't wear it, our budgets are tightly controlled. Anyone would think they were paying for it out of their own pockets," the colonel interrupted.

There was something in Delmar's manner that made Selena pursue the matter. She thought quickly, before hiding a smirk and adding, "We can always bill the Queen for it, if we play it right. I can't see her arguing—it would look bad. It's not safe out there on the streets and everyone knows it. What will the other workers and colonists think, if they see these children abandoned? They're bound to be getting worried about their own families, if something should happen to them. You know as well as I do that once trust is lost, it's hard to get back again. Besides, look on it as more positive publicity for us."

Delmar eyed her curiously. "You have a point. But what do you mean it's not safe out there?"

"I have a feeling. Just something that Jas said, that apart from the killings, some of these youngsters are going missing."

The colonel ran a hand over her head, shaved bald apart from a thin and short black strip of hair running front to back. Much of her visible skin was covered in black tribal tattoos. She wore a thin black strip of cloth across a feeble excuse for breasts, her ribs and shoulder-bones protruding. She assessed Selena thoughtfully. "You're right. Okay, we'll do it. I'll get security to organise things."

"Okay, but I'd like to be kept in the loop."

"Your liaison will be Corporal Baron." Delmar's paused and considered her. "Getting a bit soft in your old age, are you? Looking out for youngsters."

"Not at all. I'm concerned about the ones that are going missing and what's happening to them, that's all. It could be related to the ForeRunners and, if so, we need to keep our fingers on the pulse."

"Hmm, very well. I'll tell him to keep you updated. In the meantime, reinforcements have arrived, so I'm giving you the troops you've requested. Four squads of twenty, plus you already have the search teams—those that are still alive. A few of them died in Ephesus."

When Selena asked how many teams she'd have, the colonel shook her head. "What with the few Lenars who've re-joined us, we'll be lucky to field twelve teams—excluding yourself and your friend there." She eyed Shadow.

Selena ruffled Shadow's fur again, eliciting something akin to a low rumble and a warm feeling. "Shadow says the Lenars don't trust the Queen, that there's a darkness in her heart. Many of his kin agree and have dispersed deep into the forests to seek safety, but he brought all that he could with him. They're barely enough to help us for the time being, and runners have been despatched to try and recruit more."

A door to one side of the room led into a compact cabin. Through a half-ajar door Selena could see a hologram of a naked, pirouetting and dancing well-oiled woman on a desk next to the bunk and recognised the woman as one of the regiments physical training instructors. Selena ignored it but the colonel had caught the look. A half-smile played over her lips.

"Okay, we'll make do with what we have in the short time," Delmar said. "But we need those other teams up and running, and I mean soon. Other worlds in the Alliance have heard about them and are now demanding teams of their own. After all, they're facing the same threat as ourselves. As for now, you have a job to do, so go and get on with it."

"There's one more thing," Selena said, ignoring the dismissal, and how the colonel's eyes deliberately flickered over her figure. "Jas stays with me when I'm here, and with her friends when I'm not."

"Really? Okay, agreed. Now get out and find the killer, I've work to do."

\*\*\*

A new physical training facility had been set up in the outskirts of the city, just inside the walls. It didn't take Selena long to get there and she opened Staff's office door and entered without knocking.

He didn't seem surprised at her appearance and his sky-blue eyes considered her. She noticed his cropped dark hair was starting to turn gray, as he half rose and threw her a haphazard salute

"I understand from the grapevine, that we got the men you asked for," Staff said. "I hope you don't mind but I swiped two physical training instructors I know from other units, and they'll probably create hell. I'll need these people to help me run this place efficiently. After all, you can't expect me to do it all on my own."

"That's fine," Selena replied, ignoring the sloppy salute. "But make sure you ask next time. You're going to need a higher rank due to our rise in numbers, so I'm promoting you to Sergeant with immediate effect."

He remained silent, not even saying thank you as he watched her.

"You don't approve?"

"It's not that. I just don't want to be here, even with the additional rank."

"Don't like it? Tough," Selena growled. "None of us have a choice where we are sent, perks of you being a bad boy in the past. You've a job to do, Sergeant, so make sure you do it well. Because if you don't, or if you piss me off even more—and that includes by not saluting properly—I'll bust you right down to private, hang your balls up as an ornament in my office and ensure you're shipped somewhere nasty. Do we understand one another?"

"Perfectly, Ma'am. I note from Daily Orders that you've put me directly under Lieutenant Philips, he's a good man. But I hope you or he don't think I play favourites, I can't be seen to. I'll treat you both the same way I do all the others. It's the way I do things."

"I wouldn't have it any other way," Selena replied

"Good. Now get your arse outside, Commander. You're late for training."

Selena stepped outside the office and into the changing rooms next door. Stripping off she selected running kit and went back outside, joining the five lines of soldiers. No-one said anything, or even acknowledged her. They knew the drill. In physical training, they were all the same. There were troops from various sections, plus her team lining up facing the office. A few moments later Staff came out, accompanied by two much slimmer female physical trainers.

Hands behind his back, he stood at ease and surveyed them, the other two behind him, his lips curled in disdain.

"Most of you know me. For those who don't, I'm Sergeant Moore; you can call me Staff. Behind me on my left is Corporal Tracy, more commonly known as Dick. On my other side, you'll see Corporal Al Kharsi. Address him as Kami. If I hear any of you call him Shithouse, you'll answer to me personally. Do we understand one another?"

"Yes, Sir!" they chorused.

"I didn't hear you," he sneered.

"Yes, Sir!" Their reply was much louder this time.

"Good." Staff radiated contempt. "Each of your lines is a team. Behind all of you there are wheeled trailers full of axes. I want each team to split into two and take one trailer. The first half of each group are to be at the front pulling or behind pushing, with the remainder tabbing and keeping pace. When I say 'change over' you do so immediately. Now get to your posts and follow me. Move it!"

Selena found herself in the front of their trailer with three others. It was hard going, even with those pushing from behind. They pushed and pulled their contraption for ten minutes before Staff shouted at them to change, then they jogged in formation behind their replacements.

"Change!" Ten minutes later they switched again, and so it went on.

How long they battled through along a well-worn dirt track into the forest Selena had no idea, but she breathed a sigh of relief when they were finally told to stop.

"Everyone grab an axe," Staff bellowed. "Each team chop down a tree as selected by one of the instructors. How you do so is up to you. Trim and chop the trunks into logs. When you've done that, load everything back aboard the trailers. Those who finish first get a rest. What wrong with you shitheads, are you waiting for a written invite? Move!"

"Staff, these axes are pretty dull. Can we sharpen them?" one of the new troopers asked.

"Aw, dear me… No, you goddam can't! Get on with it, before I stick my boot so far up your arse it'll make you choke."

Selena and her team surrounded a tree pointed out to them by Dick. One after the other, they began to swing the heavy blades. At first her axe hardly made a mark but as they continued they gradually worked their way through the trunk. Selena shouted a warning as their tree fell with a crash into the undergrowth, and then they began to hack away at the branches.

"Leave the bark on the bole," Dick growled.

Selena had recognised her earlier. She was the pirouetting model on the colonel's desk.

"Something funny, Ma'am?" Dick growled, eying her, jaw jutting forward.

Selena was struck by a faint smell of perfume. "Not in the slightest."

"Good. Now cut those trees into logs and load them into the trailer. Come on, we haven't all day."

Her arms aching, Selena chopped in turn with the others, before carrying the heavy logs and dumping them into the trailer. She had no idea how much longer it was before the trailer was finally fully loaded, but she could see the utter exhaustion on her teammates faces. The first to finish, they sank to the ground, leaning their backs against the trailer. It seemed like only a short while later that the last team finished and the PT staff were shouting at them to get back onto their feet.

"Don't we get that rest Staff mentioned?" Singh asked.

"You just had it, think yourselves lucky. You don't get another rest until we get back. Get a move on, before I have a sense of humour failure," Dick replied.

When they were finished, they dragged the contraptions back to where they'd started.

The gasps of relief from the troopers at the sight of Capulet City was a collective sigh. As they approached the city gates. Staff's shout tore through their hopes, like a scythe through corn.

"Who told you to go into Capulet? Run parallel to the city walls. Call yourselves Commandos? I've seen children with more guts than you! Hey, Commander," he sneered at Selena, "if you evade that man who's collapsed in front of you I'll kick you in the crotch so hard you'll think you've been gangbanged by the entire regiment. Pick that man up and chuck him in the trailer. Pain, people, is character building—it's just weakness leaving the body!"

Eventually they made it into the city and back to the training base. At Staff's command, they left the trolleys and lined up, hardly able to stand, their hands bleeding, torn and blistered.

Staff stood in front of them, hands clasped behind his back, complete distain on his face. "How you people even passed basic training is beyond me. Get the hell out of my sight." He turned and strode back into his office, slamming the door loudly behind him.

Once Dick had dismissed them, Selena staggered to her team's dorm. She eyed herself in a mirror, shocked at the vision in front of her. Her face was stained with sweat and dirt. Blood dripped from her hands, and there was a small cut on her forehead that she didn't recall getting. Her limbs were leaden and she could hardly stand. Here the accommodation and amenities were mixed. Stripping off, Selena staggered into the showers. Her muted gasps of agony joined the chorus from the others.

As they soaked their aching bodies, Staff strode into the showers and stood there fully clothed in the tumbling water, watching them. "Aw, hurts, does it?" he sneered. "You bunch of pussies. Lieutenant Lacey, if you look at me like that again you'll be very sorry, Sir. Thirty push-ups, now! Yeah, right there in the water. Ahh dear, sorely hands have we?" He looked at one of the females. "Problem, Private? You need to sort yourself out, before I shove my arm so far up your gash you'll be using sheep as tampons. Commander Dillon, with respect, my office if you will when you've finished." With a final sneer he turned and walked out.

Selena struggled to hold her hands overhead, as she passed through the wall dryers. Satisfied, she dressed— watching those who'd joined the line waiting for medical treatment, almost wincing herself as the medics dressed torn hands, feet and other wounds. When she was ready, Selena jogged briskly to Staff's office. She knocked hard and heard the command to enter. Doing so, she went in and stood at attention in front of the sergeant, who rose fully this time and saluted her smartly.

"Please relax Ma'am, take a seat."

Selena did so. "A little hard, weren't you? These are seasoned troops."

"We've talked about this, I don't make exceptions and I'm not here to make friends. What I care about is getting them fit, mentally and physically, so they stand more chance of survival in the field. That's why I'm here, remember? You did well today, as you usually do—not that I'd normally say anything. Sorry if I riled you, but by not rising to the bait you showed good leadership and that's what's needed.

"Your team, plus Alpha and Bravo are released to do as you see fit. Charlie and Delta will stay here—they need a bit of work but they'll have it easier over the next few days, now I've made my mark. I'll slowly ramp it back up again before long—but nothing overly strenuous. I've checked and that's in line with your calendar. I trust that's agreeable?"

"I'll double check to make sure, but it should be fine. I want everyone coming through here on a rotational basis, but I don't want them so burnt out when they get back that they can't work. Do we understand one another?"

Staff nodded. "Perfectly." He stood and poured two cups of coffee from the silver-coloured urn behind him. The pungent aroma made Selena salivate. He offered her one of the cups and she took it gingerly. The strong brew burnt her mouth; she pursed her lips and blew gently.

"You and I are both aware," Staff began softly, "that when our troops come out of basic training they're top of the line. Trouble is, there's often little follow up. It's all left to individual commanders. They get soft, and we really can't afford that. Our troops need to be fit to fight, and I don't want the deaths of these soldiers on my conscience because I didn't do my job well, and that they weren't prepared to the best of their ability."

Selena nodded. "My thoughts exactly. Keep up the good work, Sergeant, and thanks for the coffee."

# Chapter Four

The wall screen chimed, waking Selena. Jas remained asleep on the brown leather-like sofa a white throw covering her, warm and comfortable for the first in a long time. She tossed and turned, muttering unintelligibly, her voice rising and falling. Selena donned a robe and activated the screen. Jenks, more dishevelled than usual, looked back at her.

"Sorry to disturb you at this hour, Commander, but I've bad news, I'm afraid."

*He looks flustered,* Selena thought, surprised.

"There was an electronic pulse a few moments ago, just like the one before the destruction of Ephesus. Something big's going down. I'm in the control room, best you get here quick. I've informed Colonel Delmar and she's on her way too. All units are at action stations."

"I'll be there shortly. Did you track where the signal came from?" She sent a silent alarm to her troops, warning them of impending action.

"Yes. It's about eighty miles south of Rousillon, our city at the North Pole. We've sent them a red alert, letting them know of an imminent attack. They're at action stations and are evacuating non-essential personnel, just in case. The ships in orbit have blasted the area the signal originated from right down to the bedrock, but knowing the ForeRunners, anything is possible and it certainly doesn't mean we got them."

"Good, well done, Lieutenant. One moment, I need to speak to my troops." She switched screens. Singh, Jessica and Kes looked back at her anxiously, alerted by her silent alarm.

"What's up, Commander?" Kes asked.

She updated them quickly, and then said, "Jessica, I want all search teams that can be spared out there, now! Kes, you go with her, I want that city locked up tight. Singh, you remain here with me. Any questions?" When they shook their heads, she dismissed them and brought Jenkins back online. "Sorry for the delay. Extra search teams are being despatched as we speak. Better safe than sorry."

"Thank you," Jenks said. He looked relieved and ran his fingers through his greasy-looking hair. Like her, he'd obviously been sleeping when the emergency came through, judging by the bags under his eyes. He continued, "We need to nail these guys and soon, before they can get away. I'm hoping the ships got them with their strike but they're slippery bastards, and God knows what technology they have to protect themselves."

Selena dressed, left the building and was at the control room within ten minutes. "News?" she demanded as she entered, then saw the colonel sitting in the command and control chair, a position she herself had once held. "Excuse me, Colonel. I didn't see you there."

"I gathered that, Commander," Delmar replied tartly. "As to your question, there's nothing further as yet. Your teams are about forty minutes from the—"

One of the many wall screens flashed, glared whitely, and then went completely blank.

"What the hell?" Delmar demanded.

Jenks paled. "That was Elsinore, the city on the opposite side of the planet. It's gone, we've been had. The enemy must have placed the pulse close to the North Pole, so we'd think the target was Rousillon. Instead…"

"Jennings!" The colonel snapped rising to her feet, her face white with fury. "You should have foreseen this. We've lost another city because you God-damned *assumed*! Call the extra search teams back, there's no point in wasting their time now. And get me some satellite images of this … disaster."

Jenks made the call and pulled up images onto the main screen of where it was estimated that the bomb, or whatever it was, had detonated. The city itself had vanished. All that remained were clouds of dust and debris drifting on the wind over an exceptionally large crater. The forest around it had been flattened for miles all around. They zoomed in to various parts of what once had been a city and its surrounds. There was nothing left at all.

Jenks pushed back the hair from his brow and looked guiltily at his senior officer. "Ma'am, I—"

"Not another word," Delmar grated. "You and I will talk later. After I've had a tongue lashing from the queen, no doubt. Take it from me, Jennings, you'll be lucky to still be here in the morning."

There was another brilliant flash on a screen, and then that one too died.

"No…" someone gasped.

"Rousillon," Jenks replied, his voice suddenly husky. "It's gone," he glanced at Selena. "Along with all inhabitants and your teams that were there. I'm sorry, Commander."

Selena went cold. "What about the backup teams? We just recalled them."

He looked to his screens and tapped at his keyboard. "Lieutenant Philip's team has been downed. Robert's skimmer is okay and reports they've turned back to search the area for the others. Luckily, Roberts and her crew had taken off a little later than Lieutenant Philips, and so were further away from the city when it blew."

Selena patched herself through to Jessica. "Roberts, report!"

Over the speakers her voice sounded harassed. "Sorry Ma'am, busy! I'll call in when possible."

"Carry on, Lieutenant. Take the time you need, just find them."

"Will do, Ma'am. Out."

"Commander, cancel that. I need those troops of yours back here, right now!" the colonel snarled.

"Then you're going to be disappointed, Colonel. They'll be back once they've found my people. You can court martial me later."

Was that a glimmer of respect in the Colonel's eyes?

"Very well. Keep me updated."

"Indeed, Colonel. In the meantime, I'm bringing our training wing back here to fill in where they can."

Delmar nodded. "Good. I'll be in my cabin, if I'm needed."

Selena came to attention and saluted as the colonel left. Damn the woman, despite her flaunting the rules with her personalised top. Selena was actually starting to like her. She turned to face Jenks, who looked as if someone had run over his cat. "Okay Jennings, what the hell happened? You dropped the ball, and you certainly had enough warning. How long between the first signal and the explosion?"

"Seventeen minutes, Ma'am."

Selena considered. "Okay, clever of the enemy to distract us like that. But the time delay from the first pulse suggests they deliberately delayed the explosion to try and get the teams we sent out in response. They know we're a threat to them. Jenks, I need your thoughts— now."

Jenks stared at her. She could almost smell the stench of his grubby, unwashed clothes and the sweat stains under his arms. He looked thoughtful, paused for a moment, and then said, "In my opinion, I don't think we got them. They'll have known we could track the signal to its origins and would take the appropriate action. If I were in their place, I'd have put the transmitter somewhere well away from us and controlled it by remote or delayed action."

Selena nodded. "I agree, so find and eliminate them. If you don't, I've no doubt the Queen will consider shooting you personally and, knowing her, sending your family the bill for the bullet—if she could find them."

That said, Selena turned and left the command centre, returning to her room where Jas was still asleep. She knew that she had to be rested and fully competent for when things really kicked off, so ensuring that the line to Jessica remained free she laid on her bed, fully dressed, and closed her eyes. She wasn't going to disturb Roberts as she searched for the man she cared for. Selena knew how it felt to lose someone you loved. Besides, Kes was one of her closest friends and as far as she was concerned Jessica could have all the time and resources she needed. Screw the Queen and her demands.

She was awakened by the screen beeping to let her know that a call was waiting on a secondary line. It was Staff.

"Commander, the training team and I will be landing in Capulet City shortly. Sorry for the delay, some of the guys were out on exercise and we had to go find them, pick them up and get them sorted with their gear."

Bearing in mind his aversion to the Lenars, Selena said, "Okay. I want you patrolling the outside of Capulet City. Be visible. I want you there both as a deterrent and to reassure the population."

"Roger that." There was a slight pause. "Ma'am If you could update us with any news about Lieutenant Philips and the others, we'd really appreciate it."

"Will do. You're his second in command, so keep an eye on things for him until he gets back. Any problems, you call me immediately."

"Understood."

When Staff had signed off, Selena realised that getting further rest was out of the question, so she wearily made her way back to the control centre, where she sat in silence watching Jenks working away at the screen. Three mugs of coffee later he turned to her.

"Good news, they've found your guys. The pulse had interfered with their trackers, but they're working perfectly now and Roberts reports that there's no serious injuries. Luckily, they were flying low when the pulse took out the skimmer's engines. They've only bruises, mild concussions, sense of humour failure, that sort of thing."

Standing, she said, "Jenks, you need to find those ForeRunners. We're fast running out of cities—and people, come to that."

Knowing there was nothing else she could do, Selena returned to her quarters. It was still dark outside, and she watched the pale glow of the moons rising over the city. Entering her accommodation, she found the soft snoring coming from Jas strangely comforting. For a moment or two she watched silently, until it was interrupted as Jas turned over on the couch and muttered yet again. The blanket had fallen to the floor and as Selena picked it up and gently replaced it, wondering how long it had been since Jas had slept so peacefully.

In the morning, Selena contacted Jenks "What news?" she demanded

He looked back at her from the wall screen, his hair in the usual disarray. "Your team is fine and they've all been released from hospital. The doctors recommend rest but they're ignoring that. They were incredibly lucky—had they been travelling at a different height it might have been a completely different story."

"They can rest when they're dead. What about casualties in the cities?"

"Total, no survivors at all—in fact, there's nothing left but ash. God knows what kind of weapon that was, our people are still trying to get a handle on it. The civilian population here are beginning to panic and are already leaving in droves."

"And you're surprised? We need to give them some good news. Find something, anything, but above all I want those responsible found. Oh, and stop all outgoing civilian flights for the time being—we don't want the enemy escaping. If people ask why, tell them it's a security matter. You'd better let the colonel know; perhaps she could talk to the queen about incentives for the workers to stay here. Financial rewards usually work—perhaps the queen can offer bonuses."

Jenks ran a hand through his goatee, a habit that was becoming more apparent each day. "That'll be the day, but I'm on it. I have some more troubling news for you. Corporal Baron called me last night, about an hour after you'd left. Said he had to keep you updated on a few things, but he'd heard what'd happened to the cities and thought this could wait until morning, given priorities and all that."

"For heaven's sake Jennings, just tell me what he said."

"Two bodies have just been found in Capulet, both girls, both about fifteen or so —twins most likely."

"That's all we need," Selena said with a wince, as if a weight had just fallen across her shoulders. "Where were they found?"

"In a back alley, not far from the arena. The only way to describe it, he said, is that they've been ... filleted." His lips twisted and he clenched his eyes shut for a moment.

"How the hell can someone do something like that, especially to children?" Selena said.

"If you like, I'll ask him to meet you there."

"Tell him to send the details of where it happened to my hand-held, I'll be there shortly," Selena replied.

Collecting Singh and Shadow, Selena found Baron waiting for them when they arrived. To her surprise, he was wearing the uniform of the Royal Bodyguard.

"Nice to meet you at last, Commander," Baron said, saluting as he led the way. "A shame it's under such circumstances. Like many here, I've followed your exploits. Tell me, is it true you once fed an enemy their own pets and didn't tell them until they'd finished their meal?"

Selena gave him the once over. "No, but it's an idea. Why, do you have any pets?"

He gave a half smile. "Ah, we're far from enemies Commander, despite my uniform. I want this killer caught as much as you do. And no, I don't have any pets, thankfully."

Baron was a tall but slim man, his gray hair crewcut with a large balding area on his crown. He looked wrinkled and haggard, tired beyond belief. Yet his green eyes were kind and his voice soft.

She eyed his uniform. "You're a member of the Royal Bodyguard. How come the colonel put you forward for this?"

"I believe that Her Majesty thought it a good idea and had a word. I can advise on protocol and other such matters."

Putting her distrust to one side, they followed him, and passed through the military cordon and under the high white-stone arch into an alleyway that was so narrow daylight struggled against the gloom. The rough concrete buildings around them were obviously some of the first made by the colonists when they arrived, their ancient machines churning out concrete from native material to quickly provide the housing and protective walls needed for the settlers.

Shadowy doorways beckoned, boxes were piled against the walls, amidst occasional pools of water. Cats and rodents slipped through the gloom while rubbish scampered over the flagstones, driven by the soft breeze tainted with the stench of refuse.

"You look familiar somehow," Selena said to Baron, after a while. "Do we know each other?"

His bottle-green eyes remained on hers. "No, but I was born on this world so we could easily have bumped into one another. We may even have mutual friends. You never know. I pop up in all kinds of places and work all hours, but when working exclusively for the queen I mostly do nights. I like the way the moons dance."

Selena froze as he uttered the last phrase, recognising it as a rebel recognition code. Knowing the others will have noticed the phrase was slightly out of place, she just gave a slight nod of acknowledgement. At that moment, they stopped at a doorway and her eyes slid over the blood splattered wall and passageway. "Can you tell me what happened?"

"A citizen came through here late last night and found them. They've been eviscerated—gutted if you will. There's not a single organ remaining, not even their brains or eyes."

"There was just their bodies?"

"Aye Ma'am. They've been taken to the morgue. We've never had anything like this before, I think we're a bit out of our depth."

"What about the other cities," Singh asked. "Anything similar?"

"Nope, nothing at all. It appears these killings only happen in Capulet City, which obviously points to someone living here. The other murders we've had recently have been pretty much the same."

Selena looked at Baron's gray-bordered, scrunched-up expression, wondering whether his parents had grabbed his face and squeezed hard when he was a child. He looked like he was sucking a mouthful of chilli. "How many murders are we talking about, Corporal?"

He looked away. "With these two, twelve in total that I know about. All girls."

Singh's jaw dropped. "Twelve females killed like this, and all kids?"

"Yup," Baron said grimly. "The powers that be have been keeping it quiet— they didn't want a panic."

"Okay," Selena said, after a moment. "I want constant drone surveillance on these alleyways and anywhere else this fiend could hit. The orphans are to be rounded up and brought to the citadel. Baron, liaise with Lieutenant Commander Singh here. If the children aren't out here exposed to danger, they can't be killed. See to it." She turned away and left the alleyway, Singh and Shadow beside her.

They remained silent on the way back. Selena's thoughts flickered back to Baron. Well, well—the rebels hadn't given up. The fact they had someone so close to the monarch meant they could pick their moment. She suspected that they hadn't done anything so far was itself because of the conflict, and while the Queen was acting in the planets' best interests.

Jas was waiting when Selena returned to her quarters. "I hope you don't mind, I was hungry and thought I'd make myself something." She took one look at Selena's face and put down the slice of burnt toast she was munching. "What's happened?"

Selena told her about the cities and the murders. As the young girl's face fell, Selena said, "Jas, I need your help. I'd like you and I to pop out this evening. I want us to get all of your friends that are hiding in the alleyways, and anyone else, back here. Singh's working with the Colonel's P.A, to arrange safe quarters. They'll be warm, fed, and well-looked after. But most of all, they'll be out of danger."

Jas stood instantly, food forgotten. "I'm on it now."

"No, you're not—like I said, we'll go out later tonight. Singh will be here before long and he'll update us on the accommodation, so we're armed with the latest information. Also, I don't want you going anywhere at night without an escort, at least until we find the killer. Is that clear?"

Jas nodded.

"In the meantime," Selena added, looking at her meal, "it looks to me like I'll have to show you how to make toast."

# Chapter Five

"What is it?" Jas said, yawning as Selena woke her by sitting next to her on the couch. The girl was still dressed in the tattered and torn all-in-one Selena had found her in, the still-grubby quilt held tightly to her cheek. She looked quickly around the room and then relaxed. "I'm still tired after roaming around the alleys last night."

"Well, it was a good job done. Like you said, all your friends are safe now. I've transferred some credits to your account," Selena said, tapping the data chip embedded in Jas's right arm as she made a mental note to wash the quilt, wrinkling her nose at the fusty smell. "Spend it carefully, I'm not loaded by any means, but I can top it up if need be. I have a few things to do this morning, so why don't you go out into the city and buy yourself some clothes and shoes—or whatever else you need. Do you feel up to that? If you'd rather I came with you, we can do it tomorrow."

Jas shook her head.

"Okay. Speak to Singh and get him, or a guard, to go with you."

Jas eyed her warily. "I'm not a child, you know. It's daylight, the murders are all done at night."

"I'm well aware of that, but I want you to promise me you'll take someone with you and spend these credits on what they're for, and not anything stupid or illegal. Oh, and here's a list of a few things I'd like you to pick up. I thought we could cook a meal together tonight." Selena handed over a small sheet of paper, which Jas glanced and stuffed in a torn breast pocket.

"I can't imagine you cooking."

"Why?" Selena laughed. "I wasn't always so hard-nosed. My Aunt taught me well. It's just something I don't have reason to do very often."

The girl studied her. "Why are you being so kind to me? I've heard about you, everyone has. Scary bitch, I'm told."

"Just buy the clothes and the food, Jas … and grab a shower while you're at it, you could do with one," Selena said, her good humour vanishing. "I'll be back later today. In the meantime, the door has your handprint and voice recognition, so it'll open for you. By the way, you don't need to worry about your friends. After your help getting them out of the alleys last night, they're all being well taken care of and you'll be able to see them soon, once all the data work has been sorted. We'll talk when I get back, okay?"

Jas nodded, laid back on the sofa and closed her eyes, clutching the quilt to her face once again.

"Just one more thing," Selena added. "Those knives of yours, keep them with you. Just in case."

\*\*\*

Sitting in Colonel Delmar's office, Selena noted that this time the door to her bedroom was closed. To her surprise the Colonel was in full uniform, which in her opinion was far more appropriate than the garments she'd worn the last time Selena was here. Dark tattoos peeked from under the sleeves on her wrists. Flat-chested Delmar seemed almost boyish. Her ghoulish black eyes regarded her as Selena spoke.

"Good morning, Colonel. I thought I'd take the chance to update you on the situation as I see it. The loss of the two cities, tragic as they were, has released the teams I'd just allocated to them. Consequently, they've been redeployed to begin a systematic search of the areas surrounding the remaining bases. It's all we can do at the moment, although I'm obviously open to any suggestions. I don't suppose your people have come up with any ideas?"

"Not a thing," Delmar replied. "With all the traffic being checked, along with the frequent street patrols and building inspections, I don't think the enemy are hiding here in the city—they'd have been picked up by now if they were. We just need to figure out where they are, and how the hell they're moving around without being detected. I've asked Skar if he can help but he says he doesn't have the equipment he'd need. He also said that they only have a few remaining ships that could detect them, and can't spare any at this moment in time. He did say something rather odd though."

"Ma'am?"

"He said it won't matter soon. They are coming."

"Who is?" Selena asked, eyebrows raised.

"Skar wouldn't elaborate, and, as I'm sure you know, the Manta are hard to read." Delmar paused before saying at length, "As to our other problem, I have wondered if the murders are down to organ smugglers."

Selena shook her head. "If they were there'd be nothing left of the bodies at all, they'd have taken everything. People still need limbs, muscle tissue, skin— that sort of thing. They'd probably keep the bodies alive as long as they could, and then farm them to order. These murders are either a scare tactic by the enemy, in which case I don't understand why just here in Capulet City and not anywhere else, or we have a real psycho loose."

Delmar nodded her agreement. "My thoughts exactly. Personally, I think we've a serial killer on our hands. But why take their organs? All we seem to uncover is more and more questions." She rose from behind the desk and moved across the room to a percolator. "Coffee, Commander?"

"Yes, black please," Selena said, pleasantly surprised. "We've been out rounding the vagrant children up. According to Jas, we've all of them already. Corporal Baron has found accommodation and civilian staff to look after them. I guess we have to figure out how to bill the Queen for it all now."

Delmar's thin lips spread to a smile, as she placed two mugs in front of them and sat in her chair, rocking backwards. "Oh, I wouldn't worry about that. It's taken care of. I simply pointed out to Her Majesty that if she doesn't take care of these waifs then the settlers will up and leave, and others won't come here. No sane person would risk their children being left to starve out on the streets. This reassures the workers that their children will be well taken care of, if something untoward happens. That, and the offer of bonuses, seems to have calmed things down."

Delmar ran the fingertips of her right hand on her desk, her alloy nails making a light drumming sound as she contemplated Selena, her lips twitching. "When all this is over, and you've finished your sentence, you should seriously think about a political career."

Selena snorted. "How many ex-cons do you know have done that? Besides, it's the last thing I'd think about doing."

"Why?"

Before Selena could reply, the colonel's screen chirped. She instantly swung to face it and said; "Delmar. Speak."

A fresh faced young male officer, looking flustered, appeared and said, "I'm sorry to disturb you Colonel, but there's a Sken vessel approaching and it's asking permission to land."

Another screen switched from displaying the forests to the black, amoebic craft swinging into orbit.

"Did they say what they want?"

"Yes, they're demanding an immediate meeting of all the races. Apparently they contacted Skar first, he's already waiting in the conference room."

"Very well. Permission to land granted, and prepare the room. Inform Admiral Van Pluy, send him my respects and ask him to attend via screen. You'd better inform the Queen too, she likes to be kept in the loop, but stipulate that it's a military-only meeting." She turned the screen off and added, "Commander Dillon, you better come along."

They waited for a moment, watching the screen silently as the Sken vessel slipped into orbit and the organic craft elongated. A piece detached and floated majestically towards the surface, fluidly changing shape as it came.

"I can never figure out if those ships are alive, or not. There's something almost … surreal about them." Selena mused.

"Well, well, Commander," Delmar replied with a half-smile. "Something that actually flummoxes you. Come on, we'd better get ready to greet our guests."

Skar was indeed there waiting when they arrived, but despite their greetings, the hulking insectoid ignored them. Delmar and Selena glanced at each other and shrugged, deciding silently to emulate the Manta's welcome. Shadow stood at Selena's side and through him she could sense the raw emotion flowing through the room, from the guards' alertness and the Manta's strange expectancy, to Delmar's curiosity and excitement.

The door slid open and three Sken fluttered into the room. Thrumming wings suspended their cat-sized translucent bodies, while their many eye stalks twisted and coiled around each other as they took in their surroundings. They constantly changed colour; the belts interlacing their bodies looked almost like stripes. Selena and the colonel watched, nonplussed, as the Sken stopped and hovered over chairs. The wall screen came on and the Admiral Van Pluy joined them.

"Greetings," Colonel Delmar began, with a nod to the admiral while addressing the Sken. "While it's always a pleasure to see our allies, at such short notice this must be important."

"It is so," a Sken's voice replied in their minds.

Selena knew it was the middle one who had spoken, and wondered whether they'd somehow inserted an identifier into their 'speech' to allow this.

"We are here to tell you," it continued, "that it is almost time. Soon there will be a battle between ourselves and the Cetra, those you call the Forerunners. You will not be involved."

"But we're already involved," the colonel said, "and what do you mean, it's almost time?"

All three Sken faced Delmar. "Exactly that. This battle was predicted long before your race, but until now our forces have been spread thinly due to our explorations and it has taken time to assemble. We have travelled great distances to be here but have finally gathered ourselves for what must come. This is between ourselves, those you call the Manta, and our common adversary. You Humans are diverse. Some of you are fighting on the side of the enemy, so having you there could be confusing. It would be unfortunate if there were some ... misunderstandings."

Finally, the bulky shape of Skar's face swung towards Selena and the colonel. An orange orb appeared above its right shoulder and span into life. There it remained like a swirling blood-moon. "Before they went away, the Sken warned the enemy to control themselves. The Cetra ignored this and we were forced to engage them in the Sken's absence, to protect both the other races and ourselves. Eventually they were defeated, but have now grown strong again by using your people. We intend to stop them. Now, once and for all."

"We would like to be of help," Van Pluy said. "I'm sure that—"

"No!" Small as the Sken were, the power of their answer reverberated in Selena and the others' skulls, causing them to wince. "You will *not* interfere. No mercy will be shown to any human vessels in the area."

"Shadow here agrees with what they're saying," Selena said, addressing her superiors. "The Lenars advise us to stay well out of the way."

"He speaks for all of them?" Colonel Delmar asked.

"He does."

"It appears we have no choice," Van Pluy said, chewing at his lip while his reddening face displayed his frustration. "I'll inform the Assembly of Worlds that we are to stay out of this, and are only to act to defend ourselves."

"You will be held to that," one of the Sken replied, wings fluttering like those of a hummingbird. "Do not disappoint us, for we will not take responsibility for any Human casualties or vessels destroyed. You have been told."

"While you're here," Selena said, breaking the sudden deathly silence, "we have a problem you might be able to help us with. We believe the Forerunners have a base hidden on this world. They've destroyed some of our cities, and, while we have the means to detect individuals up close, we need to find out where their headquarters are and eliminate them, before this happens again. Could you help us locate them?"

"The matter is already in hand," the Sken said. "We detected them as we entered this system."

"Could you let us know where they are?" Selena asked, hopefully.

"As I said, the matter is being dealt with. We know you fight them, and so on this one occasion we are being merciful to you."

"What's that supposed to mean?" Delmar's eyes flashed. "We're supposed to be on the same side. We could lose another city at any moment!"

Without another word, the Sken rose a foot or so and, as one, turned and fluttered through the suddenly opened door, much to the consternation of the guards in the corridor outside.

"Did you see that?" whispered the colonel. "How the hell did they open the doors? Only we have access to the controls."

Selena shrugged. She had more important issues to worry about.

Skar stood and followed the Sken out. But at the door, he paused and looked back. "Do not stand between the Sken and the enemy, for their rage is absolute."

"Skar, we are also enemies of the ForeRunners," Admiral Van Pluy said. "We'd like to help."

The huge Manta faced the screen. "You are descendants of the Cetra and others of you are allied to them. You are lucky the Sken have not exterminated you and obliterated your worlds, as is their right." Skar paused, as if to consider.

"The Sken, ourselves and the Cetra were once the guardians. We nurtured emerging civilisations and guided them into the light of true consciousness. There was peace in the universe and mostly all got along, until the Sken decided to leave us and explore the deep. It was then that the Cetra changed. They began exterminating many of the new races. We tried to protect them but were almost destroyed ourselves, for the Sken had taught the enemy well. We defeated them in the end and peace reigned once again. Hibernation was called for. We were exhausted."

Selena found she was holding her breath, heart hammering. "We disturbed you."

"Yes. You, a fledgling race born from the ashes of our old enemy. We believed you were the Cetra returning, but now we know better. Advice, do not anger the Sken."

Like the others, she knew if the Jellies wanted they could destroy them easily, and there was nothing they could do about it.

Colonel Delmar faced Van Pluy as Skar lumbered from the room. "Sir, what do you make of all that?"

"I say we're damn lucky the Sken weren't around when we were battling the Manta in the first place. I don't think we'd be here now, if they were."

"Or maybe they would have told the Manta we weren't the ForeRunners, and stopped them attacking us," Selena said. "It could have gone either way but my money would be on the former."

They watched on the screens, as the Sken flew slowly into the sides of their vessel and it lifted from Capulet's spaceport. It rose rapidly and merged with the orbiting mothership. Without warning the oil-black amoebic vessel spat three small globules towards the planet, a pause and then three more. That done the craft swerved out of orbit, speed increasing rapidly.

"What the hell," Delmar gasped. "Shields up!"

Selena shook her head. "I don't think we need to worry, Colonel, I've seen this before. Besides, those projectiles aren't heading towards our cities."

Even as the shields glimmered overhead and sirens sounded, flashes lit up the sky as the globules impacted in the wilderness. Screens switched to show orbital images of the swathes of destruction, forests flattened and what had been an entire mountain turned to a cloud of settling dust and tumbling rocks. One of the projectiles had hit on the coastline, where a basin was now swiftly filling with sea water.

"Can someone tell me what just happened?" Delmar asked.

Shadow looked up into Selena's eyes and she felt what he knew.

"Our ForeRunner problem is solved. After all, we did ask the Sken for help. Shadow here tells me they have destroyed an enemy base, plus two of their vehicles. I have a feeling that the Sken are going to find the enemy, no matter where they hide. Somehow, I feel almost sorry for them."

They watched as, with no visible sign of propulsion, the Sken craft disappeared from the system.

The colonel straightened. "Let's hope you're right. We'll get some teams out to those sites to poke around. In the meantime, I know it's unlikely but there could be one or two of the enemy or their agents still about, so keep security at maximum. Admiral?"

"In my opinion, the commander is correct," Van Pluy answered. "The Sken used those weapons when we carried out a joint attack on an enemy world, having travelled there via the Eden tunnel system. Commander Dillon saw it happen, she knows what she's talking about. Having said that, there's something about this whole scenario that I don't like. I have this nagging feeling they're keeping something from us."

Delmar looked at Selena, questioningly.

"I have to agree with the admiral, Ma'am. But I'm more than happy for us to stay out of it, that way we won't incur any casualties or lose any ships. Let them battle it out amongst themselves, while we wait and see what happens."

As the admiral signed off, Selena turned to the colonel. "Ma'am, to change tack, is there any news about the murders?"

"None. All we know is that all the victims are all young females and this only started a few months ago. We've been unable to trace any victims prior to that."

Selena looked at the colonel. "Doesn't mean there weren't any, or that we just that we can't find them? If what you say is true, it could be the killer is one of the new colonists or workers. I'd like to review the records of all new arrivals for the past six months."

"Very well, let me know what you find."

Moments later Selena found herself walking down the stark-white corridors of the citadel's main building, noting how many who saw her coming stepped to one side. *Scary lady*, Jas had said. She wondered if people really saw her that way and, if so, why? She was only doing her job, they all were. Entering a lift, she got out at the ground floor and left the building through the white-framed glass doors, walking slowly back to her office. Her feet crunched on the dull-gray chips of stone that graced the pathways, while small clouds of dust rose with each step to coat her boots. When she arrived, Selena was surprised to see Singh sitting in one of her office chairs waiting for her.

"What are you doing here?"

"I thought you might like to come with me, to see Braxis," he replied, black-booted feet swinging back and forth.

"Did you?"

"Yup. I'm betting he doesn't get many visitors and I'm sure he'd appreciate it."

She glanced at the bag he was holding. "What's that?"

"Grapes."

"You're kidding me. You're actually going to give them to him?"

"No, I'm going to throw them at him."

She snorted and briefly eyed the brimming coffee pot waiting on the side. Pushing the temptation away she said, "Okay, let's go."

"I heard about the Sken vessel," Singh said, as they walked. "Any new developments we should know about?"

"We don't have to worry about any more cities being destroyed. The Jellies picked up the ForeRunners hiding here from orbit, and got rid of them for us—a bit like pest control, I guess."

Singh grinned. "That's damned good news and a lot off our minds. Are we sure they got them all?"

"Positive," Selena said. "I've a feeling they knew exactly what to look for, and could pick up a flea hidden on a planet. They got the ForeRunners all right. From the impression I received earlier, they hate them and would have made sure of it. That said, the colonel wants our units to remain in place. You never know, others could slip in."

When they arrived, Braxis was sat up in bed, a huge pink cocoon covering his new left arm, chest and shoulder. A servo-med stood next to him, flickering lights and odd sounds monitored his vital signs while the machine itself administered whatever meds were required via the tubes plugged in here and there. On seeing them, his eyes lit up, then he looked concerned. "Hey, how you doing? Umm, everything's all right, isn't it?"

"We've not discovered any of your scams, if that's what you're thinking," Selena replied. "Singh simply suggested that we pop in and say hi, see how you're doing."

"It's all good," Braxis said. A smile tugged at his lips, as he caught the bag Singh lobbed at him one handed before peeping inside. "Hey grapes, thanks." He looked to where a nurse hovered nearby and whispered conspiratorially, "You see that cute blonde over there?"

They looked, noticing how the nurse had been covertly watching them while she tapped at her hand-held. At their glances, she quickly averted her eyes and turned to attend the other person in the double room, reddening visibly at Braxis's smirk.

"Tell me you didn't," Selena said, eyebrows rising in surprise. "Not in your state, surely?"

The big man's grin broadened. "Takes more than this to keep me down, Ma'am."

"It's true, Commander," Singh interjected. "I've known that nurse for a long time and we spoke briefly in the café earlier, when I asked her if fuck nuts here was up to seeing visitors. She said yes, it would be good for him. She also told me it's the best sex she's had since she was a man."

Braxis' face went slack, his eyes widened and his breath released audibly. The smile vanished and his lips moved but no words came out.

"You're obviously doing well," Selena said, straight faced. "I guess we can look forward to you re-joining the unit before too long." She patted his good arm and they left the room, unable to stop their snorts of laughter echoing down the gleaming white corridors.

\*\*\*

When Selena entered her flat she saw that bagged items had been flung around the room. The percolator lay smashed on the floor, coffee painting everything around them.

"Jas, what's going on?"

"I thought that with me being with you, things would be different," she replied.

"In what way? Tell me what's happened."

"I hoped that people would treat me decently, leave me alone. But oh no…"

"For heaven's sake, sit down and spill the beans!"

Jas threw herself onto the sofa and stared up at Selena, tears in her dark brown eyes. "I bought the food, like you asked and was really looking forward to cooking a meal with you. Then I went into the clothes shop next to that new haberdashery, the one catering for new build houses out in the wilds."

"Okay," Selena said, sitting next to her and speaking softly, in a reassuring tone. "And then what?"

"I didn't see anything I liked, so the owner showed me some holographic items that had my image modelling them. I saw some that looked fab and ordered them. That big fat slug asked me to come back in an hour, saying that's when they'd be ready. When I returned, he told me to go into the changing room and try them on. I didn't hear him when he came in. I had my back to him and my arms up in the air trying to put this dress on. He came up behind me, grabbed my breasts and rubbed himself against my ass."

Selena clenched her fists and said tightly, "Then what?"

"I turned and shouted at him, pushing him away from me. He fell out through the changing room curtains. There was someone else in the shop, so I dressed in my own stuff and walked out, calling him a pervert and throwing his items at him."

"I'm surprised you didn't stab him with those knives of yours."

"I'd taken them off to try on the clothes and hidden them in my shoes, I didn't want anyone seeing them. Besides if I had stabbed him I'd have ended up like you, sentenced to twenty-five years in the Penal Regiments just because some paedo bastard grabbed a handful of tit. But he's got it coming. He'll get his, don't you worry about that."

"You did the right thing but leave it be," Selena said quietly, trying to control her breathing. "Revenge can leave a bitter taste in your mouth and cause more trouble than it's worth, particularly at this moment in time when we're trying to get the local authorities to take care of you guys. I'll talk with them, and word will spread. Here, help me pick this lot up off the floor and tidy up this mess."

When the kitchen was a lot tidier, Selena handed Jas a kitchen knife. "I have to go speak to Baron, and tell him about what's been happening with the Sken. They got the ForeRunners on this world, they're all dead; so no more destroyed cities, at least in the short term. While I'm out, you start prepping dinner. Peel the potatoes and wash the other vegetables too. The last thing we want is food poisoning."

"I'll be fine," Jas replied, busying herself with the veg while wiping away a tear. "Just don't be long."

Selena came back forty-five minutes later, gave Jas a hug and looked at the vegetables. "Hey, good job! What we do now is steam those and mix them with the mince, garlic, a few herbs and—"

The wall screen chirped and Selena groaned audibly. "On," she commanded.

Colonel Delmar looked at her intently. "Been busy, have we, Commander?"

"Don't know what you mean, Ma'am."

"Don't lie to me! Can you tell me why you went into a hardware store in town a short while ago, bought a hammer and a handful of very large nails, and then nailed the owner of the shop next door to the outside of his premises by his scrotum?"

Jas looked at Selena, eyes widening.

"He sexually assaulted Jas. I won't have that, I was just sending a message."

"And what might that be? You also stripped him and carved *paedophile* across his chest and stomach—had those cuts been any deeper, his guts would have fallen out."

"I don't like paedo's and that scumbag got what he deserved," Selena said, calmly. "People will think twice about such things from now on, and whoever is killing these children now knows that I'm after him."

"Him? Well, I've no doubt that message was received. Just so that you know, the medics were unable to get the nails out of the wall. In the end, they had to cut the heads off of them and pull him free, leaving the rest of the metal there. There's still blood and pieces of his flesh on the wall. I'm guessing you'll want that to remain."

"Indeed, nothing like a little reminder. Now, if that's all Colonel, we're in the middle of cooking dinner."

"No, that is not all, Commander." Delmar looked angry for a moment, and then awkward. Taking a deep breath, she hurried on. "I've had a complaint from the Queen's Council. It appears two of your staff, Lieutenant

Roberts and Philips, have been seen cavorting in public. The Council has pointed out that relationships are strictly against our regulations."

Selena stared at her. "Are you serious?"

"Of course I am. Look, you and I both know it happens, just tell them to keep it quiet."

"Or what, charge them both with misuse of government property? They're not the only ones 'misbehaving', are they Ma'am?"

"Commander," Delmar said in chilling tones. "Mind your place! As your senior officer, I'm duty bound to ensure you resolve this and it's your responsibility to take what action is appropriate. Are we clear?"

"Perfectly, Colonel. Thank you, I'll deal with it."

When the wall screen had blinked out, Jas said quietly, "Talk about sending a message…"

Selena smirked. "He did make a bit of a fuss. Men, huh?"

"Yeah," Jas replied. "Men."

# Chapter Six

*"Can't we increase speed?" Selena demanded.*

*"We're at full throttle now and still accelerating, Ma'am.'" Bryn replied.*

*"They're on the surface," Arthur informed them through the speakers. "Some of their ships have gotten through and landed." At his command, the image on one of the screens changed to show the Dutch Lady's frozen outer shell, where the Manta vessels could be seen landing and disgorging bugs draped in some sort of protective suits. They watched in dread and fascination as the enemy stalked the surface, looking for a way in.*

*"Ugly fuckers, aren't they," Kes noted, raking them with fire from several of the many Gatling turrets. But more and more of them were filing from the alien craft and returning fire at the weapon emplacements.*

*"Guys," Za'an said thoughtfully, "if they're letting their troops off, won't they have to drop their shields to do so?"*

*There was a moments silence from Kes and Za'an and then the guns retargeted. Rounds of ammunition and powerful beams slammed into the enemy ships, blowing them to smithereens. The countless explosions didn't even make the Dutch Lady wobble, but the shrapnel from the exploding ships sliced through the enemy ranks, like a scythe through corn, heavily depleting their numbers.*

*Alarms burst into life, their clamour deafening.*

*They're in the ship!*

Selena awoke, screaming. Jas was on top of her, trying to hold her shoulders down with her body weight as she tossed and turned, keeping Selena's deadly hands trapped beneath the bedcover.

"Wake up, it's me, Jas! You're having a nightmare!"

Selena went rigid, and then forced herself to relax. Her body slackened as she realized that Jas was right, it was in the past, their battle to destroy the Manta's home world. The memory of Bryn dying hit her again, and she couldn't stop the tears. Jas held her until her sobs subsided and then she let her go, silently sliding off the bed.

"Sorry, yeah like you say, it was just a nightmare. I get them, sometimes," Selena said, wiping fruitlessly at the river of sweat drenching her face, and putting her walls back up.

"I'll go make some coffee, that'll perk you up," Jas replied, padding barefoot from the bedroom.

"Okay, I'll be there in a minute." Breathing deeply Selena closed her eyes and focused. Just a nightmare, that's all. She breathed deeply; the thudding of her heart slowly subsided, the feeling of weight on her shoulders and chest eased and gradually she found herself breathing normally. As the scent of fresh coffee perfuming the air she left her bed, threw some water over her face and put on a thin white dressing gown colourfully hand-embroidered with local birdlife, belting it around her waist. She wondered how things were going but it was still far too early to call in. Besides, if there had been any news she knew that someone would have called her, despite the hour.

"Good morning. I know it's only six but, given we're both awake, I've made breakfast," Jas said, as Selena entered the kitchen. "Well, toast ... and it's a bit scorched."

"Sorry if I woke you," Selena said.

"You didn't. Listen, I know this isn't the best time to tell you, what with your nightmares and all, but I've had some bad news that you need to know about. I had a call from the hospital, which is what woke me up, to tell me my friend Lucy has been admitted. Another girl, called Sebo, has been murdered and Lucy saw what happened and flipped. We all carry a contact list and that's how they got hold of me." Jas poured the coffee and offered her a steaming mug.

Selena wrinkled her nose at the acrid smell and took a tentative bite of the toast lurking on the plate Jas put before her. "I'm sorry to hear that. How is she, and are you okay?"

"I don't know much, and yeah, I'm fine. I spent all my tears a long time ago."

Selena forced herself to swallow. Although she was concerned about Jas's friend, she was secretly pleased that Jas had taken on the task of making breakfast. It was a win-win situation and she'd get the hang of it. Jas now had a regular task and she herself woke with a meal. "So, tell me about Lucy," she said, putting aside her plate. "I thought you'd said they'd all come in."

"I'm sorry, but I lied. There were a few who didn't want to, including these two, and I couldn't break their trust. They were scared and who can blame them? Afraid they'd be forced to come in and find themselves trapped in a room. Ironic, isn't it? They thought they'd be safer outside, where they could run away if need be. Lucy was with Sebo, a friend of hers who wasn't feeling well; and while she stayed in the doorway, Lucy went to get them both something to eat."

Selena sized Jas up. She'd bulked out a bit, but even so still looked skinny. "What else did the hospital say?"

Jas continued to avoid her eyes. "That Lucy was found babbling and crying by a woman out shopping late at night, to avoid the rush hours. When the medics arrived, Lucy told them that when she'd returned she saw someone bent over her friend, cutting her open. As she was telling them about it, Lucy started screaming and didn't stop. They had to sedate her and take her to hospital, which is when they found the contact list. That's all I know, apart from when they found Sebo a short while later she was already dead, gutted like all of the others."

"Okay," Selena said. "Try to relax, you're safe here."

"But it could have been me!" Jas cried. "I know that sounds awful and that I should be focusing more on what happened to them, and I am, but … me?"

"Yes, it could have been you, but it wasn't. That's what you need to keep telling yourself. Look around; see the things in this room? Go and touch them, are they rough or smooth? Taste them, smell them – and remember you're here now and that you're safe."

Selena slid her right arm around Jas, who leaned into her. "I'm going to see this friend Lucy. I'll try not to be too long, but don't worry if I am. You can call me if need be and I'll be back as quickly as possible." She knew that there was only one hospital in the city, so Lucy should be easy to find. "I'll let you know how she is when I get back. In the meantime, remember, stay here."

Jas fought back tears, clenched her fists and compressed her lips. She said slowly, "I don't think anything could make me go outside at the moment anyhow."

Selena hugged Jas again, and took a swig of her coffee. She swallowed and said. "Listen, it'll all be over soon. Trust me, we'll catch the person responsible."

At that moment, the door chimed and Selena wasn't surprised to see Jenks on the viewer. She let him in, saying, "It's okay, I already know. In fact, I'm going to get dressed, then go to the hospital, you might as well tag along." In no time at all, she'd zipped her all in one right up to the collar and led the way.

Selena eyed him as they got into the lift. "As the saboteur issue's settled, I guess you coming here means we're working together on these murders."

"We are. Do you want to know what I think?"

"Do tell."

Jenks turned to face her. "I think the ForeRunners are behind these killings. They can't reproduce, remember? This way they get reproductive organs, to try and fix the issues they have."

"I've considered that, and the possibilities top of my list. With the ForeRunnerrs not able to bear children, it means race diminution. Got to stock up from somewhere I guess. But then they were all killed by the Sken, and these murders were last night, which means the killer is human." Selena wafted a hand in front of her nose and grimaced. "Hey, what the hell is that smell—is that you?"

Jenks nodded. "Yup, it's the latest from 'Salam'. Apparently, it's Phenomes women can't resist."

"In that case," Selena said. "Trust me, you were robbed. You smell like gorilla piss. If you turned up on a date smelling like that, I'd stab you."

Jenks looked confused. "What the hell's a gorilla?"

"Think of Braxis, only much hairier."

"Uh, okay. And another thing. If I turned up for a blind date and found it was you, you needn't worry. I'd stab myself."

They were at the hospital within thirty-five minutes, facing a wary-looking human receptionist instead of the expected robosec, much to Selena's delight. Above and behind the battleship of a woman there was a white sign with bright-blue lettering, declaring *Human receptionist, we care for humanity.*

"I'm Commander Dillon from the Regiments. A girl was brought here by ambulance, name of Lucy. Where is she?"

"Ayuh," the woman replied. "Lucy Wilson. Are you a relative?"

"Do I look like a fucking relative?"

"I'll take that as a no," the receptionist said coolly, eyeing Selena's black uniform and matching eyes before visibly shuddering. Smoothing both hands along her too tight dark-blue nurses top, as if to clear away any dirt, she said, "In which case you can't see her."

"Now you listen here," Selena snarled, leaning forward across the sparkling-white worktop that melded perfectly into the wall. "I'm working on these murders and need to see this patient, and that means immediately. There's a lot of dead kids so far, and more dying by the day. So, tell me where she is right now or I'll come over there and beat the info out of you!"

The middle-aged woman stepped backwards, eyes widening. Jenks flashed a badge at her.

"Pardon my friend, she hasn't had breakfast," he said. "You'll see I have clearance at the highest level and we two work together. Now, as the commander says, we need to see Lucy immediately."

"Zed ward, room five," the receptionist said hurriedly, obviously relieved at finding a way out of the situation. "First floor, you can't miss it."

"Tetchy this morning, are you?" Jenks murmured as they walked to the lift.

"Sod off."

"Roger that," he replied, looking both surprised and a little hurt.

When they got out of the lift a signpost pointed them along to the left. In the long white corridor, which stretched into a curve until it disappeared, there was little décor—apart from an occasional chair or two besides ward entrances, placed at regular intervals. When they reached the ward they again faced a human guard, who was sat at his desk reading from what looked like an antique E-Reader. Above the door, a sign proclaimed in large red letters, "Secure Unit, Zed Ward". Selena eyed Jenks, who shrugged.

Again flashing his badge, Jenks' said, "We're here to see Lucy Wilson."

The guard huffed noisily and put down his pad. Taking Jenks' ID he scanned it in a leisurely fashion and opened the secure door by pressing a button hidden beneath his desk. "The doctor is with her at the moment," he said in a disinterested fashion. "She's in room five, which the third on your left as you go in. Please, wear these at all times." Without barely a glance he handed each of them a self-adhering lapel badge and went back to his book.

"Thanks," Jenks said, holding the electronic door open for Selena, as they attached their hospital badges and passed through.

A few steps later and they were outside the room they needed. Through an open door, they saw a blue-coated doctor bending over a small patient, buried beneath stark-white sheets. On the other side a servo-med stood guard, bleeping regularly. Gesturing for Selena to wait by the entrance, Jenks went in and talked quietly to the small, Asian-looking doctor. Together they came over to Selena, as she waited with fingers tapping on the door frame.

"So, how is she?" Selena asked.

"Not in a good place, as you can imagine," the doctor replied peering up at her, his hair and beard in a hygiene net. "She's under sedation."

Selena bit back a retort at his short response. "Has she said anything that might help us find the killer?"

"All we've managed to get from her is that she and a friend had been sharing a doorway in a secluded back alley, not too far from a well-known food outlet. One who was kind enough to give them whatever leftovers they had. Lucy went to get food and was on her way back when she heard the other girl screaming."

Selena sighed, resisting the urge to grab hold of the man's beard. "And?"

"Lucy says that's when she turned a corner and saw her friend Sebo laying on the ground, trying to fight someone off. There was blood everywhere and this person was bending over her. I'm afraid Sebo was already dead when our paramedics reached her."

"Look, tell us something we don't know."

The doctor raised one eyebrow and continued. "She initially thought the killer had been trying to help. It was only when Lucy ran over to see what was happening that she saw the blood and realised her friend had been stabbed, or rather that her stomach had been slashed open. Then, she says, the demon who did it turned towards her, a bloodied knife in hand."

"Did you say demon?" Selena asked, finding she was holding her breath.

"That's right," the doctor replied, eyeing Selena up and down. "Dressed all in black apparently. Holes in the face where the eyes should be. 'A shadow that moves in the dark,' she later said."

"Say what?" Selena asked, eyes narrowing.

"I guess the killer looked like you, or rather…"

"My God, it's one of us," Selena gasped. "Someone from the Penal Regiments has been doing the killings!"

"That makes sense," Jenks replied, raising his eyebrows. "Trouble is which one? There's thousands of you guys here, it could be anyone of you."

Lucy stirred feebly and tried to rise to her elbows. Her eyes opened, focused and widened. She gagged and scrambled backwards up the bed, pushing herself into the wall, where she began shrieking at the top of her voice.

"Demon, demon! *Please … help me!*"

The doctor rushed back to Lucy, along with two nurses hurrying from adjoining rooms. The nurses tried to hold the girl down as the doctor administered meds. The doctor said something to one of the nurses who practically ran to the door and shut it in their faces. Selena and Jenks faced each other, neither saying anything.

Behind the closed door, they heard Lucy's shouts turned to sobs. The ruckus quieted abruptly, as they turned and left. Selena and Jenks went through the ward entrance and returned their passes to the disinterested guard.

"Well I guess that gives us something to work on, Commander," Jenks said briskly and they retraced their steps. "Looks like you've a wolf in your midst. All we need to do now is track it down."

"And exterminate it," Selena concluded. "That's a pelt I want on my wall, no matter what the cost or what the law has to say about it."

\*\*\*

"Are you certain of this?" Delmar asked in astonished disbelief.

"As much as we can be, Ma'am," Selena replied, Jenks nodding silently beside her.

"That's … rather inconvenient."

"Inconvenient, are you mad? People are dead!" Selena said, harshly. "We've no idea why these murders started, let alone why it's children who are being chosen."

"From what Lucy said, it's quite clear that it's someone from the regiments, probably a new arrival," Jenks said, calmly. "Which would explain the why now. We can easily trace them, but we need to run a check on what they were sentenced for."

"Could be anyone," Selena replied. "Take me, for example."

"Hardly," Jenks replied. "You've been here many times, were born here, and there's no record of such events during those periods—or any others while you were at other posts."

"My God, you've checked me out, haven't you!"

"It's my job to be thorough, Commander. Someone of power, such as yourself, would in an ideal position. I know it's not you; your sense of integrity also rules you out. Now, all that aside, the question is what time frame do we consider recent—a couple of months, maybe five or six? After all, whoever it is might not have started killing immediately."

"I'll look into it," Delmar said. "Target all troopers who arrived three months prior to the first killing. If it *is* one of us, we need to find who and stop them, fast. Word will get out, no matter what we do, and soon. After all, people talk. Particularly civilians such as the medical staff, and we can't have this disrupting our recent good press. The description Lucy gave fits all of us to a tee, so go find us our killer, Commander. Do whatever it takes."

"In that case," Selena said, "I need to check what those people were convicted of, personally. There might be a lead there and you've too much on your plate as it is. To do that I need your permission."

"Ah, what you're saying is that you want access to their personal records. That's not the way we do things in the Regiments Commander, and you know that. Only the officer in charge of each unit, and their direct seniors, have access to the records of the troops under their command. Those are the rules."

"With respect, Ma'am, screw the rules. They're made to be broken."

"Oh really?" Delmar said, lips thinning and black-tinted alloy nails tapping away at her desktop. "I'm not going to change procedure just to suit you. They're on a need to know basis for a reason, confidentiality. Once a trooper's sentence is served they're released back into society with a new identity, if they wish it. It's only on that release that they discover there's a five-year reserve time, which means if they commit another crime it's activated and added to any sentence. Quite a deterrent against re-offending, wouldn't you say?"

"For heaven's sake!" Selena exploded. "I need to see those files, you've put me in charge of this case and I can't do my job properly with my hands tied behind my back. If that's going to be the case, with all due respect, I suggest you get someone else to do it—or do it yourself."

"Careful, Commander," Delmar replied in a deathly voice. "You don't get to vote on this in a room full of happy-clappy citizens. You will do as you're told. Despite what you obviously think, you follow orders—the same as everyone else." She took a deep breath and fought to calm herself. "But I concede your point. I'll grant the access to the files. To both of you."

"What, to Jenks?"

"Yes, you're working on this together, remember? He's also in the Intelligence Corps and has access to areas that you don't," Delmar said. "And unlike you, he's never been convicted of a criminal act in his life. Now both of you get out, and get on with it."

"Very well," Selena said stiffly, coming to attention and saluting. "We'll let you know when we get anything." She turned sharply and left Delmar's office biting her lip, Jenks at her side.

"Don't take offence," Selena said, as their boots crunched across the parade ground. "None was intended. I'm just trying to limit access to personal data, that's all."

"Don't worry, I've a thick hide," Jenks replied. "Let me buy you a coffee."

Entering a café, Jenks ordered lattes, while Selena selected a sofa with its back to the wall and a clear view of the room. A small wicker table stood in front of it, like a barrier to the inquisitive. There were few customers in the place, and several of those got up and left when they walked in.

Selena graced Jenks with a slight smile as he returned from the bar with their coffees. "Sorry if I was a bit off, I'm a tad tetchy. In a previous mission one of my team turned out to be a serial killer up to his old tricks again. The killer, Za'an, was a really sick bastard—a hired assassin who used to keep bits of his victims for a snack."

"I didn't hear about that part," Jenks replied, visibly shocked.

"Yeah, well I guess they kept it quiet 'for the good of mankind'. We were heroes, apparently. Despite how many of us died, and we didn't know until right at the end that our mission was simply a diversion. Sure, we blew up the Manta's world and drew attention while another ship hit their sun and destroyed the entire system. But a nest ship escaped and command didn't get our message about it, so the bugs survived. What a waste of lives."

"I wouldn't say that, Selena. What you did was hellishly brave."

"Huh, we were told the enemy couldn't live without the crops they grew on their home world, something to do with minerals in the soil. The Manta didn't know about that little bit of information, until they captured one of our ships and accessed their files. How ironic is that?"

Selena found herself biting her lip again, realising it was becoming a habit. Aunt May would have soon sorted that out. Annoyed at herself, she continued.

"Za'an eventually got his. The wife of Arthur, another member of our crew, was a victim of his. Arthur was a genius and he'd wrangled his way into the team just to get even with him. I found out about his plans during the mission and we struck a deal. He wasn't to touch the killer until it was all over, then he could do whatever he chose. Arthur kept his word, bless him. He killed Za'an when the lifeboat crash landed, saved me a job."

Selena shook her head trying to clear bitter memories, the gunfire and horror of the crash still echoing in her ears. This was far too close to home. An image flashed to mind of Samantha laying on the floor, stomach ripped open and her guts hanging out as she clutched at Arthur's hand, staring wildly into his eyes, tears trickling down her cheeks even as she died.

Their lifeboat bucked as it ploughed through the atmosphere of that unknown world. Brilliant crimson flames roared past the port holes, the deafening atmospheric scream rising in their ears. Their craft pitched and turned over, and then … nothing.

Bryn. Bryn was dead.

She felt a hand on her shoulder, and someone shake her gently.

"Commander, are you all right—*whoa!*"

Selena had grabbed Jenk's hand and twisted it into an arm lock, slamming him face down onto the table top, spilling their drinks. Her knife was already pressed against the side of his throat, blood trickling in a thin line onto the table from its pressure against his bare flesh.

"Commander?" he said, tentatively.

Slowly Selena came back to herself and looked at the frightened barista and other patrons watching them. Thinking quickly, she sheathed her knife, pulled Jenks back by the scruff of his neck and dumped him back onto the sofa. Dusting him down, she said loudly, "Guys, you'd think he'd know better."

"No shit," Jenks coughed, as he struggled to regain his composure. "You broke my nose!"

Selena reached forwards. "Hang on. Brace yourself, I'll reset it."

At the horrible grating crunch and accompanying gasp of pain, several more patrons got up and left.

Selena gave him a serviette, which he held to the blood flowing from his nose. Gesturing to the barista, she said, "Let me get some fresh coffees, you seem to have spilt the others."

With the serviette now a deep red, Jenks changed it for another and touched his fingers to the slight cut on his neck. "Jesus, remind me never to piss you off."

"Sorry," she murmured to Jenks, somewhat abashed. "Word to the wise, don't grab hold of me like that again."

"Really?" he replied, sardonically. Regarding her quietly for a moment though pain filled eyes, he said. "You know, even though your eyes are as dark as the night, and hard to read, there's something quite chilling in them. I take it you don't get out much."

"As it happens, no, I don't."

They looked up as the man replaced their drinks and swiftly stepped back.

"It's on the house," the fellow managed, as Selena simply looked at him. "As always! Can I offer you anything else?"

"Just some space. Get lost," she said, sharply.

Jenks watched the rapidly retreating man. He coughed again, this time into the back of one hand. Eyes watering, he leaned closer. "Are you all right, Commander?"

"Peachy," she replied. "I think your nose is better that way, although you always looked like a very bad boxer. Now, don't be a baby and let's take a look at these records." Using their hand-helds, they paged through the files of troopers who'd arrived on Capulet in the past few months.

Jenks reached for another serviette and then froze. "Hey, this guy looks good."

"Who is it," she asked, eyes widening as she put down her hand-held and grabbed his. She snorted. "Staff? No way."

"Do you know that for sure?" he asked, his gray eyes looking into hers searchingly. "We can't screw this up. If you're one hundred percent positive, then we'll move on. If not, then let's get him in and check him out. Says here he was an enforcer for organised crime, was caught red-handed battering someone who owed his boss gambling money."

Selena was surprised. She took a taste of her bitter-sweet coffee. "Staff an enforcer for the mob, seriously? Guess that explains his bad attitude. Not that I suspect him but I'll get surveillance bees to monitor him, just to be sure. He's unlikely to notice them at a distance, or in the dark. But none of this makes sense. He's afraid of the Lenars because they remind him of the big cat that killed his sister, so it's unlikely he'd come into the city where he could run into them. Given all that, how could he have killed those girls?"

"You have to remember it could all be an act," Jenks replied. "It won't hurt to check him out, and there's no mention of his sister's death in any of the records. Tell you what, let me look into him." Jenks rubbed at the graying stubble on his chin with a soft rasping sound. "If there's anything there, I'll find it. Should be relatively easy, I'll get right onto it."

Just then Selena's hand-held bleeped. She looked down and snorted.

"Good news?" Jenks asked.

"Depends which way you look at it. Braxis has been released from the hospital, light duties by the look of it. I can't see him standing for that."

\*\*\*

"Come in." Selena looked up at the sharp knock from her temporary desk in the training camp. Apart from Staff, they'd only found three other possible suspects, but they were still looking.

To her left, Jenks glanced at his handhold and said, "Sorry Commander, I've got to go. Duty calls, so if you don't mind I'll have to leave you to it." He stood to one side as the door opened and Staff marched in. Then he left, closing the door behind him.

Standing to attention in front of Selena, Staff saluted. He looked straight ahead, eyes cold, fists clasped at his sides. "You asked for me, Ma'am?"

"So's to speak. Tell me, Staff, I know I've no right to ask under our current rules and regulations, but I have to. Why were you sentenced to the Penal Corps?"

"You're entirely correct," Staff grated, obviously trying to rein in his temper. "You have no right to ask me that. But as you're my Commander, you'll have seen the official records. You need to know that they don't reflect everything. I didn't volunteer for the regiments, unlike some of our members, I was sentenced for committing a crime."

"Which was?" She waited.

"One that I was guilty of, that's all I'll say. I deserve to be punished for what I did. They gave me forty years' servitude, and when I get out I'll not re-offend. I'll be an old man, if I live that long."

Selena looked him up and down, lip curling and all respect lost. "Don't try to hide behind your rights and sympathy seeking. I've been given access to all necessary files because of necessity, including yours. Apart from being a mob enforcer, you're a paedophile. You were sentenced for abducting and killing young boys. Isn't that correct?"

His fists tightened, eyes spitting fire. "Partly."

"You were caught in the act."

"No, I was framed," he said, with a smirk.

"Don't fuck with me, Staff, I'm not in the mood. Why did you kill these girls?"

His eyes widened and abruptly he laughed. "Girls? I don't kill girls. Don't you read the information that's in front of you? It was young boys I did in. I admitted it and I've been punished accordingly. But it wasn't paedophilia, so get your facts right. Don't you think I'd have killed girls beforehand, if that was my want?"

Selena didn't flinch. "Not necessarily. So, why boys?"

"Because those little bastards I did in deserved it. Each of them were from my sister's school. They bullied her constantly. Apart from beating her up, they sexually molested her on a daily basis, until she ran away. I didn't know anything about that until it was too late. She must have been desperate because she knew where she tried to hide was a tiger sanctuary. It was in one of the few areas that had survived the devastation from the Independence Wars. Those creatures ate her, they ate my sister..."

Selena was shocked to see tears in his eyes. One trickled a lonely path down his cheek.

"My parents and I only discovered what had been going on when we found her note. I couldn't save her from the tigers, but I made sure she was revenged. By doing so I saved other girls from similar treatment at those monsters' hands. Unfortunately for me, their parents were very well connected, so my sister's death was hushed up and I was framed as a paedophile. They threw the book at me and I have never hurt a girl in my life. So why would I now? If anything, I'm your least likely suspect."

Selena was silent for a moment or two, giving him chance to settle down. The memories were obviously hard for him. Eventually, she said, "I had to ask because you were a killer in civilian life. Our witness says the murderer wore black and had pitch-black eyes, 'like a demon's', she said."

"Who said?" Staff asked, looking confused.

"I told you, a witness."

"What did this witness say exactly?"

Selena told him, watching as he turned the information over in his mind. "So, let's get this straight. There was you and Jenks in the doorway, the girl sees you and all hell lets loose."

"That's right," Selena confirmed.

Staff stared at her. "It seems you're missing the obvious. The person in black was a woman, you. Which says to me that you aren't looking for a man, your killer's a female."

Selena felt sick, how could she have missed that? A woman, the killer was a woman! She leant back in her chair. "Holy shit!"

Staff's stance relaxed, his face softening. "For some reason people always assume serial killers are men, and given the averages over the past hundred years or so, who can blame them?"

"Staff, I'm—"

"Sorry, yeah, I know. But you're only doing your job. You're a damned good officer, Commander, and for your information, you've seriously pissed me off—but I understand that you need to find the killer and will do what needs to be done. If anyone ever asks whether I said any of those statements, I'll deny it. The question now is, what can I do to help?"

Selena's hand-held beeped. She picked it up. "Dillon, what is it? I told you I wasn't to be disturbed ... what?"

Stunned, Selena put down the hand-held and stared at it.

"Something wrong?"

"I'm sorry, Staff. The witness ... Lucy, she's dead. So is the duty nurse and the security guard outside the ward." She had a sudden vision of the guard studying his ancient E-Reader.

"Surely the security cameras will have caught the attacker."

"No," Selena replied with a frown. "For some reason they were all turned off, which is odd. Says here they're always on, which means someone must have had the facility to tamper with them."

"So, who do you know who has the access codes and authority to do that," Staff replied. "May I?" he gestured to the chair.

Selena nodded for him to sit down.

"Let's recap, Commander. You're looking for a female trooper, who has high security access. Who do you know who fits that description?"

"Only one, Jessica Roberts."

"Lieutenant Roberts, are you kidding me? I don't know what she was sentenced for, but she's no cold-hearted killer. I'd know."

Selena looked at him with despair, so much for men's intuition. "Staff, shut up. You've no idea what you're talking about. We're missing something and I can't quite put my finger on what it is. Let's go through the evidence together again. What do we know?"

"That you were stood in the doorway and Lucy shouted 'Demon', or whatever. The killer has access to high security and is probably a Regiment trooper."

Selena played the information over and over again, then she froze. Oh, my, God! "Staff, what if Lucy didn't shout 'demon' because of the black uniform but because she recognised the killer? It's not a woman, the killer's a man. Your law of probabilities was correct, and there were only two of us there at the time."

"Yes, you and … Jenks? He left as I came in, I saw him from the corner of my eye."

"But he has gray eyes, not black."

"Get real, Commander. He could wear contacts short term."

"That's true, and now our only witness has been killed. He must have known that Lucy recognised him at the door and that he had to silence her. It'd be easy for him to get one of our uniforms, and find out where the patrols in the city were whenever he needed, so he could skirt around them and kill at will. He must have bypassed the security protocols in the hospital and killed Lucy and the others. Staff, you're with me, now!"

Selena contacted Colonel Delmar via hand-held and informed her of their suspicions. As she and Staff ran outside they found her skimmer was missing. Luckily Staff's lay next to where hers had been and they quickly leapt aboard, with him at the controls.

"Colonel, can you find out where Jenks is right now?" Selena asked, shouting into the hand-held above the rising whine of the craft.

"Hang on."

The skimmer rose and Staff accelerated the craft to maximum speed, something to be avoided in case they hit something mid-flight, but now they had little choice. Selena watched on the hand-held's small screen as the colonel did something on her desk, no doubt tracing Jenks via his personal tracker and facial recognition software.

"That's odd, he's in the barracks. Seems to be approaching the accommodation block."

"He's going after Jas," Selena said jaw clenching, as the skimmer braked harshly and landed. She leapt over the side to run the short distance, followed by Staff.

As they ran, Selena alerted Singh and the others, telling them to meet her at the accommodation block.

She prayed they'd be in time.

Kes and the others arrived just as they did. "It's Jenks," she said. "He's the killer and he's after Jas— we have to stop him! Kes, Singh, get the building secured. The rest of you come with me."

They halted outside her apartment door. Holding a hand up Selena stopped the others. "Jessica, guard the door. Staff, you're with me."

Keying the room door open, she and Staff rushed inside and froze.

Jenks held Jas against the far kitchen wall, a knife pressed to her throat.

"Selena!" Jas gasped with relief.

"Shut it!" Jenks snapped, turning to glare at Selena and Staff, his face contorted with rage. "Stay where you are, or she dies."

"You were going to kill her anyway. The difference is, now we know that you're the killer, you don't stand a chance. This building is locked down and my troops are outside the room. You've nowhere to run, Jenks. I'd give up if I was you."

His steely-blue eyes shot back and forth, looking for a way out. But those eyes always came back to Selena, standing in front of him. His bearded jaw tightened and his unkempt mousy-hair shook as he spoke. "But you're not me, are you! It was going so well until you decided to interfere. I'm going to kill this kid, unless you let me go."

Staff's bottom lip jutted and he raised his sidearm and cocked it, his free hand pulling free a long wicked-looking knife from his knee-sheath. "If you hurt that girl, Jenks, I swear I'll cut out your eyeballs and skin you alive."

Selena glanced at Staff. *My God*, she thought, *he means it*. Staff was literally shaking with rage. "Hold on guys," she said soothingly, "let's all calm down. There's too much testosterone in this room for my liking."

"Aye," Jenks sneered, "and most of it's yours."

"Tell me," Selena asked, ignoring the jibe. "Why did you kill all those girls?"

"I gave you a hint, you stupid bitch. The Forerunners made me do it. I've no idea how but they'd discovered I'd murdered women in the past and had gotten away with it, so they blackmailed me."

Without warning, Jas kneed him in the groin and, as he gasped and doubled over in pain, she whipped one of her knives from her sleeve and rammed it into his left cheek, up to the hilt. As he screamed and reached up to claw the wound, she pushed him away and darted to safety, behind her friends.

Maddened with pain and shock, Jenks tore Jas's knife from his face. Still bent over and ignoring the blood gushing from his wound and mouth, he swung the knife in towards Selena as she advanced towards him. She ducked backwards, allowing the knife to pass her by. She quickly stepped in and her left hand dropped over the inside of his elbow, her right-hand slammed into the gripped knife, forcing the weapon back in and up towards his throat. Unbalanced, he stumbled backwards, finding himself trapped against the wall in the young girl's place.

"Get her out of here," Selena grated.

Behind her, Staff quickly escorted Jas out of the room, to the troops waiting outside, while Jessica came in and covered Jenks with her sidearm.

"Tell me what they wanted with those girls' body parts, Jenks. What did you do with them?"

When he replied, blood spattered from his lips and flowed down the ruins of his face. "The ForeRunners couldn't come into the cities themselves because they'd be discovered by the Lenars, so they forced me to do the work for them. They need those parts to try and find a cure for this affliction of theirs that stops them procreating."

He coughed and spat a mouthful of blood to one side. His tongue darted about his lip, the blade had obviously missed it. then he continued. "It's done that way to scare you, to make you wonder who's next. Sure, the ForeRunners on this world were eventually killed but others will come. In the meantime, the body parts they need are right here waiting for them."

He spat blood again and continued. "In case you're wondering why the Lenars didn't pick up on me, it's because their empathic abilities include a feel for different types of beings. They can tell aliens from humans. The ForeRunners taught me how to shield my feelings, so those creatures you now call our friends never caught me out.

When the Sken arrived the drugs the Cetra gave me knocked me clean out. The Jellies couldn't latch onto me."

"Where are the body parts?" Selena demanded. "Tell me!"

"They're in the freezer of a rented apartment. You'll never find it."

"Is that it? You killed those girls because the ForeRunners threatened to expose what you'd done in the past?"

"No, that's not the only reason. They told me they're going to attack Bernard's Star. My family are there and they said they'd spare them if I complied. I can't let them be killed. It's my mother, father, my sisters…"

Selena felt her stomach do a flip. "They're going to attack Bernard's Star … you know this for a fact and yet said nothing?" Watching Jenks carefully, she keyed her hand-held. "Colonel? Warn Bernard's Star—they're going to be attacked. Tell them to go to full alert and inform the fleet."

"How the hell did you know?" Delmar's voice squawked. There was silence for a moment. "I've only just found out myself. You're too late, Commander. The entire system's gone. The Forerunners hit them a few hours ago and took out their sun. There's nothing left now but plasma; seems they took a lesson from what you did to Mantis. God knows how many people we lost, billions I'd imagine. Then there's the bases, shipyards and the fleet that engaged them. It's-it's just horrible. Have you got Jenks?"

"Yes, we've got him Colonel. I'll call you back." She faced Jenks squarely. "It's too late. Bernard's Star no longer exists. You could have stopped that, Jenks. You could have prevented those losses and saved your family, but you did nothing."

"They'll be safe," he babbled. "My family, the ForeRunners promised…"

"You cut those young girls up!" Staff said in a choked voice from behind Selena, having come back into the room.

"You're a fool, Jenks," Selena snarled. "The ForeRunner's used you. Now we've lost billions of people, let alone those children you butchered for them."

"They insisted it was young girls. I had no choice!"

"There's always a choice." Selena said. Then she jerked the knife and twisted it, pushing the blade up against the underside of Jenks' jaw, making him climb up onto his tip of his toes. His eyes began to look haunted and desperate. "Guess that just leaves just us now, and the question of what to do with you," Selena continued. "Tell me, did the Queen know what you were up to, was she part of it?"

"Hell no, that evil cow would have killed me on the spot. You two are so alike. Bitches, both of you."

"Please, let me," Staff begged from besides her, his eyes almost standing out from his face. "Let me! I want to kill him."

"Oh, I'm afraid not," Selena said. "He tried to kill Jas, and that makes it personal."

Jenks' realised what was about to happen. "Wait, you don't need to do this…"

"Oh, but I do." Looking deeply into Jenks' widening eyes she gave a slow, chilling smile, and with another jerk Selena shoved the blade up through the soft underside of his jaw, crunching through the bone and up into his brain. His eyes bulged, feet tap-danced on the floor and his hands beat agonisingly against hers. Selena watched calmly as his life slipped away, and only then did she release him and let him fall to the floor. He hit knees first, before face-planting with a sickening slap.

The others filed into the room at the noise. There was silence for a while, eventually broken by Jessica.

"I take it there was a struggle," she said, her face grim.

"Indeed. Unfortunately, the knife went off in my hand."

"Is that right, Staff?" Jessica asked.

"Yup, the bastard slipped in his own blood, fell and impaled himself on the knife the commander was holding. All rather sad really, can't you see the tears in my eyes?"

Jessica put a caring arm around Jas, who was trembling and staring down at the dead body. "Selena, you'd better go see the colonel. We'll take care of this little lady until you get back."

"Thanks," Selena replied. "Nothing personal but, if you don't mind, I think I'll have Staff look after her. I can't think of anyone better suited."

# Chapter Seven

"So," Delmar began, studying Selena carefully as she stood in front of the colonel's desk. "Jenks fell on his knife during a struggle and died. Is that correct?"

"No," Selena replied. "If you want to know the truth, I killed him deliberately by shoving his own knife—no doubt used in his murders—up through his jaw and into his brain. But my official report will say it was an accident. You *did* tell me to deal with it by any means possible, and this was my way of ending the matter. I didn't want that bastard getting off, or escaping somehow."

She paused for a moment, considering. "The problem, as I see it, is that Jenks worked for us. You naming him as the killer could cause real issues."

"I disagree. We need to be upfront and honest. The truth could come out somehow, which means we could end up with egg on our faces." Delmar picked up a stylus from her desktop and fiddled with it, lips pursing. "His demise will reflect that the culprit was caught and killed during the arrest, as you suggest. The Queen threw a head-fit when we told her he was the killer but, thankfully, she seems to have calmed down now."

Delmar put the stylus down, her eyes lifting to watch Selena carefully. "I understand she has a new beau and that it's getting serious. Rumour has it they might even be getting married. What do you think about that?"

"I feel sorry for him, but she's of no concern to me. Jenks exonerated her of anything to do with the murders, which has to be a first, and I have to admit it came as a surprise. As long as she stays out of my life, I have no problems with her. Why do you ask?"

"Just checking. Incidentally, how are you, if you don't mind me asking? Jenks had mentioned some concerns. Said you were ... becoming tetchy."

"Ha, he was a great person to say that—look what he turned out to be. I'm fine, just tired and of course I've been concerned about Jas, but everything's all right now. Any more news about what happened at Bernard's Star?"

Delmar sighed and shook her head. "All we know is that several ForeRunner vessels appeared and that the fleet engaged them. There were just A.O.W. ships there at the time, and there was one hell of a battle from what we can tell, but we've obviously heard nothing since they hit the sun. Losing our headquarters has been quite a blow, but Admiral Van Pluy tells me they're activating the reserve HQ on Loreen."

She leant back, the chair automatically changing its contours as she squirmed into a more comfortable position. "Your old ship, the *Vampyre*, was engaged in the action and badly damaged. Luckily, she was sent away from the battle to seek repairs. Many of her crew were killed and, due to the ongoing battle, she was denied permission for repairs in system and told to seek help here. They left shortly before the destruction of Bernard's and managed to arrive safely. She's now at the City Port, undergoing repairs.

"*Vampyre*'s here?" Selena asked, with delighted surprise.

"Yes, she's being rebuilt and upgraded. Crew replacements will be needed when she's finally ready, and no doubt she will be thrown back into the fray. In a way, she was lucky. Not many ships got out."

"Sounds to me like we're getting a bit of a battering."

"We give as good as we get," Delmar replied. "Or we would, if we knew where their worlds were. We could destroy them the same as we did Mantis, and the ForeRunners are now doing to our worlds."

"It was bad enough when we bashed each other with rocks or clubs," Selena said, "then it was arrows, missiles, nuclear and chemical-biological weapons— anything else we could lob from a safe distance. Now we destroy entire planets and even solar systems. Where will it end?"

"That's not for us to ask. Our task is to fight the enemy, how and when told. As for you and yours, Commander, you're to continue with your current task until further notice."

"But Jenks told us there are no ForeRunners remaining on Capulet, that they were all killed. So, why do we need to carry on with what we're doing?"

"Because I want those teams of yours on top form, just in case," Delmar said. "After all, one of the enemy agents could slip through any time and we can't afford to drop the ball now."

Selena found herself nodding in agreement. "Makes sense. But you don't need to worry, they're on the ball."

"And find that flat Jenks mentioned. Recover the victims' missing body parts and let's give those kids a decent burial," the colonel continued. "It'll put people's minds at rest and give any relatives closure. By the way, I've sent the remainder of Jenks' team off-world. It's not healthy for them here at the moment. It's down to you and your team now."

"Okay," Selena replied. "We're on it."

\*\*\*

Entering Jenks' ID into the facial-recognition software allowed Selena to track his movements. She was soon able to narrow the location they were after down to two possibles. He'd visited both immediately after each of the killings. The first one turned out to be a simple clean-up pad, somewhere he could wash and change his clothes without arousing the suspicion of those in the military by his blood-splattered uniform, which he could have gotten from anywhere. From there, he'd moved on to the second address, where they hit the jackpot. When they raided the flat they found the parts of at least seventy people in strange looking translucent tanks, far more than those reported missing.

"What the hell?" Selena said, peering into the third packed tank. It resembled a very long freezer that ran almost from one length of the lounge to the other. The flat had three bedrooms, kitchen, bathroom and lounge. Each, except the bathroom, was jammed full of the devices.

"This is bizarre," Kes said. "There's nothing wired in, no internal power source that we can see or any such wireless device. There must be one—where is it?"

"They're a lot more advanced that we are," Selena said. "It could be anywhere." She called Colonel Delmar on her hand-held, to give her the good news.

"Are all the bodies accounted for?" Delmar demanded.

"Kes, what's the body count?" Selena shouted.

"At least seventy-three, Commander. But that's just by counting heads."

"Heads? Christ, did you get that, Ma'am? Seventy-three. That's a lot more than reported missing. Guess it's down to the pathologist to determine which are from our girls, and who the other parts are from. I'll give you a call once we finish up here."

It was then that the local enforcement arrived. They looked around the room, stunned, with two leaving instantly. The sounds of their throwing up in the corridor outside didn't help matters, but at least they hadn't contaminated the room, Selena reasoned.

"Hey," Selena said. "Can we get DNA tests arranged on all of these? And I want to see all of those reports."

"Already in hand, Ma'am," one of about ten officers replied. He wiped sweat from his brow with the back of one hand and looked both shocked and scared as he stared at the bodies. "These could be from anywhere. Let's face it, people go missing every day, hundreds per year—in every city. This fellow Jennings could have been storing them as a stop gap for other worlds, who haven't even realised yet what was going on."

"Okay, this is your bag of chalk now. We're out of here." Selena pulled her team out. "Go get some rest, guys. Leave it to the locals."

As they streamed out of the building, Selena used her hand-held to call Delmar back again. "Colonel? Yes, confirmed. Far more than we imagined. Local enforcement believes it was a holding area from other outposts. Yes, he must have brought them in somehow. There could be other killers in the colonies that we know nothing about, might be worth sending an alert."

"Well done, Commander," Delmar responded. "I'll get that actioned. In the meantime, I've had some news of my own. The ForeRunners have gone on the offensive. We lost three other colonies so far, same as Bernard's Star— the enemy took their suns out. They've also attacked Loreen—they must either see it as a strategic world or know about it being the backup headquarters. The battle's been going on for two days now. Nice of them to tell me. So far we're holding our own, although it's costly. Trouble is we're having to protect the sun there too, which takes a large number of ships. Wait, there's another report coming in."

Selena heard disbelief in the colonel's voice. "For God's sake, now the Manta have attacked us on two worlds."

"But … but they're supposed to be our allies!" Selena gasped. She felt sick. Shuddering, she apologised to the colonel and paused her hand-held for a moment. Calming herself, she resumed the call. "I'm sorry, Ma'am, something came up. You were saying, the Manta?

"Yes, they've attacked several outposts. Our 'so called friend', Scar, says they're from a splinter group, a hive who've failed to assimilate their data properly due to a technical hitch. They view the ForeRunners and ourselves as the same race, and are ignoring all updates and the command to desist."

"The Manta attacking us…" Selena spat, biting back anger. "There's a surprise."

"From what we can tell, Scar's own forces are engaging them. It's now Manta against Manta." Delmar's voice still held that tone of disbelief. "They're attacking them *en masse*, taking out all of their ships and slaughtering their forces. I've never seen anything like this."

"Let them kill each other," Selena snarled. "Fuck them all. I hope every last one of them dies, it's the only way we'll be safe."

"Hang on," Delmar said, and was silent for several moments.

*She's confused*, Selena thought. *Past it. Let someone new take over her post. Someone with enough fire in their belly to dampen out this alien menace, once and for all.*

"The Sken are also attacking the Manta insurgents," Delmar said, at length. She firmed up and once again became the Colonel that Selena had come to admire. "Let's sit back and see what happens. I'm with you on this. I hope they wipe each other out, but we both know that's unlikely to happen."

Still intent on her call, Selena the entered the citadel. She gestured for her team to follow her. she needed to update them.

"Two other worlds aren't responding to any communications, either," Delmar continued. "I have a horrible feeling that they've been obliterated, just like the others. Listen, about those bodies you've found. I'm going to send specialist teams to work with the local authorities and examine the enemy equipment. There may be something that could be of interest to us. We also need to cremate the remains, as soon as possible."

"Okay, I'm standing my teams down for the time being. They could do with a rest."

"Then best you call them back up again. There's been a change of plan."

Selena had just reached the lift in her accommodation block. Exhausted, she leant back against the wall and closed her eyes for a moment, touching the first finger of each hand to her nose. Kes and Singh raised their eyebrows and sidled closer to listen in.

"Go ahead Colonel, I'm all ears."

"You and your team are to report to the *Vampyre*, where you'll take command. Intelligence suggests that the enemy might be planning an attack here too, and we need to be ready for them. Have Lieutenant Roberts take over the search teams. She's done it before and knows the ropes. Get her to speak to the Lenars and let them know what's going on. I've a feeling they'll be fine working for the lieutenant, they seem to like her."

"Okay, I'll call the others and let them know. We'll report aboard ship once we've cleaned up. What are our orders?"

"To get her up and running—the dockyard workers are dragging their feet. Conduct any necessary shore-side trials, including full checks of all systems and generators. She's a relatively small ship and has limited supplies, so until she's ready you'll live in your current accommodation."

"Understood. Dillon, out." Selena had one more call to make. Baron answered immediately and she told him of their discovery and that the killer had been found.

He was pleased, but appeared distracted and offhand. "That's great news, Commander," he said. "I'll let the children know that they're safe now, although I'll advise caution nonetheless."

"Baron, are you all right?"

"To be honest, no, I'm not. Someone tried to kill our beloved Queen earlier today, an explosive-poison bomb. Luckily she survived, although her latest consort and a handful of guards weren't so lucky. All hell's breaking loose, so I'd better go and help find the culprit."

*He knows the call is being monitored*, she thought, and chose her words carefully. "I've no doubt the assassins will be long gone by now. Let's face it, they'd be mad to remain anywhere near the palace. You know the Queen, she's bound to find those responsible and I wouldn't want to be in their shoes when she does."

Baron nodded. "Aye, you're right there. I have to go, but well done on cracking the case. Her Majesty will be delighted."

They signed off and Selena couldn't help hoping that Baron had taken her hint and was going to get the hell out of there.

***

Much to Selena's surprise and delight, she learned next morning that the Queen had given approval for an orphanage to be built. One specifically designed for those youngsters whose parents had died in the cities. It was to be a tall, white, imposing building named Ephesus House, and financed directly by the Queen herself. Selena broached the subject with Jas one morning after breakfast.

"I see your friends from the destroyed cities have been earmarked for the new house. It won't take long for it to be built, perhaps a week or so at the most – what with the rapid-build technology." *Amazing really*, she thought, *houses designed and built quickly in factories. Taken to site and put together with final polishes, all done by machines in a few days.*

Jas looked at her cagily. "At least they'll have somewhere to live again, and they'll be off the streets. I can't help wondering why she'd do that, not like her to be so considerate. More coffee?"

"Yes, thanks. How do you feel about moving into Ephesus House, to be with them?"

"I've been waiting for this," she replied, avoiding Selena's eyes. "I guess it would be for the best. After all, you don't want me hanging around for the rest of your life. Do you."

"Look, you know that once this current situation is over I can be sent anywhere at any time, and it's unlikely that you'll be able to accompany me. As it is, we're waiting for *Vampyre* to be space ready and that speaks for itself. This is a penal unit remember, and there will be no-one to look after you when I'm gone."

"Admit it, Selena. You just don't want me around, I can understand that."

"You're wrong," Selena said, teeth grinding. "As it happens, I quite like having you around. It's nice to be able to go home to somebody, but we have to do what's best. Besides, what choice is there?"

Jas looked down at her empty plate on the table. "I want to stay with you."

Selena breathed out slowly, a warm feeling replacing the tension in her chest and neck. "Okay, let's see what happens. We're here for the time being, but if I get drafted at short notice you can go stay at the House until I get back. How does that sound?"

"As good as I'm going to get," Jas replied with the hint of a smile, and leant over the table to hug Selena.

\*\*\*

"From what information we have," Selena told a packed debriefing room that included her own team, "it appears that the ForeRunners blackmailed Jenks into working for them. They also taught him how to protect his mind, so that his misdeeds wouldn't be picked up by the Lenars, and also an ability to hide from the Sken by being comatose." *That was a bit of an eye opener. It also brings into question whether the Sken could miss people after all*, she thought. "That would explain why they didn't pick up on him during their last visit. Some of you may recall he was notably absent at the time."

"I think all of us here trust each other," Kes interrupted. "We're Penal Corps, we're all we have. To us, that counts for everything."

"You're missing the point," Selena replied. "Yes, we can catch the ForeRunners, but what if enemy spies *have* managed to infiltrate us using this mind blanking ability the Lenars can't pick up on, how would we know? Yes, Jenks was Regular Forces Intelligence working for Admiral Van Pluy, so he wasn't really one of us. But nonetheless, we need to bear in mind that there could be other enemy agents around.

"This brings to mind Lieutenant Arthur Jones," she continued. "He was part of my team's first mission and was killed in action, yet the ForeRunners somehow managed to recreate one of themselves in his image, with his memories. He lived amongst us for quite a while before he was outed as an enemy infiltrator. What I'm saying is, we need to watch our backs."

"What's the way ahead for our team now, Ma'am?" Braxis asked. "We should be out there, kicking ass."

"As much as I sympathise with your comments, Corporal, I've spoken with the colonel about this and she quite rightly says there's no reason to believe they won't be back. While we're working on the *Vampyre*, she also wants us to stay around to keep the Lenars happy. That said, Lieutenant Roberts is now in charge of the Search Teams. We need to show our faces, remain alert and keep the cities safe – all the while working on getting the ship back into the fight. It's business as usual, everyone. Back to our posts until we get new orders. My immediate team stay here— the rest of you can go."

When the last of the others closed the door behind them, Selena gestured for them to sit. "Look, I'm as frustrated as all of you but the colonel has a point. Yes, we know that Loreen is under attack and God knows what's going on over there, but our job is here. All we can do is pray that our friends and new home will come out of it okay."

She knew by the looks on their faces that they all remembered Loreen had granted every member of the Penal Corps citizenship on completion of their service. In turn, Loreen gained a citizenship of veterans that could easily be turned into a professional army at a moment's notice. No other world could match that. Unwanted anywhere else in human space, penal veterans had flocked to the relatively new colony and made it their home.

"I have a message for you from the Colonel," Singh interrupted. "She says that the Sken have joined the battle at Loreen. Their ships came into the system a short time ago and have engaged the ForeRunners. There are Manta ships with them too. She asks you to call her when the meeting's over."

"With any luck one of our ships will take the bugs out," Braxis growled. "Accidentally, of course. The two-timing, backstabbing bastards that they are."

Selena held up a hand. "Stop right there. I'm not fond of them either, but think about it. We humans are descendants of the ForeRunners, and we're fighting on both sides. It's the same with the Manta. We can't accuse them of being traitors when our own people are acting the same way."

"Aye, Ma'am. Guess you have a point there."

Selena's hand-held bleeped and vibrated. It was Colonel Delmar.

"Colonel, just finishing up here," Selena greeted. She put it on visual as she flapped her other hand towards the door, in a gesture to the others that their meeting was over.

"Commander, things are changing quickly. Information has come through from intelligence; they believe Capulet's going to be attacked."

"What, here? Damn, that's all we need. How can I help?"

"Focus on the *Vampyre*. Get her up and running quickly, and I mean *damned quickly*! As long as your team can breathe and she can fire her weapons, she'll do. I don't care if we have to drag her out there by tug. Is that clear?"

"Perfectly."

"We have little time left, so do what you must."

"Very well, Colonel. I'll keep you updated."

Delmar paused for a moment, as if deliberating. "One more thing. You know that fellow Baron you were working with on the child killer case? Well, it appears that the Queen had him and his entire family executed. The reports I have say she put his family through an industrial disintegrator right in front of his eyes, trying to force information about the revolutionaries from him. He was the last one to go in. I suspect the news was leaked deliberately, as a deterrent to others."

Selena closed her eyes. If only he'd listened. She mumbled something and broke the connection.

"Are you okay, Commander?" Kes asked, a worried look on his face.

"I'm fine. Word has it the ForeRunners will be here soon. Tell everyone to get their kit on board the *Vampyre* immediately, we're living on board as from now. I'm going home to grab my own gear, and give Jas the bad news."

\*\*\*

Jas knew something was amiss, as soon as Selena opened the door.

"Hi, how does a cup of ... what's wrong?"

"I need you to go to go and be with the other kids, Jas—and that means now. No arguments, just go. The shit's about to hit the fan, but you'll be safe there. Well, as much as anyone can be."

"Why, what's happened?" Most of Jas's belongings were already packed, a habit she'd kept from her time on the streets. Grabbing the few items she'd hand washed from the dryer, she pummelled them into the bag.

In the mirror, Selena saw Jas add her E-Reader before following her into the bedroom. "Well, are you going to tell me?"

"There's a good chance the enemy are on their way here, and the Colonel needs all available ships in orbit," Selena said, packing quickly. "And that means the *Vampyre*."

"I heard what happened to those other colonies. If they manage to destroy our sun, then being in the house won't make the slightest bit of difference. I'd prefer to stay here, if you don't mind."

"You're going with the others, and that's final. Are you ready? Come on, I've a skimmer outside and I can drop you off."

Neither of them spoke during the short journey, but as they pulled up outside the accommodation, both of them glanced over to the almost completed new orphanage a short distance away. Jas leant over and gave Selena a hug.

"You be careful, okay?" Selena said, keeping the vehicle in hover mode. "No more shopping in dodgy stores, at least until I get back."

"I'll be fine, don't worry—and you needn't worry about that," Jas gave her a half-smile and leapt over the side of the vehicle, waving goodbye as Selena drove off.

When she arrived at the ship, Selena could see robots and men busy at work, the ship healing before her very eyes. Sleek, gray and shark-like at sixty metres in length, the ship radiated power. She paused for a moment to take in the view, remembering her first command of the vessel on Andros Prime.

She strode up the gangway, which was bedecked with long white banners either side, which had the ship's crest and the words *Vampyre* emblazoned on them in thick gold lettering. The top of the gangway was manned by two armed and attentive guards who piped her aboard in shrill whistles. Kes promptly appeared besides the guards and saluted her.

"Ship's status?" Selena demanded, as she stepped off the gangway and strode towards her cabin. "Has Singh made his assessment, as to when we'll be ready?"

"I've spoken to him and have a progress report for you," Kes replied. "He says an adequate job of refitting the ship will need a minimum of six weeks."

"He's got a couple of days, if we're lucky. Tell him to cut it to the marrow."

"Not sure if that's feasible, Commander." He followed Selena to her cabin, watching as she threw her kit bag onto the bunk and sank into her chair, gesturing for Kes to sit on the chair opposite. "We're also short on crew, and need to make up the numbers before we lift. Pointless trying to fight shorthanded."

"I'll contact the colonel and tell her if she wants us space worthy, we need the numbers. Until then, do what it takes. You're my First Officer, so it's your responsibility to make it happen." She paused, before adding, "Oh, and get hold of Staff. Tell him he's part of this crew until further notice. He'll be in the emergency party—he's the ideal person to kick ass and get things done. Dick and Kami will have to manage until we get back. What other updates have you got on the ship?"

"The engines are okay. Luckily the damage they took was easily repaired and has already been completed. The command module has been completely extracted, repaired and refitted, as have the generators. We're working on the weapon systems but, basically, we've already taken out what was left of the old ones. Most of those, plus the sections of the ship housing them, had been destroyed. God knows how so many of the ship's company survived. We can't do anything until the hull sections are rebuilt. Once we've done that, we can begin fitting the weapon pods."

"Crew's quarters?"

"Same thing, thank God for modularisation. We can skip that, if need be, and just repair what we can. The crew can sleep in the passageways for the time being, if needed."

"No, get them sorted. I need my crew as rested as possible and sleeping in a passageway isn't going to do it. We have the time while the other work's going on."

"As you wish. All being well, the rest is just covering and patching. She won't be pretty but she'll fly and kick ass. We can do quick trials once we hit orbit and head on out, but she'll need an extended refit when we get back."

There was a short silence, as neither of them said, *If we get back.*

"We'll worry about that later. Until then, crack on." Selena returned his salute and sank further into her chair as he rose and left the room. She grabbed a quick coffee from the vendor by her desk and took her time savouring the taste. Rising, she got changed into her coveralls. Removing her commanding officer's insignia, knowing it would be a distraction, she made her way from the cabin down towards the engine room, where she reported as a general hand to Chief Mathers, the grizzled veteran of many years who was in charge there. He recognised Selena, but kept quiet and immediately put her to work. He soon had her welding, behind a plaststeel facemask, sparks spitting in all directions. At the end of what seemed a never-ending shift, Mathers sent her away to get some sleep.

In what seemed like only moments later, a crewman was shaking her but, to her surprise, several hours had passed. Achy and tired, she was told that Kes had called a meeting of the Heads of Departments and she was expected to attend.

Kes was there as ship's First Officer – or X.O., Singh as First Pilot, a now relatively fit Braxis serving as Master at Arms—with a promotion to Sergeant. The Chief of the Boat—an incredibly short, fat man resembling a ball — studied Selena with a disbelieving eye.

"Problem, Chief?" Selena asked in reply to his stare, as she sat.

"No disrespect, Ma'.am, but I understood that this ship has been transferred to General Service. You and your lot are Penal Corps, in other words, criminals. *We are not.* One of our two groups shouldn't be here. General Service and Penal Corps never work together."

"Is that so? Well, given your dimensions, it's you who shouldn't be here. Are you fit enough to fight, hand to hand if need be? I understand you've all been through a lot, we all have, so I'll ignore what you've said. But don't ever question my authority again, is that clear?"

"Um, I guess so."

"Yes or no, Chief? If it's a no, get the hell off my ship. I'll have a word with Colonel Delmar and I can have all of you sweeping the streets in no time at all. That said, I'd rather have you aboard. Make your choice."

"Commander, if I may," a bespectacled sub-lieutenant of the old crew said, trying vainly to sit upright and make himself look bigger. "Like you say, we've all been through a lot. The Chief of the Boat may be unaware that you were this ship's first Commanding Officer, and saw her through those pirate incidents. As for you, Chief, I suggest you shut the fuck up."

Selena liked him immediately. "I agree. This may be a first for our two separate services to show that we can really work together. You are?"

"I'm Olding, Ma'am, your Medical Officer."

"Ah yes, I read the files of the crew on route. Chief of the Boat, take note of this man. If you speak out of turn again, you will need his services. Now listen in. Word has it that the enemy is planning an attack on this system. Colonel Delmar needs all ships available and ready for action, and that includes *Vampyre*. Yes, I know this ship's a mess and we have a patchwork crew, but your Medical Officer is right. I commanded *Vampyre* once before, and I know her well—which is why I've been re-assigned. Other members of my team have also served aboard, including your new X.O., Lieutenant Kes Philips. He'll be speaking when I'm finished.

"Fifty percent of the in-system fleet, such as it is, will be deployed in six groups ringing Capulet. *Vampyre* will be part of the remainder, which have been assigned to protect the sun. Hopefully this way, whichever angle the enemy comes in from, they'll face a fight. If it's our group they hit, we'll get assistance from the squadron protecting the planet. If it's the other way around, then the planet has had it. We can't afford to abandon the sun to help the planet, because if they take this star out, we've all had it.

Wherever they hit, hopefully we'll be able to delay them long enough for reinforcements to reach us."

Kes took his cue and continued the brief. Coughing briefly, he said, "As the C.O. says, the admiralty has staged Task Units at strategic positions. A.O.W reinforcements have been despatched. By staging our ships as we have, it's hoped we can hold the enemy off until they arrive."

"By that time this system could be dust," someone from the regulars muttered.

"Things are what they are," Selena replied firmly. "The die is cast. Now, are you all finished?"

"Yes, Ma'am," Singh said. "When do we leave?"

"As soon as this ship is repaired and ready for action, so get to it."

\*\*\*

"We're all set to go, Captain," Singh said, without looking away from his console.

"Excellent." Selena keyed the ship's tannoy. "All hands standby, set condition Alpha and prepare for launch." She visualised her crew checking systems all over the ship, hatches and valves normally open planet-side would be double checked to ensure they were closed and airtight. She closed the mic and looked over at the attentive Singh. "Launch."

Slowly the *Vampyre* rose, gaining speed as she did so. The cityscape visible through the wall screens fell away, and soon they faced the open sky. Cotton wool clouds vanished in a downward motion, the blue sky darkened and then, quite suddenly, they'd reached high orbit. Selena ordered the ship through a few manoeuvres as they moved further away from the planet, test firing the weapons once they'd passed the orbiting planetary defence stations and the moons. Once those were complete, they continued to the centre of the system, continuing to conduct trials as they went. The few glitches and a small fire were dealt with quickly, showing that her crew were highly trained veterans.

In no time at all, the *Vampyre* was ready for action and eager for the taste of blood.

"Inform all that we're en route to our station," Selena said to the Comms Officer.

Increasing speed, the *Vampyre* swept through the system and took up her post on the far side of the sun, along with *Vanquish* and *Voracious,* two other ships of the same class. Apart from themselves there were four other task units, each with three ships, placed on an axis around the sun, Selena's group being the furthest away. Capulet itself had its planet-based and orbital defences plus the home fleet, which was split into four sections facing away from the sun.

They'd not had time to test their four torpedo tubes, nor could they afford to waste those projectiles. But the three sunbeam weapons worked well, as did their shields and Close in Weapon Systems.

There was something special about being aboard a space-going vessel, Selena thought. It might be the subtle scent of lubricants, the sound of the engines, the soft silky touch of silicon or even the low hubbub from the crew's chatter as they moved about the ship. There was also the enticing scent of cooking wafting from the ships galley through the air vents, the shushing sound of hot beverages being made for the bridge crew via the dispensers, the rattle of dice and occasional curse as off-duty officers played board or digital games.

They'd been lucky so far and Selena knew it; the *Vampyre* had been repaired quickly, although the damage she'd suffered had been bad enough to warrant a major refit. Several of the other ships picketed out here had also sustained damage, although it had been limited enough not to warrant dockyard maintenance. Consequently, the *Vampyre* was relatively fit and bearing her teeth, while the other ships sat still licking their wounds, their crews carrying out what repairs they could in situ.

It was on their third day on station that a sudden and deafening *Uurgh Uurgh Uurgh* snapped Selena from a deep sleep. In pure reflex she leapt from the bed, blood pounding and adrenaline surging, and ran non-stop to the bridge.

"Hands to action stations!" Kes' voice bellowed from the speakers and again came the *Uurgh Uurgh Uurgh*. "Hands to action stations, enemy vessels closing."

Selena hit the bridge running, leaping into her chair as Kes abandoned it.

"Report," she snapped, taking her survival suit from its compartment under her chair. She pulled it on with the speed and surety that came from practice.

"An F.O.M. fleet has just entered the system. Three battlecruisers, two carriers, five destroyers, six frigates and several ancillaries. They're on approach to Capulet. Planetary fleet is manoeuvring to intercept."

Kes checked her suit, she checked his; the rest of the crew examined each other. The slim oxygen tank and rebreather on her back enabled Selena to regain her seat, watching comfortably as other reports came in.

Displays lit up all around Selena, showing that each station was prepared. "Inform Fleet Commander that *Vampyre* is ready for action and assuming command of this Task Unit." The three ships in her group made a sub task unit of the in-system fleet and, as Selena was the senior officer, she was automatically in charge. If communications with her ship were lost, the next most senior would take over.

"Acknowledgement received," someone reported.

"Ma'am," Kes said, "what are your orders?"

"We remain where we are, until ordered by the fleet commander to do otherwise. The fleet is well placed to deal with the intruders, and those ships could be a diversion to make us abandon our stations." She watched the video feed. The planetary defence had a real fight on their hands, as it looked like the F.O.M. meant business. Swarms of fighters were already erupting from the larger vessels and taking up formation, while a number remained close by to protect the capital ships in Defensive Combat Patrols.

She watched as the F.O.M. frigates and destroyers moved in closer to harass the defending ships and orbiting battle stations, while the enemy battleships engaged with their heavier weapons from a safer distance.

"They're not targeting the cities," Kes said. "Just the ships and orbital platforms. Perhaps they're trying to take them out in preparation for a landing."

"I doubt it," Selena replied." "They'd be hard pushed to do that with just two carriers, unless there are others out there waiting for the all clear before they come in. They're probably just following the ForeRunner's battle plan."

"Contact!" the ships communications officer shouted. "Two more ships have dropped into the system dead ahead. They're ForeRunners!"

"Shields up," Selena ordered. "Task Unit prepare to engage."

*A good strategy*, Selena thought. *Make us think you're planning to invade, so we throw everything we have to try and stop you and abandon the sun.*

The screens switched to show two large white featureless orbs. They reminded Selena of the Sken vessels, although those ships were organic and these looked something like porcelain. A sense of dread pervaded the *Vampyre's* bridge, as the enemy ships came towards them. Without warning, dazzling white objects spat from the craft, gaining speed as they came.

"*Voracious*, take those out!" Selena commanded. "Standby close in weapon systems." Selena knew that it took a few moments for their sunbeam weapons to recharge, and if she ordered all vessels to fire at once they would be at a tactical disadvantage.

Sunbeams shot from *Voracious,* taking out the incoming projectiles en masse. *Vanquish* fired, taking out a second salvo. At her command, *Vampyre* and *Voracious* directly engaged the enemy vessels, leaving *Vanquish* as their goal keeper, destroying the incoming fire.

"All ships, fire torpedoes!" Selena ordered, hoping that at least some of them would slip through. Tight lipped, she found herself gripping the arms of her chair and she forced herself to relax. If her crew saw her nervous, they would be too. Hearing the cough of the torpedo's release she held her breath, willing them to strike home.

At the very last minute the enemy ships released a band of multi-coloured rippling energy waves that simply absorbed the torps. Again and again beams and projectiles flashed towards the enemy as they closed, their beams splashing uselessly against the ForeRunner shields. Selena ordered all three ships to fire salvos of torpedoes in turn, but yet again they burst against the rainbow ribbons of energy.

"Damn it!" Selena snarled in frustration, as the task unit continued to fire in rotation, sunbeams intercepting incoming weapons or flashing towards the enemy ships.

"What have we got left?" she demanded suddenly of Kes, aware of the limited number of torpedoes each ship carried.

"Twenty torpedoes and four planet busters. All ships have about the same."

Again, the enemy fired. This time several swarms of those eye-searing white shapes grew in the screens as they raced towards them, before suddenly jigging this way and that. The other two ships in the task unit engaged the weapons as ordered, while the *Vampyre* focused on the enemy. Close defence weapons suddenly kicked in, the thud of beam weapons and constant rattle of Gatling guns adding to the clamour of voices and her shouts of command.

"Clear," Kes said, indicating the incoming fire had been taken out.

"All weapons, focus on the enemy ships," Selena said loudly. "Stand by. Fire!"

Beside them, the *Vanquish* suddenly blossomed into a growing ball of flame and debris, and then vanished in a blinding explosion. Another missile exploded alongside *Voracious*, the shrapnel shredding parts of the ship and disabling its engines, although it doggedly continued to spit fire at the enemy.

That's when something hit the *Vampyre*. The ship shuddered violently. Alarms went off as compartments and corridors were exposed to vacuum.

"Report," she shouted, relieved that the bridge was holding firm, and airtight. *Thank God for the battle drills on the way out*, she thought. *At least her crew had been prepared for this.*

"It was just debris from the *Vanquish*, Ma'am," Kes replied. "Defence guns took most of it out but some got through, hit us amidships. Port-side main corridor's exposed to vacuum. Repair bots are on their way, no casualty reports as of yet."

"Damage control reports life support, power and weapons are all functioning normally, Ma'am. They have teams on the way to tackle the damage and sickbay has just confirmed there are no casualties," Kes reported, relief in his voice evident.

"Get me an update on the damage, please."

"Just a big gash in our side and numerous perforations. Apart from that rent, they'll have it sorted out in no time. I'm sure glad we weren't any closer to the explosion."

"You can say that again," Selena breathed. "Continue firing." She watched as the partially disabled

*Voracious* kept up her barrage against the enemy, despite drifting listlessly.

"Nothing's getting through," Kes said, grimly, gritting his teeth as he glared at the approaching enemy ships.

Selena had an idea. "Okay," she said. "This time, fire four torpedoes. Two planet busters to follow, interspaced by two seconds. A second pair to follow four seconds later, same timing. I don't expect the torpedoes to get through but I do want to catch them off guard with the busters. *Voracious* is to follow suit by targeting the other enemy vessel, is that clear? Good. Standby. Fire!"

The torpedo tubes coughed again.

"Ma'am, the other task units are dispatching a ship each to us," Comms said.

"Negative, tell them to recall them!" Selena prayed she'd made the right call. If she was wrong, and *Vampyre* and *Voracious* lost this fight, the other people in the system would pay the price.

Barely seconds later, a third ForeRunner vessel appeared, on a separate attack path to the sun. Selena breathed out slowly, she knew it. Both the attack on her group and the one protecting the planet had been diversions. This was the main threat, their throw of the dice. Luckily, the other units had remained in place and would be able to deal with this new menace.

The two enemy vessels approaching them fired again but, as before, their missiles ran headfirst into the sunbeams, which cut through them before splashing against the enemy's defensive shields.

The *Vampyre's* torpedoes hit and exploded, as brief glints of light in the dark. Then there was a blinding flash followed almost immediately by three others, a slight pause between each. All on the bridge tore their faces away from the screens, dazzled by the ferocity of the explosions. *Voracious* had already fired, and again came those blinding flashes. It took a moment or two for Selena's vision to clear, when it did she saw that the incoming pair of ships had completely vanished. There was nothing left of them, except an expanding field of diamond dust glittering in reflected sunlight.

Only the third ForeRunner craft remained now and Selena quickly called the Task Unit commander, advising that he follow her tactic. Before he could do so, the pristine white orb averted course and vanished into the depths of space.

All around her Selena could hear cheers and cries of relief. In the respite, she looked back towards the battle for Capulet. It was chaos. Myriad beams of light flashed in the dark above the pearl of a world, the flickers of battle like constant lightning in a distant storm. There was so much debris there from shattered ships that it was impossible to tell which side they were from. One of her screens switched to a planetary feed, which showed point defence guns guttering, missiles and ships exploding. The constant blooms of silent explosions and flashes from power beams reminded Selena of the huge firework display they ran every year on Capulet, to celebrate First Landing.

"Oh my God," Comms said.

Selena caught her breath. The enemy had taken a large number of casualties and were in retreat, but now swarms of missiles fell towards Capulet like a glittering snowstorm. Many ships in the defensive fleet threw themselves into the path of the projects, flaring briefly as they died. Despite their heroics, much of the barrage got through and fell planetward.

"No!" Selena said, jumping to her feet. Fear and disbelief wrenched at her stomach, tying it in knots. "No, not Jas too. Please…"

Then planetary defence kicked and, one by one, the enemy missiles winked out of existence.

"Did any of the enemy missiles get through?" Selena demanded of no one. "Is Capulet hit?"

"No," Kes said through puffed cheeks. "Nothing got through at all, thank heavens."

*Of course, he'd be worried too*, Selena thought. *Jessica's down there, in charge of the search teams.*

In the long silence that followed, no one else spoke. Then came sighs of relief and quiet murmurings, a cheer here and there. Selena keyed the inter-ship communications. "Enemy vessels destroyed, and the remainder have legged it. Prepare to take on survivors."

*Voracious* lay drifting. Torn open. On one side chunks were missing from the ship and there was obvious damage to the engines. A few bodies in survival suits drifted nearby. Just looking at the wreck Selena felt sick, knowing there would be many casualties. How any of that crew had managed to continue fighting as they had was beyond imagining.

Selena keyed her hand-held. "Staff, get over to *Voracious* with a rescue team and see what you can do to help them."

"Roger that, Ma'am. On it."

The bridge crew watched silently as their lifeboat docked with the stricken vessel. Selena ordered the *Vampyre* moved to a safer distance from the damaged craft, as per safety procedures unless they were coming alongside to render assistance. A while later, someone put a cup of coffee in her armrest.

Her hand-held vibrated, and a small red light blinked. She took the call on the main screen. "Admiral," she greeted.

"Good day, Commander. An excellent job on destroying those ships, very intuitive." Van Pluy began. "A shame that other ship escaped. They're bound to overcome your strategy in time, but at least we have a way to destroy them for the time being. I'm damn proud of the whole Battalion, you fought like lions."

"Thank you, Sir."

"We've taken quite a few prisoners too. Many of the enemy got out of their ships in survival suits or escape pods. Your Lieutenant Roberts and a Lenar are sitting in on their interrogation'. The captives will be put into stasis afterwards, until we decide what to do with them."

"That's a great idea, Sir. We can't have any of the enemy sitting in prisons; they could get up to all kinds of mischief. What are you orders?"

"To remain where you are, under fleet command, until you're released. Then report back to Colonel Delmar."

Inwardly, Selena sighed. "Very good, sir. Signing off." She cut the comms and brought up a link to Staff. "Sergeant Moore, a situation report if you will."

"We've boarded the *Voracious*, Commander. So far we have twenty-three survivors, nineteen of which are wounded. We're unable to get into some of the compartments at this moment in time, until we can install false bulkheads to ensure there's no loss of atmosphere when we enter. There could be any number of survivors in them."

"We can't spare any more men; do the best that you can."

Staff's forehead furrowed beneath the cropped black but graying hair. "I'll send the lifeboat over with the badly wounded, and get the pilot to pick up what we need. Those of this ship's crew that can function will remain at their posts, in case of another attack. She might be wounded but this ship can still fight."

"Good. Keep me up to date and if you need anything, shout."

A short while later the lifeboat docked and the walking wounded were escorted to sickbay, the more seriously injured ferried on anti-grav stretchers. With the supplies Staff needed quickly loaded, the lifeboat was soon on its way back to the inert vessel. Selena knew that, with the *Vampyre* on hand to lend assistance, further help from Capulet would take quite a while as they'd be busy dealing with the aftermath of the battle above them.

There was nothing her engineers could do for the *Voracious'* engines, they'd been shredded. The ship was lucky their generators had survived, to provide power to their weapon systems and life support.

"Now what?" Kes said at length.

"We wait," Selena said. "A couple of days here, maybe; given there's no more attacks."

"Commander," Comms said. "A resupply ship is on its way from Capulet. They say they'll be able to take the wounded back planet-side with them."

The words had barely been spoken when their screens lit up in a startling explosion.

"What the hell," Singh gasped, shielding his eyes.

"The *Voracious*, she blew…" Kes said a few moments later, disbelief in his voice, as the shields kicked in to deflect any shrapnel.

"The lifeboat?" Selena asked, her voice flat

Kes looked at Selena. "It's gone, Ma'am. There won't be any survivors."

Selena felt crushed. The battle had cost them dear but the loss of even more close colleagues and friends hurt. To lose someone in battle was one thing, to lose them like this another.

Selena closed her eyes and simply breathed for a moment or two. Then, over the ship's tannoy, she told her crew that their shipmates were gone; that they'd died quickly, and bravely, while rescuing others.

"Kes, you have the bridge," She said afterwards. "I'm going to get some rest. Send a message to Fleet and the Colonel; tell them what happened to the *Voracious*. Shake me if needed, I'll take the next watch."

In her cabin, Selena drew a cup of coffee from the dispenser and sat on her bunk, savouring the earthy smell of the piping hot beverage. Finishing her drink, she kicked off her footwear and lay down on her bunk. When they got back she knew their weapons would need to be upgraded. They'd had little effect against the ForeRunner orbs and she was aware that newer versions of the sunbeam arrays were available, but they'd fitted what they could in the short time allowed—just to get her ship into space. It was foolish to send ships up against such a superior enemy while fitted with substandard weapons. She knew that the Alliance of Worlds had the weight of numbers against the ForeRunners, and that the enemy couldn't afford losses, but in her opinion neither could the F.O.M. The *Vampyre* would have to wait to be healed, though; she knew there would be other ships with more pressing needs following the battle.

*We're losing millions of people*, she thought. *This can't go on.*

The Colonel's calling, Ma'am," Comm's said, over her cabin's loudspeaker.

"Put her through."

Delmar's face appeared on the main screen. "Well done, Commander. I have to admit there were a few anxious people back here for a while."

"Here too," Selena replied, her face betraying no emotion at all.

Pursing her lips, Delmar nodded. "Thank God none of the enemy weapons got through to the sun. We were damned lucky."

"We certainly were, Colonel, tragic about the other two ships... Do we have any further orders?"

"Remain where you are, until relieved. It shouldn't be long. Loreen's safe—the battle there is won too. Her defences were much stronger than the enemy expected and, with the help of our allies, the enemy took a hammering.

Other members of the A.O.W. already have ships in their system and some will soon be on their way here."

"Well, if the Manta have ships there in that A.O.W. fleet, let's hope the admiral doesn't get too comfortable. I don't care what Skar says about other hives, they can't be trusted. Quite often I'd like to destroy the whole damned race, despite what I've said in the past."

"Oh, I hear you there," Delmar said. "I truly do."

\*\*\*

Two days later, a flotilla arrived and slid into orbit above Capulet. Shortly afterwards, three were despatched to relieve *Vampyre*. They'd been lucky—in the battle *Vampyre* had sustained relatively little damage and while on station had done many repairs since, but more work was needed. On their return to Capulet they remained in orbit, the docking stations there being full of other damaged vessels.

It wasn't just a case of welding over holes; work was needed on both inner and outer hulls. Then came the process of smoothing and coating of heat-reflective material, allowed for sustaining low-radar signatures and protection from the intensive heat of atmospheric entry.

When dreaming of space battles as a child, she'd thought you just needed to pull up somewhere and spray paint your vessel, but now she knew it was a lot more complicated than that. It was awkward to use sprays in space. They tended to act as a propellant, so painters could easily find themselves shooting off at bizarre angles if they weren't careful. Sealing and testing each section took time and a lot of hard work before they were finally ready. While using robots or droids was preferable, they weren't always available.

With the Colonel's and Fleet's permission, Selena gave the orders to land at Capulet City, where they could finally finish their repairs. The bridge crew came to attention as she entered and slid into the comfort of her chair, watching the city grow from a pinpoint as the *Vampyre* dropped towards it.

Following touchdown, they secured the ship and disembarked. Selena and the others were surprised to see people cheering and waving, as they walked down the gangway. Embarrassed, she gave a tiny wave back, before boarding a regular forces silver-coloured skimmer, which had drawn up alongside the ship to take her to Colonel Delmar. She had already told Kes to ensure the necessary repairs were started, to get the ship stored and ready for take-off as soon as possible. She'd given them a rotational twelve hours off, but there was to be no leave as such for the time being. They both knew that Jessica could visit him on the ship, given the opportunity.

The colonel actually grinned at Selena, when she entered her office.

"Ah, Commander Dillon. You did well. If those damn orbs had gotten through we'd have all had it, no matter how the battle for the planet was going. Take a seat, can I offer you some coffee?"

"Yes, please. It was sheer luck, Colonel, and many paid the price. Just as well the Queen insisted on having the planetary defence grid up and running, or you probably wouldn't be here either."

"Wonders will never cease," Delmar said in surprise. "Is that you praising the Queen on her defences? Not like you at all."

Selena scowled. "I'm just stating the obvious. She was safeguarding her own hide more than anything; but in the process she saved Capulet, and everyone has to be thankful for that. What other news of the war?"

Delmar told Selena that with the Jellies and Manta reinforcing Loreen more ships could be spared to Capulet, with a few of their alien allies along for the ride. The fleet had suffered dreadful losses, but so had the ForeRunners and Federation of Man. For the time being attacks had stopped completely. Skar had reported that the rebel Manta had been, as he put it, exterminated. The universe was holding its breath, as if waiting for something dreadful to happen.

"If it's not the ForeRunners, it's the damned Manta, we daren't let our guard down for a minute." Selena growled.

"I don't trust the Jellies either," Delmar said. "I have a feeling that there's something they're not telling us."

"There is?" Selena replied, eyebrows raised.

Delmar changed tack. "We captured quite a few F.O.M. prisoners, from the attack, including a Commodore. He had some interesting information. We'd noticed for some time that all of our prisoners seemed incredibly healthy, but their injured and unwell were being culled and there was nothing they could do about it. ForeRunner spies have infiltrated all levels of the F.O.M. government. No one is safe, anyone could be a spy and dissenters quickly disappear. He was reassured by the presence of the Lenars, which is why he told us what he did. Many of the F.O.M. want out, but are afraid to speak. People's families have a habit of disappearing."

Selena brightened. "Does this mean we might be able to swing them towards our side?"

"Anything's possible, Commander. F.O.M. citizens are going missing all the time, some possibly for a ForeRunner living organ bank. Their fleet hadn't been told about their plans to attack our sun, either. As far as they were concerned, Capulet was to be invaded. They see now that they're expendable, nothing but cannon fodder.

"Seems to me," Selena grinned, "things are beginning to go our way. Let's hope we can find a way to broker a truce between our two human factions. If we get the F.O.M. on board, we stand a much stronger chance against the ForeRunners."

# Chapter Eight

Selena returned to the *Vampyre* noting, as she walked up the gangway, that the repairs were now imperceptible. Having more ships in system meant more time could be taken. Consequently, the weapons had been stripped, upgraded, and put back together. The magazine housings were extended and crew areas reduced. Robots of all shapes and size scuttled back and forth amidst their myriad tasks. Sparks flew while chunks of battered, scorched and torn segments were lowered to the ground using anti-gravs – or in some cases, simply dropped.

In the background, men swore amidst the clanging of metal, the buzzing of machines, and the drone of mechanical voices. There was that special warming smell that Selena found so welcoming, like heated ozone, which came as a matter of course with ship repairs.

Luckily, the puncture wounds and deep gashes in the ship's side hadn't caused major damage. Modules were replaced and secured, which sped up the ship's healing processes. Stores were trundled on board, up along the gangway and conveyor belts to vanish into the depths of the ship.

*Funny how we still think of ships as a 'she'*, thought Selena, as no doubt captains of vessels had for thousands of years.

She found Kes and Singh in the galley, the communal come-dining area for crew members aboard ship, as opposed to the wardroom for officers. At her quizzical look, Kes told her that the wardroom was currently being used as a ready-use storeroom, while work on the ship was underway. She sat beside them on one of the padded benches which, like the silver-rimmed white tables, slid into the bulkheads during time of action. This left valuable space available to muster boarding or repair parties, and an emergency first-aid post. Selena announced that she'd be speaking to the ship;s company in an hour or so, but for now what she needed was a shower and a chance to freshen up.

Making her way to her cabin, Selena locked the door behind her and stripped, dumping the black garments into the recycling bin where they would be automatically selected for cleaning. Grubby and unkempt, she desperately needed a scrub. Padding the few steps to her tiny ensuite, she turned on the shower and luxuriated in its stream of hot water. Finished, she turned the shower off, watched the apparatus vanish into the wall as she was blasted by a stream of hot air from the walls many vents. She was soon dry and slipping into a fresh uniform. Sitting at her desk with a sigh of contentment, Selena put her feet up onto her bunk, drew herself a cup of mocha and blew gently on the steaming chocolaty brew before taking a sip.

The weight of the past few days began to lift from Selena's shoulders and sleep tugged and urged her towards her bunk, but she shrugged the exhaustion aside and began flicking through the countless reports on her desk screen. Finally putting down her cup, and clearing the last of the reports from her screen, she keyed her hand-held.

"Listen in, this is the Captain. I've just returned from speaking to Colonel Delmar and she's informed me that the enemy's attack on Loreen has been beaten off. You'll also be pleased to know that, like us, they've received reinforcements from the colonies. Loreen sustained heavy military losses but very few civilian.

"Our job now is to get *Vampyre* repaired and back into the fray. While we've received some ships from the A.O.W., others are still in transit, or have yet to be despatched. Only when they've been received, and this ship is cleared by the maintenance crew, will a short period of leave will be granted. That is all."

She stood and opened her cabin door, preferring to leave it open whenever possible, but as she did so Kes appeared and saluted. At her invitation, he entered and sat on her spare chair.

"Glad to hear about the shore leave," he said. "The crew could do with it. I've posted a duty rota, which will update automatically to the dates applicable. The ship will split into four parts. Two of those will be on leave during a twenty-four-hour period; the remainder will take alternate six-hour shifts. At that rate, and with shore-side help, we'll have the *Vamp'* up and running in no time."

Selena felt her lips twitch. "Good. You'll work on opposite shifts with Singh, reporting directly to me wherever I may be. I need to keep an eye on the training wing and find a replacement for Staff. Then there's the search teams to worry about. Coffee? I'd offer you something stronger but, until the work's completed I want a dry ship. Can you make that known to all hands? Ensure that no alcohol or stimulants are issued until my say so. Anyone infringing this can stand by."

"Selena, can I speak off the record?"

"Sure, go ahead."

"I'm getting really concerned about the Manta. Yeah, I know they've been working on Capulet with us on a cure for the Lenars' disease, but they're not to be trusted. For them to attack our worlds when they're supposed to be our allies, it's as though they're waiting for this war to end so they can start another and settle their argument with us."

Despite herself Selena felt herself nodding. "Those are my feelings too, but we have to follow orders and can't afford a war on two fronts. Things are hard enough as they are. Let's just hope we're wrong, and that things will quiet down and pan out between our races. Have you spoken to Jessica?"

"Yes, I have and she's fine. She has Shadow and Jas with her, and says they'll all be pleased to see you. From what she says Shadow and Jas are becoming inseparable."

\*\*\*

The first leave party disembarked within the hour of the new ships arrival. Selena took a few days off too. Leaving Singh in charge, she took Jas on a camping holiday in the wilds for a couple of days, leaving a message that she was only to be disturbed if absolutely necessary.

With permission from the Colonel, Selena was permitted to use her skimmer, but was aware it was against the rules and suspected Delmar had only allowed it so that she could return at short notice.

"Do you like it here?" she asked Jas, as their craft landed softly in tall grass at the side of a river. In the background mountains jutted from the forest against a deep-blue sky. The slow pace of the river's clear waters was a gentle murmur, as it ran around white rocks protruding from the shallows.

They watched as Shadow padded off into the forest, knowing intuitively that he'd be back when they were ready to leave.

"Yeah, it's nice," Jas replied. "But why have you bought us here?"

"Thought we could take the opportunity to get to know each other better," Selena said. "The things that make you tick, and how we can improve things for the other orphans. Besides, we don't get much chance of a break, so let's make the most of it."

Their time was spent exploring, fishing, gazing at their readers, cooking over an open campfire and staring up at the night sky, trying to name the constellations behind the overhead fleet of ships that glittered so in reflected sunlight.

"You remind me of myself," Selena said one night, as they sat around a fire staring up at the stars. We've both lost loved ones in tragic ways."

"You've told me about your aunt and your parents," Jas said. "I'm surprised the Queen's still alive, given your reputation."

"She's very well protected, and sometimes you just have to forgive. If you don't, then you risk becoming sick, bitter and twisted. Doesn't mean you forget though, now does it."

"That's true," Jas said.

"I don't want you to make the mistakes that I did. Show yourself a bit of compassion. It's a bit late for me."

Jas remained quiet for a moment, prodding the fire with a long stick and watching the vermillion flames brighten in the gentle breeze, fragrant with the scent of wild flowers. "How long before you finish your sentence, and what happens then?"

"I've served longer than my sentence now—those twenty-five years passed quickly. I remained in because of the war. Besides, what would I do outside in the civilian world? When I leave, I'll probably go to Loreen and see that house they built for Bryn and I. Might be what I need, we'll see."

Jas watched her for a few moments longer, remaining silent. She went back to prodding the fire.

As the days passed, Selena found herself being drawn closer to the youngster. She and Jas talked about what could be done to help the orphans, to find ways to ensure procedures were set in place, so that if such tragic events occurred again other children would never find themselves in similar circumstances.

It was soon time to return, and as Shadow joined them again, a message flashed up on Selena's hand-held. It was from Colonel Delmar, telling her to report to her office immediately.

***

Having dropped Jas at the orphanage, it didn't take Selena long to get back to her ship, and from her cabin aboard the *Vampyre* she contacted the Colonel via wall screen. To her surprise, Delmar answered at once.

"Have a good break?" she enquired, dryly.

"Yes thanks," Selena replied. "Just what I needed, to get away from it all. I had a message that you wanted me to call?"

"That's right. A.O.W. ships are now arriving in large numbers. It appears the Commander-in-Chief is building a fleet ready to attack one of the ForeRunner worlds. Enough ships will remain behind to protect this system, including *Vampyre* when she's ready. You'll remain in command of her for the time being but keep her docked landside until needed; things are crowded enough up there as it is. I also want you down here keeping an eye on the search teams. Lieutenant Roberts is doing a good job and has things under control, but I want you running things just in case something goes wrong. We need to keep the Lenars and the Queen sweet."

"Until when, the end of the war? Roberts is more than capable, she doesn't need me peering over her shoulder."

"This isn't a choice, Commander. You follow orders, the same as I do. You're an important liaison between the Lenars and the Regiments, and with the people of Capulet too. They trust you and while I agree that you and the Queen may not get on brilliantly, at least you respect each other and know where you stand."

"I'd like to *stand* on her throat, as I'm sure you well know."

"Be that as it may, the decision's been made. You're staying here and will be in command in my absence. Yes, I've been assigned to the fleet."

Selena found herself gritting her teeth, a bad habit she'd picked up. Changing the subject, she said, "Acknowledged and good luck, I hope it all goes well. How big a fleet are we talking?"

"Difficult to say. We'll be fielding at least four hundred A.O.W. ships, the Manta thirty-five or so, the Jellies ... well. Their damn ships keep splitting up, so how the hell are we supposed to know? One moment we could have three ships the size of a planet, the next twenty or thirty more moon-sized ones – and then of course, how big is a moon?

"The Jellies have given us knowledge that will further advance our shield technology and torpedo yields. Unfortunately, the attacking fleet won't have the chance to implement these updates until they get back. Those remaining behind, including ships under build, maintenance and patrol, will have them installed—or at least a substantial portion of them."

"Can't you wait until the Fleet's been updated? Our beam weapons were no use against the ForeRunner Orbs, nor our torpedoes, come to that. The fleet will be in a similar position; C.I.C. will be sending them to their deaths."

"Commander, I've advised waiting too. But what do I know, I'm just a colonel."

Selena looked into Delmar's eyes, the blackness within them bottomless pits. "Well, let's hope we're wrong, but I've a horrible feeling we're about to get our asses kicked."

***

Four days later, Selena and the others heard that most of the fleet had been wiped out. Everything had gone well until they dropped out of hyperspace in the enemy system. Somehow they'd been expected, and the slaughter was unimaginable. Only twenty-six A.O.W. vessels got away, and most of those were damaged.

The fleet's loss was felt heavily. Grim and gray faces met Selena everywhere she went, for it had been a shocking and disastrous defeat. Everyone now had to face the fact that although the ForeRunner race was depleted, they still carried a terrible punch. Selena had known this and had tried warning Colonel Delmar. Attacking one of their worlds with substandard weapons had been foolhardy.

Of the Sken vessels, only a dozen or so survived. The Jellies were besides themselves with rage. You could feel it everywhere, an oppressive and palpable dread. It was like a subdued tingle in the skin, as if a storm of unbelievable power were about to break overhead. The surviving Sken vessels remained in orbit about Capulet with the A.O.W. ships as an ominous, brooding and troublesome presence.

Delmar had survived, much to Selena's relief, for she'd come to understand and trust, to a degree, her senior officer.

A few weeks after the disaster, the colonel informed everyone that something odd was happening. Stars at a great distance were being blotted out. Something immense was moving towards them and they had no idea what it was. Throughout the news of this threat the Sken remained silent. It was only when the A.O.W. were about to despatch ships to investigate that the Sken revealed they were responsible for the strange phenomenon.

Concerned, Delmar despatched several small spy ships anyway. When one sent back a video feed, she looked stunned, as she called Selena and shared the view. Sitting in the Captain's chair on the bridge of the *Vampyre,* Selena put it onto the main screen and gripped the arms of her chair tightly. Like the rest of the bridge crew, she was mesmerized by the site before her. The video displayed an unbelievable armada. Even at long range, the fleet filled the screen. There were countless Sken vessels the size of planets, others larger than the most massive of suns. Together they formed a vast, unbroken field. They gleamed, twisted, changed shape and colour.

It was the sheer number of such ships that was blotting out the stars and, according to the spy craft, this fleet would pass worryingly close to Capulet. The armada consisted of millions of the huge vessels. Sometimes they melted into each other like liquid metal; other times they simply absorbed another, all the while continuing onwards.

There were many smaller craft with them, the number beyond count, flitting one way and another, as if by random. They streaked off at unbelievable speeds before stopping instantly and reversing course, or moving off at a sudden ninety degrees without even a pause. Some of them scattered from their larger kin in a shotgun effect, as if preparing to fend off approaching adversaries.

This wasn't the only such fleet. Many others were reported, some even dwarfing the one approaching Capulet. The sight was utterly alien, sending shivers through Selena's body as she gripped the armrests tighter and tighter.

She felt helpless, and knew that if the Sken turned on humanity, nothing would save them. Mankind would be destroyed. Utterly. For the first time in her life she was afraid. Her entire bridge crew stood awestricken, watching the monstrous sight marching across the heavens towards them, sucking up light from the stars as they passed. Many stars dimmed and went out, others guttered like flames in a breeze before valiantly fluttering back to a lower brilliance.

She faced Colonel Delmar on the screen. Neither of them spoke. What could they possibly say?

After a long moment, her voice broken and hoarse, Delmar finally said, "This is going A.O.W. wide. Whatever it takes, we mustn't anger them and we're going to comply with whatever they want. We don't have any choice."

Selena was in total agreement.

\*\*\*

A few days later, the Sken fleet diverted course slightly and skirted Capulet's system. Everybody that could possibly do so watched, breathing sighs of relief as the huge vessels sailed majestically past. Everyone had been concerned that their sun was under threat. The Sken and Manta vessels in system slipped away to join the armada without comment.

It took days for the fleet to clear the heavens, for the stars to begin to shine through once again. Yet even at that great distance, their sun dimmed, creating an enduring twilight. It became bitterly cold and within days the low temperature broke all records. Pools, ponds, reservoirs, and rivers froze. Globs of ice began to be seen on the seas and the moonlight faded. At the end of five days, just when people were beginning to fear the seas would freeze over, the sunlight began to increase.

Reports came across Selena's desk from other systems, including Loreen. They told of other such armadas that had come and gone like shadows in the night, sweeping up their kindred ships before moving on.

For a long time, nothing happened. There was a long palpable suspense; and then, without warning, all hell let loose. The skies filled with distant blinding flashes which made those looking skyward shield their eyes. Within those sudden glares, worlds and entire solar systems died. Space warped and time bent, bringing with it those flashes almost as they occurred. Ships, moons, and asteroids vanished, as they were sucked from existence and hurled into oblivion. Ships venturing into, or caught between, these odd parallels were never seen again. Humanity watched in awe, humbled.

One colony reported a huge amoebic ship approaching. It engulfed two of their moons and vanished without a word, leaving the colony to deal with the catastrophes that came as a direct result. Tsunamis swept those distant shores and earthquakes shattered whole continents. Any human habitat on those moons vanished with them. One moment they were there and the next they were simply … gone.

People huddled in their homes, not daring to go out in case they were struck down. The Alliance of Worlds mustered what strength it could, just in case. They waited, knowing that against the vast forces being unleashed they stood no chance at all.

***

A call from Loreen startled Selena from her reverie. It was Franks, her friend back on Loreen who now headed the local populace. "One of those Sken bubble-ships just came and snatched Hope," he said. "They just … took her. Can you help us?"

"Woah, slow down. What do you mean, snatched?"

"Exactly that. We were eating a meal when Hope just stood up without a word, as if she was in some kind of trance, and walked out the door. We were calling her name and asking what was wrong as we followed her into the garden, but she didn't answer. One of those weird amoebic things, appeared out of nowhere and floated down onto her. It…it just enveloped her. Swallowed her whole, and floated away again."

"Have you spoken to Admiral Van Pluy?"

"Of course," Amanda said, peering over Franks' shoulder.

"What did he say?"

"He's trying to contact the Sken to find out what's going on. Is there anything that you can do?"

"I'll do what I can, which isn't much at all, to be honest. Van Pluy's your man and he'll be doing everything possible, you can trust me on that. I'll speak to Colonel Delmar and see if we can raise them from here."

"We lost her once," Franks said, "Getting her back was a miracle in itself. We can't lose her again. Please, you have to help us!"

She promised to get back to them if she received any news and broke the connection. Then she called the Admiral, who said he was indeed doing everything he possibly could, but he couldn't promise anything as the Sken weren't even answering his calls. They were a law unto themselves, and only contacted the A.O.W. when it suited.

Selena called Franks and Amanda back to let them know what had been done but said that, for the moment, there wasn't a lot anyone could do. Breaking the connection with her friends left a very bad taste in her mouth.

Selena recalled how Amanda and Hope had gone missing down the Rabbit Holes, that strange warren of tunnels buried under a hill on Loreen that somehow led to other worlds. She remembered how Singh had discovered the ForeRunner machines, which they'd called the Caretakers, would follow his orders. Out of sheer boredom after watching them marching back and forth endlessly with those silly woven baskets on their heads, gathering food before disappearing down further tunnels, he'd stood and asked one of them to bring him an apple. He'd only been mucking about at the time and hadn't expected anything, but had been stunned when the Caretaker had stopped and done exactly what he'd asked. Summoning Selena, he told her what he'd done and demonstrated it again. Out of sheer desperation, Amanda had followed his lead and asked the Caretakers to find Hope.

All of the machines had stopped, turned around and disappeared into the forest. Their mutual disbelief had turned into astonished delight, when the machines eventually reappeared with Hope sitting upon them in a lotus position. The broken bones Hope had suffered in an accident had not been repaired but instead somehow replaced by the same glass-like alloy that the ForeRunners used, leading to speculation that she'd been cloned, much like their old shipmate Arthur had. Yet, although she'd been watched closely since and apart from an incredible growth rate, she'd given no reason for them to doubt her.

On reflection, Selena realised that if Jenks had been able to hide what he was from both the Lenars and the Sken, then perhaps Hope had too. May she *was* a ForeRunner agent, but if she had those abilities, then how had the Sken discovered and kidnapped her? And what's more, why? Nothing seemed to make any sense. All they could do now was wait to see what happened.

That and pray.

\*\*\*

Selena and Jas often sat together by the window in her room, with Shadow besides them, all three watching the firework display in the heavens where fleets, worlds and creatures were dying in their millions. But it had been almost two weeks since the last explosion lit the heavens, and they couldn't help but wonder what was going on out there, in the endless ocean of the cosmos.

"So much for the power of mankind," Jas said, looking up at the sky one morning. "Those battles made us look like children, watching as adults perform tasks they know nothing about. Is it over, do you think? There's been nothing for ages."

"Maybe," Selena replied. "If so, we can only pray that the Sken won. And if they did, let's hope they decide to go back to wherever they came from."

Jas regarded her with those solemn brown eyes. "I can't help but wish things could go back to the way they were, before the Manta came."

Selena found herself agreeing. "All we had to worry about then were cruel monarchs like our Queen, pirates and other such criminals. Now we also have the ForeRunners, Manta, and the damned Sken too. Those Jellies can brush us aside whenever they like."

Selena was so frustrated she felt she was about to explode. "Whichever way you look at it, humanity is screwed. The universe has gone mad!" Realising what she was saying, she gave Jas a hug. "Don't worry, it'll be all right. Everything pans out in the end."

Comfort flowed from Shadow, easing into their senses. He assured them that Selena was right, the Sken would soon depart back to those dark places they'd been summoned from. Selena stroked the soft fur on his head, sensing rather than hearing a satisfied purr.

They were sat waiting for the other members of the team to arrive, so that they could go and have supper aboard the *Vampyre*, when Selena's hand-held vibrated. The message was from Colonel Delmar. Short and sharp, it summoned her to the control room immediately, and said that her team members had been told to report there too.

Trying not to show her consternation, Selena stood and said, "Jas, stay here. Shadow needs to come with me, but we'll be back as soon as we can."

Jas raised her eyebrows but said nothing. She simply nodded and gazed back up towards the heavens as they left.

It didn't take them long to get to control, where Colonel Delmar sat on the edge of her seat, staring up at the screens. She wore the all-in-one standard black uniform, and the black strip of hair across the middle of her head, from front to back, looked freshly trimmed and possibly dyed.

"You called, Colonel?" Selena asked.

"Just watch," Delmar replied, noting Shadow at Selena's side with a quick sideways glance, before nodding towards the main screen in the control room.

It was only moments later that alarms sounded and a Sken vessel flashed up on their screens. The visual was being sent by countless bots the size of pinheads, scattered throughout their system. The ship arrowed past towards Capulet, then slowed on approach.

"We picked it up on long range sensors," Delmar said. "Looks like we're about to get an update on the war."

"They're asking permission to land," Comm's said, loudly.

"Permission granted. Escort them to the conference room." Delmar turned to Selena. "Well, this should be interesting, Commander. Care to join me?"

Selena, the colonel and Shadow were already there, waiting along with several others, when a single brilliantly yellow-coloured Sken arrived and was shown into the room. It fluttered over to the huge wooden conference table and just floated above it, wings beating rapidly. The groups studied each other, then the humans bowed their heads slightly. Except for Selena—she'd always said she would bow to no one. Besides, she suspected the Sken had no understanding of bows, handshakes or any other such greeting or signs of respect.

Selena sensed through Shadow that the Sken was exhausted.

"Greetings," Delmar said. "I see you're alone today. What news of your battles with the ... Cetra?"

The Sken's words whispered through the corridors of their minds.

"There have been a great many battles. In their fight with you the Cetra withheld many of their abilities which we knew nothing about, and so once our battle was joined we were taken by surprise. Their physical numbers were limited but they had built a large fleet and automated them.

We managed to turn them against their builders and so, finally, the battle was won."

"Drones," Selena said. "Is that what you mean, that they used drones?"

The Jelly ignored her. "Afterwards they used these unknown weapons. Ones that killed our living ships. The enemy had prepared well for the event, for they knew that without our ships, we are nothing."

"Symbiotes," Selena said. "Does it mean that one of you cannot exist without the other?"

"You are somewhat correct, Selena Dillon," the words echoed in their minds. "We … co-exist."

A subtle scent filled the room. It was floral, but indescribable in its complexity. Somehow it spoke of the Sken's horrendous losses, and brought with it a great sense of loneliness. Selena wondered suddenly if this was part of their communication, something they'd all missed. Perhaps the Sken communicated with smell as well as telepathy, as a means of conveying their feelings. She felt an unexpected sense of sadness wash over her from Shadow.

"Sounds like they used biological weapons," Delmar said, thoughtfully.

"Makes sense," Selena added. "Look what they did long ago to the Lenars."

"Many of our ships were hit but were not destroyed, and we wondered why. They seemed well and continued fighting and tending us. They merged with others, and with others again—as is our want. Unexpectedly, these weapons began to trigger. Those ships died … horribly, and our interstellar cities with them. We felt their agony in our minds as our great ships died, and our people were cast into the void even as their craft shrivelled."

"Mines," Selena said to Delmar. "A weapon of old that could be set to ignore several ships and explode after a certain number has passed, or even target a specific vessel by using propeller signatures. Sounds to me like the

ForeRunners used a similar technique, with the biologicals triggering after a certain number of mergings, to ensure the kill rate was maximised. They've used such weapons before remember, against both the Lenars and the Manta."

"My God, this is terrible," Delmar said, her mouth hanging half open. "The enemy prepared well, yet you are so many. Surely they didn't destroy all of your vessels?"

Despite the colonel's tone, Selena thought she saw a brief sense of relief flit over her face.

The Sken turned vermillion and ignored the colonel, aiming its next comments at Selena. "Your conclusion is correct. Your friend Shadow is sad because he understands, whereas you cannot and never will. We lost our ship brothers beyond number; and as they died, we died."

"Is there anything at all we can do to be of assistance?" Delmar said carefully. "We are highly versed in biological engineering, as are the Manta. Surely between us there's something we can do?"

The Sken turned to face the colonel, its colour changing to a burning amber. "It is too late; the contaminated are as dust. The battles were momentous and, while the Cetra were defeated, we ourselves are ... diminished."

"What do you mean, defeated?" Delmar asked, excitement tingeing her voice. "Have they surrendered?"

"They are ... no more."

There was an uncomfortable silence as the information sank in, then Selena asked, "Can you elaborate? We're also concerned because there are reports of your ships attacking our colonies. Why are you doing this?"

"The stain of the Cetra has been removed from this universe, completely. This includes from their hidden bases on the worlds you claim as your own. They tried to use your presence as shielding. We were not fooled, though we let them think that we were. Any loss you have suffered as a consequence was necessary; you were warned not to stand in our way."

Selena licked suddenly dry lips and bit back a retort.

"We would have been unaware of these hidden bases," Delmar said, the words grating. "Had you informed us about them instead of attacking us, we would have gladly dealt with them with your assistance. A great many lives would have been spared."

"There was no time for such niceties."

Clenching her shaking fists, Selena rose to her feet, but before she could speak Delmar reached over and put a hand on her shoulder, pushing her back into her seat.

"Sit down," Delmar whispered. "It's already done. There's nothing we can do now, except save what we can of humanity from further action."

Simmering, she obeyed the colonel, realising with a start that one of her fists had opened and now rested on her sidearm. The Sken was staring deep into her eyes and she felt somehow naked and afraid. Exposed, as if it were looking deep into her soul, and she pitied it for whatever was found there. Suddenly giddy, Selena felt herself falling into a deep dark place, in which the shadows of unknown creatures slinked. With a start, she snapped out of it.

The Sken's many eyes continued to study her without a word, as if waiting for a move that would change many things. Selena forced herself to relax. Breathing out slowly, she put both hands on the table in front of her and laced her fingers together. She matched the Sken's calm gaze for a while longer. Then it looked away, and the moment was broken.

A steward interrupted the meeting. He entered through a side door to offer around trays of refreshments. There were fresh fruit, juices and water in large crystal jugs. The multitude and myriad colors of the items on offer somehow surprised Selena, for half of them she'd never seen before. It was a blatant attempt to discover what their alien guests might find palatable, yet all were declined. Selena took an extra-strong coffee, grateful for the caffeine that surged through her system, as she blew and took mouthfuls of the hot brew. The colonel was eyeing her and she looked straight back as the gentle voice in their heads continued.

"The Manta also suffered great losses, although their numbers were limited. All of their ships, bar a few, were destroyed. Those that remain are being repaired. We have advised them that it is best they leave this area, to find another more distant place where they can rebuild their civilisation once more."

"Rebuild..." Delmar began but was cut off by a bizarre *fsszzt* sound from the Sken, which sounded very much like an interruptive dismissal.

"If they remain, the risk of conflict with you humans will grow. Particularly now that the Cetra are no longer a threat."

*True*, Selena admitted, silently.

"You will provide escorts for their safe passage, for they will travel close to your worlds and we wish there be no ... misunderstandings. You will ensure their journey to the borders of your territory goes without mishap. There you will leave them. Where they go then is not for your concern, but it will take them many lifetimes to reach."

"Like hell we will," Selena growled.

"Commander!" Delmar said, the coal-black of her eyes boring into hers. "Enough!" She turned to the Sken, her voice soothing. "Yes, we will do this. Our ships will happily escort them from our space."

"That is ... acceptable."

"Good, we are in agreement." Delmar said. "We humans sorrow for the losses you suffered."

The Sken hissed again. "Many human vessels fought on the side of our enemy. Some of us demanded your race be annihilated, but they were overruled. Those human ships on our enemy's side were destroyed, along with the worlds that sent them."

Selena's stomach flip-flopped. "But, most of the people on those worlds were innocent! They had no part in it."

"Then they should have moved."

"What on Earth, our people's home world?" Selena asked. A weight descended on her shoulders as she held her breath for the answer. "It's not long been re-colonised, it was of no threat."

"It was one of the worlds punished. It is no more."

For once words deserted Selena. She sat staring at the Sken, stunned beyond belief. Earth, the cradle of mankind, gone. While sparsely populated, it had been one of the most fortified systems in mankind. Yet Earth had raised its hand against the Sken, and for that it had been destroyed.

"I believe this meeting is over," Delmar said, choosing her words carefully. "Send us the details of where and when the rendezvous is to take place. We will comply with your request."

"We will be watching," the Sken said, turning to leave the room. "We always are."

"Wait!" Selena called. "One of my friends is missing, her name is Hope Franks. One of your ships took her from Loreen. Her parents are worried about her; do you know if she is all right?"

The Sken paused mid-flight. "Yes."

"Yes, you know if she's all right, or yes she is?"

"She lives."

"Well, that's a relief. Tell me, did you take her because the ForeRunners—sorry, Cetra—repaired her?"

"What makes you think they did that?"

Shock flooded Selena, her mind blanked. "But, she had a transparent alloy replacing her injured bones. Only the Cetra do that."

"Is that so?" the Sken said in her mind, then turned and left the room.

"What the hell do you make of that?" Selena asked.

Delmar, who simply shook her head. "Damned if I know, Commander."

Her mind swirling, Selena and the others watched the monitors, as the Sken was escorted to its craft by the troops waiting in the corridor outside. She changed tack. "Do you think they meant it, that they're watching us? And, if so, how?"

"Oh, I believe they're watching all right," Delmar said. "Ever catch a movement from the corner of your eye but when you look nobody's there? Do you get the feeling that someone's watching you, but not know who, why or where from?"

"All the time, but I'm sure I'm not the only one. As George Orwell* said, 'Big Brother is watching you'," Selena retorted. "I thought that would always be the military and relative governments, not the Sken."

"Maybe they've been watching us for a lot longer than we know," Delmar replied, tactfully.

Selena held her head with both hands, leaning forwards with her elbows on the table. "All those worlds, gone. Billions of people, dead," she muttered.

"War always brings loss," Delmar said. "I'll hear no more on the matter, sounds like the war's over and we have to look to the future. All we need now is to get the Manta away from us. I think that the Sken came here specifically, to tell us what happened and what they want now. Their coming here to Capulet tells us that it's this planet's responsibility to arrange the escort. Consequently, I'm giving that responsibility to you."

"Me? You have to be kidding. There's plenty of other officers who'd be more than happy to do this."

* George Orwell (1949). *1984*. London: Secker and Warburg.

     "I've no doubt about that, but you're the one I want on this job. You get things done, Selena, and we can't afford any unpleasantries, now can we?"

# Chapter Nine

"Inbound ships, Ma'am," Kes said, eying his screen." Five Manta plus our escorts."

"All as it should be," Selena replied, reaching down to fondle Shadow's fur as he lay beside her chair. Admiral Van Pluy had carefully selected those A.O.W. ships and their crews himself. All of them were Penal Corps veterans, and many were people she knew personally. The *Vampyre* was to join the group here on the outskirts of Loreen's system, where she'd assume command of the task unit.

Her orders were simple: to get the Manta the hell out of human space. She was hoping there wouldn't be any incidents. If there were she would have to deal with them herself, and God help anyone responsible for any such 'mistakes'.

"Commander Dillon, of the *Vampyre,* speaking," she said keying her hand-held, so that her message carried over their task unit-wide communications. "As you know, the ForeRunner War is over. To facilitate the withdrawal of our Manta allies, Admiral Van Pluy has agreed that we escort their vessels safely out of our space, so they can find a new home a great distance from our worlds."

Several people's voices were raised in the corridors behind her, followed by senior's shouting at them to "shut the hell up."

Ignoring it, Selena continued. "It's our job to ensure they get through safely, no matter what any personal feelings we may harbour. To that end, we've taken station on the edge of Loreen's system, awaiting the other ships. Once the bugs reach our boarder limits, our ships will return to Loreen.

"I'm sure that you'll all be delighted to learn that, when we get back, I've obtained permission for all ships to land and attend the victory celebrations. Leave will be granted to each of us in turn, but, in the meantime, keep alert. We can't allow anything to interfere with our mission. We have to get it right first time, so there can finally be a peaceful co-existence between our races in future years. That is all, Dillon out."

Selena looked at Kes, as she switched off her hand-held. "What's the status of the Manta vessels—are their shields up, weapons armed?"

"Shields were up but they dropped them on approach. Their weapon systems aren't armed. It appears they're reassured by our presence, or rather *your* presence. Oddly, it appears that they trust you."

Selena snorted. "What's that supposed to mean? I hate them as much as anyone else, and our unit's certainly killed more bugs than any other. So why on Earth would they trust us, or even me come to that? Tell the escort ships to assume an arrowhead formation around the Manta— *Vampyre* will take the lead. All ships are to follow our pre-arranged course."

As they departed the system, the private message icon flashed on Selena's hand-held. It was from Admiral Van Pluy and was marked 'Eyes Only'. To her astonishment her hand-held did a quick retina and DNA scan, before the message could be opened. It hadn't done that before. She read it, paused, and then reread it more slowly. When she'd finished, Selena pressed delete, watching as the letters fluttered away on the screen like leaves in a strong wind.

She sat thinking about what Van Pluy had said and, after a while, found herself listening as Kes issued her orders and the escorts assumed formation. In the background. Braxis, meanwhile, was grumbling about a previous visit ashore in Loreen.

"You got us all banned from that establishment, if I recall correctly," Kes said, a few moments later. "Now we need to find somewhere else to cool off, thanks to you."

"Really? That's a shame, it certainly wasn't my fault," Braxis continued. "Damned marines, always too big for their boots."

"I didn't hear about this," Jessica said. "What happened?"

Selena heard Kes chortle in the background, as Braxis began his tale.

"I hate the bloody marines. On this occasion one of them was saying how they went in with us on the strikes on Demos and Mecca Prime."

Jessica grimaced and nodded. "I was there, we sure kicked the hell out of the bugs then." She looked at him in puzzlement. "So, what happened?"

Braxis took a deep gulp of his drink, wiping his mouth with the back of a meaty hand. "Well, he said the marines pulled our arses out of the fire – which is blatantly untrue. Then he said 'but when we were outnumbered on Anderson Five, where were you then, eh … where were you?' I told him that we thought the bugs were doing all right by themselves. Holy crap, you should have see it. Did the shit hit the spinning blades, or what?"

Selena's chuckle dried up as her eyes narrowed and she felt Shadow tense. Instantly alert, she asked, "Kes, why are our escorts manoeuvring closer to the Manta ships? Tell them to keep their distance and to assume formation as ordered."

Selena sank into her chair and tried to relax. It was all coming to an end. The ForeRunner war was over, the Manta were leaving, and much to everyone's surprise humanity had endured. All that needed to be done now was to get these ships out into the deep zone, far from the threat of further conflict. Using her hand-held she ordered a coffee.

"The escorts say that they are complying with your last message, Commander. You ordered them into close escort formation."

"I did no such thing," Selena said, puzzled. "Tell them to resume their previous positions, and look into the matter. I want to know what they're referring to."

"The escorts aren't responding," Kes said, after a moment.

"Try again, all frequencies."

"I have, Ma'am. They're still not responding."

Premonition weighed on Selena's shoulders and settled heavily into her stomach. She caught her breath. Feeling as if someone was standing on her chest, she tensed and said, "Hands to actions stations! Warn the Manta to raise their shields!"

There was eye searing flash across all screens. It was so brilliant that it temporarily blinded them. Even though Selena had automatically shut her eyes, and turned away, the glow was still visible through the forearm she'd thrown up to protect them. When she could see again Selena demanded, "What the hell was that?"

"All systems rebooting," Kes said. "We were too close to the explosions and our shields were down, just about everything's shorted. It'll take a moment or two. Standby, backups are kicking in. We'll be up and running … here we go."

"The ships, Ma'am," Jessica replied, "They're no longer there! Everything's gone, both our escorts and the Manta. We're all that's left, along with a field of expanding debris. Looks like our ships blew themselves up, taking the Manta with them."

"What … why the hell would they do that?" Selena said, her jaw going slack.

"No idea, Ma'am."

"Any survivors? Scan the debris!"

"Hang on, my sensors have picked up a signal pulse that was sent just moments before the explosion," Jessica said.

"Track it, I want to know where that signal came from—and quickly!"

Jessica turned to look at her, face grim, "Ma'am, it originated from this bridge."

Selena looked from one of her crew to another, as she drew her sidearm. "Okay, what's going on—who's responsible? All of you, stand up and move away from your controls—and each other come to that. Hands up, in plain view."

Looking at each other in disbelief, her team complied, all except one.

"That means you too, Singh. Hands in the air, now!"

"I think not," he replied. "You know we couldn't trust the Manta. Sooner or later they'd be back, no matter their or the Jellies' promises. They even started attacking us again before the damn ForeRunner war was over! A *mistake* they said. Ha, as if we're supposed to believe that. If we hadn't killed them now, while we had the chance, it would only be a matter of time before they returned. Then we might not have been able to stop them at all."

"Singh, no…" she moaned.

Ignoring her, he continued. "Now, I'm pretty damned sure that the admiral gave you orders to destroy those ships, if they showed the slightest wrong move, hence the bombs planted in their armouries. I'm right, Selena, aren't I?"

"My orders are of no concern to you, Lieutenant," she replied, gathering herself. "Have you any idea what you've done? You've executed the last of the Manta, not to mention our own people in the escorts."

"They were volunteers. I'd spoken to all of their captains prior to this mission to sound them out about my plan. They agreed to it, as did their crews. They were heroes, every last one of them."

"What are you talking about, have you lost your mind?" She held up her right hand, forestalling the other bridge crew members from doing anything.

"Quite the opposite," Singh replied. "I'm the only sane one here. This had to be done and no one else would do it."

"What the hell, Singh? The Sken are watching us all of the time! How they do it we have no idea. They'll have seen this … needless slaughter, and they're going to be royally pissed. There's no way we can possibly win a war against them, and the chances are they're going to kick the living shit out of us!"

"No, they won't…"

"Of course they will! You're a bloody fool, Singh. You've just doomed what little's left of the human race. If the Manta had tried to attack us, that would have been different, we could have defended ourselves. And yes, I had contingency orders from the admiralty in case of Manta betrayal, hence the bombs as you say. But they didn't attack us, did they? The bugs kept their end of the bargain. We had peace for the first time in God knows how long. You've doomed us all, Singh. For pity's sake, why?"

He finally stood up and moved away from the others, hands raised. The expression on his face was one of sadness. "Because if I hadn't, you probably would have, if you knew the truth. You see, there are things you don't know. Things that were deliberately kept from you."

"Enlighten me."

Singh's eyes were locked onto hers and, despite their black pits, she knew he was telling the truth. He'd never lied. "The Sken told us that the Earth had been destroyed, didn't they?"

"Yes, it's awful, but that's history now. We have to look forward. For the human race to survive we have to accept that things happen in war."

"Yes, things happen. But you see it wasn't the Sken that destroyed Earth, it was the Manta."

"You're lying." But Selena knew that he wasn't—his eyes were baring his soul.

"We destroyed their world, you, Bryn, me and the others—and finally they got their revenge."

"You're talking nonsense."

"It's true."

"And you know this how?"

"Kotes told me. He and the Magellan were on a scouting mission nearby and saw the attack as it happened. When he informed Admiral Van Pluy, he was told to keep it quiet. The Admiral believed mankind would go berserk it they knew, and demand an immediate attack on the Manta—even though they're technically our allies."

Selena stared at him. Could this be true?

"The admiral also said you weren't to be told about what really happened to Earth. He believed you were the right person to get the bugs to safety, but feared that if you discovered the truth you might act differently and attack them yourself. I couldn't let that happen and did what was necessary. They killed Bryn, Selena, the man we both loved. And then they destroyed the Earth."

Selena's ears buzzed, the room swam and she felt hot. She shook her head to clear it but didn't know what to say.

Singh continued. "Maybe Kotes told me so the decision was mine whether to tell you or not. Who knows? The Manta killed Bryn's family, remember? He and I found what was left of them in the ruins of their home, back before we met you."

Selena remembered Bryn telling her this, when she'd pegged him as a loose cannon and he'd begged her to keep him on the mission which they'd believed was a one-way trip. It was his chance for revenge, and so she'd let him stay and had eventually fallen for him. And yet, at the end, their love had paid the price. Even now she could feel the pressure of his lips on hers, the tender touch of his fingers caressing the side of her face, the love shining from his eyes and their love making … all gone. For he'd died during their lifeboat's crash landing on an unknown alien world. She blinked back a tear, as Singh continued, bringing her back to the present.

"He and I broke into a prison holding alien prisoners and killed them, I just couldn't let him do it alone. Unfortunately, those bugs were the only prisoners we'd managed to capture alive and they were still being studied. We were caught, and that's why we were sentenced to service in the Regiments. But, you know what? It was worth it."

He swallowed, choking back his sadness. "Maybe you're right, Selena. Mankind can't win a war against the Sken, even with their numbers depleted. But I know in my heart that if I hadn't stopped the Manta right here and now, our people would pay the price later on—or our children would. If whoever carried out this act has to die, then it's better me than it is you."

"What do you mean?" she asked.

"Think about it. The Admiralty can truthfully deny all responsibility for what happened. You have to go on, Selena, Jas is waiting for you. And, if I remember correctly, you have a score to settle with that bitch Queen of yours."

Singh slowly began to lower his right hand towards his sidearm.

"Don't!"

Singh's eyes were on hers as his hand crept slowly towards his pistol. "If you're right, Selena, and the Jellies *are* watching us, they'll see that you punished the person responsible. Mankind will be safe."

"Singh, don't make me do this!"

"It's okay. Remember, they didn't attack the Manta when they attacked us the first time, or more recently, did they? Instead, they let them resolve it themselves. The Sken are an understanding race and only interfere when there's no choice. Let's face it, without Bryn I've no reason to go on. But you do." He pulled the sidearm free and slowly raised it towards her. "Goodbye Selena." He cocked the weapon.

"Singh, stop...don't!" Her pistol barked once, twice.

Singh was thrown backwards onto the floor, dropping the pistol as he landed on his left side before pushing himself up against a console to face her. Blood dribbled from the side of his mouth, as Kes and the others stared down at him in horror. "It's okay, Selena," he coughed. "At least I'll be with Bryn now."

"Give him my love," she said, wiping a tear from her left eye. Then she aimed and pulled the trigger again.

# Chapter Ten

"I guess I should ask for your weapon," Kes said, his voice breaking the shocked silence.

"Negative," Selena replied, voice harsh as she pushed back her emotions and holstered her side arm. "We both know I'll be exonerated, which means you could end up on a charge of mutiny and face a court martial. I'll deal with any repercussions on my own, thank you."

Kes lowered the hand he'd stretched towards her for the weapon, and looked over to Singh's body, shock evident on his face.

"Is it true what Singh said, about your orders?" Jessica demanded.

"Take your seats," Selena said to the others, and used her hand-held to pipe over the ships intercom, "Clean-up crew to the bridge!"

She paused for a moment to gather her thoughts, and said, "On this ship you'll address me as Captain, Lieutenant. In answer to your question, yes, although I only received them a short time ago. Singh must have known about their contents in advance, and exactly how concerns me. In that message, Van Pluy's instructions were to destroy the Manta vessels if they became a threat, but only then. That was the first I'd heard about the mines on those escorts. He said that he'd personally chosen volunteers to man those ships, and their Commanding Officers knew that planet-busting bombs had been placed aboard their vessels. They had control of those devices, but they'd also been set for remote detonation by me in case the ships were compromised."

"Selena…" Kes interrupted.

She held up her hand to quieten him, and continued. "My orders were to kill myself immediately afterwards, to demonstrate to the Sken that while we'd been prepared for such an eventuality the person responsible had been punished. Just as Singh took the punishment himself."

"The irony is," Braxis said, "it was humanity who betrayed the Manta for a change, and not the other way around."

Kes spoke again. "Singh was right, he had to die to save us all. The fact that we're still here and talking about it means the Jellies witnessed Singh's self-punishment and understood. They're already mad at humanity, because some of our worlds had been aligned with the ForeRunners."

"But, Singh was your friend," Jessica said. "*Our* friend."

"Yes and, trust me, I did all of humanity—including us—a favour."

"Are you *sure* the Sken are watching?" Jessica asked.

"Absolutely, they even told us they are. But like I said, what we don't know is how they're doing it."

"Well, I'm pretty sure from what I've heard that they're against genocide," Jessica said.

"Oh, really? Then what about the Forerunners?" Selena said.

"That was their last resort," Kes said. "Let's hope they give us a chance."

"Commander, I'm detecting a vessel moving away from the debris field. It's a Manta landing ship and it's approaching Loreen at high speed." Jessica said, interrupting.

Selena felt as if her stomach had fallen through the floor. "Are you sure?"

"Positive. I didn't see it before, it was hidden in the debris. They must have suspected something when those escorts closed, and ejected just before the bombs detonated."

"What's happening now?" Selena demanded.

"That one contact's split into five! What the hell? They've slipped through Loreen's defences, they must have been blinded the same as us. Looks like they're going to land near the Gateway to Eden."

"Shit! Kes, take the helm. Get after those ships. Jessica, get me Admiral Van Pluy."

"Commander," Van Pluy said, his face appearing on the screen. "What the hell's going on? I'm getting reports of a massive explosion in your vicinity and numerous Manta ships approaching Loreen."

"Tell the defences not to fire, Sir, we're after them and closing fast. Singh got control of those mines you'd planted on the escorts, and detonated them himself. Hopefully we can stop this from getting further out of hand."

"I'm dispatching reinforcements to the site and putting them on full alert. Whatever you're planning, Commander, it better be good."

"I'll report in as soon as I can. Dillon, out."

"We're through the outer planetary defences," Kes reported, teeth gritted. "Traffic Control are telling us to reduce speed, planetary rules and so forth."

"Sod them," Selena snarled. "Tell them they can bill me and in the meantime, they can use their regulations as a suppository. Now get us the hell down there!"

"Weapons online and ready," Kes said.

"Do *not* fire," Selena replied. "Stand down weapons, that's a direct order. Land us close to their ships, Kes, but not too close."

Even as the *Vampyre* screamed through the planet's atmosphere, Jessica shouted, "The Manta have landed, Ma'am! There's reports of them storming the Gateway, I can hear gunfire in the background!"

"They're trying to get away," Selena said. "That gateway is the only path now open to them."

"Well, they can't just set up a camp anywhere. Without the minerals they need for their crops to grow, they've had it." Kes replied. "Perhaps if they can get to Eden through the gateway they can use the Rabbit Holes there to reach the worlds, allocated to them by the Sken. Seven minutes until we land," he added.

"Personal armour on, people. No anti-gravs, the bugs will probably be waiting for us and will pick us off like flies. We're going to have to get up the hill to the Gateway the hard way. Shadow, I want you to stay with the *Vampyre*. You don't need to get involved with this."

Shadow agreed. Turning his back on her, he disappeared into the depths of the ship.

Her troops were lined up, inspected and ready before the ship braked sharply and kissed the ground. As the gangway whispered to the grass, the twin hatches opened and they raced down it and took up defensive positions.

"Clear!"

Selena relaxed for a moment and, leaving the defences set, she mustered the others in front of her. They could hear the rattle of gunfire from atop the hill, and the *crump* of explosions; the banshee shrieks of beam weapons and the hideous screams that followed. Before she could start to give orders several skimmers, each filled to the brim with Penal Troopers, appeared and pulled up next to the *Vampyre*. Soldiers leapt over the sides of the craft and reinforced her defensive positions, as a burly crew-cut woman approached Selena.

"Are you Dillon?" the woman asked, her voice sounding as if she smoked sandpaper.

"Commander Dillon, yes," Selena replied, saluting.

"I'm Major Huxton. This area's under my command. I have jurisdiction here, so you'll follow my orders." She returned the salute. "Now, tell me what's going on. All I've been told is that the Manta are here and they have a major bastard on, thanks to you."

"Contrary to what you may believe, Major, it had nothing to do with me. The long and short of it is we betrayed them and destroyed their last few ships, instead of escorting them to safety as we'd promised. Their only escape now is through the Gateway at the top of that hill, which you may or may not know about that."

Huxton's jaw and lips twisted, as if she were chewing a mouthful of jalapenos. "Of course I know about it, and as you have trouble following orders, you can remain down here and establish a perimeter. Just in case the bad guys decide to come down and pay the locals a visit."

"Listen Major—"

"You have your orders, Commander, now get on with them. While you're at it, take out those Manta landing ships. We don't know if their weapons can be remotely controlled and I don't want to get toasted from behind. We can apologise to them later."

"You can't leave me here," Selena began.

"I can, watch me. I'm going to stop the fighting, one way or another. Oh, and see if you can contact the guards at the Gate. Tell them not to detonate the mines in the Rabbit Holes, those tunnels that lead to the alien worlds. I want the Manta to go through them, we need to get the bugs off this planet. If we can do that, then we can resolve matters on the other side, one way or the other. Besides, if we lose access to Eden we also wave goodbye to a lot of resources. And we have people on the other side too."

"On it," Selena said, through gritted teeth.

The major split her troops into a column two-troops-wide behind her and led the way, tabbing up the steep forested incline.

Selena found herself grinding her heels into the grass. "Kes, you heard the major, blow those bug ships."

With the muffled explosions thumping in her ears, Selena growled, "Fuck this for a game of soldiers. Kes, detail that lieutenant over there to look after this post. Tell her no bugs are to get through, then follow me."

"And where are we going?" Kes asked. "The major said—"

"I know what she said, but Huxton can kiss my baby maker if she thinks I'm staying here. It's getting dark and there's a storm brewing, we need to move now."

As Kes hurried over to the lieutenant and gave him his orders, Selena selected her team and a few others to make up a total of ten. When Kes returned a few minutes later, she took the lead as they began trotting up the slope.

After twenty minutes Selena began to feel the punishing pace in her armoured suite but carried on up the steep incline nonetheless, knowing the troops behind were not only suffering too but watching her every move. Clouds gathered overhead, blotting out the stars beginning to peep from the heavens. From nowhere rain blew into their eyes and quickly turned into a downpour. They dropped their visors to protect themselves against the stinging liquid tattoo but the incline soon became a muddy, slippery hell. They stamped onwards through the sudden brown rivulets that quickly developed into gushing streams. They slid, stumbled, and fell to their knees, but they got up and continued on.

Memories of Staff's training methods flashed into her mind and a grim, fleeting smile stole over her as the foul-tasting mud got in their mouths, despite their visors' protection. Three of her people slid over the edge of the incline and disappeared with chilling screams. Lightning flashed overhead. The drum of thunder crashing in their ears adding to the sound of battle and finally, after what seemed an age, they reached the top. Desperately trying to gather their breath, they reformed and double checked their weapons.

The facility had been lightly defended, a point Selena remembered picking up on with the admiral during a much earlier visit. Van Pluy had told her it was because the more heavily defended the facility, the easier it would be picked up from space. She remembered that, at the time, it had made sense. Now, she wished she'd stood her ground.

When they reached the cave at the top of the incline the gunfire had long since ceased. The silence was only broken by the moans of the wounded and the dying. The acrid smell of chemicals from projectile weapons, mixed with the dank stench of blood, caught the back of their throats.

There was no time for the enticing ocean view that tossed and turned below them, made visible through the lightning-lit treetops; nor any to spend investigating the shattered and blood-stained rock as they entered the cave. The few lights that still hung from the ceiling flickered, while the remains of the once daunting silver-coloured barrier, derived from ForeRunner material, glimmered in their weapons' torch beams. Yet now the barrier lay ripped apart like torn foil. The intimidating auto-guns were no longer there, their emplacements completely destroyed. Even the encoded keypad hidden in the rock had been smashed beyond repair.

They clambered over the bodies that lay piled atop each other, both human and Manta. As Selena and the others picked their way through the shattered metal, rock and torn bodies she suddenly realised that the rabbit hole that led from here to Eden was still intact. Somehow, amidst the carnage, her message must have gotten through. Suddenly they saw living troopers huddled on each side of the rabbit hole, which was filled ankle-deep with a foul soup of blood, minced flesh and bone.

"What the hell happened here," Selena demanded of one of them, "and where's Major Huxton?"

"She led the way through the tunnel, Ma'am," the private said. "There was an explosion, some kind of flechette weapon. One moment there was a group of them there, the next they were a red mist. Even got most of those out here, standing in line waiting to go in."

*Fuck,* Selena thought. *Manta air mines. If it hadn't been for the major, that would have been me.*

Stepping over the fallen, she recognised Sergeant Baines, who'd served under her command when she ran things here at the Gateway. Surrounded by dead bugs, his lips were drawn back in a snarl and his sword was buried deeply in the side of a huge Manta. The creature's maw was filled with flesh ripped from his shoulder. Baines' innards adorned them both, like some form of bizarre and morbid jewellery.

"Shield!" Selena said.

Braxis came forward with one of the new portable units that was generally used for overhead cover, but which could be turned to a great many uses. It may not protect against beam weapons, she knew, but it might help against fletchettes from the air mines.

"Don't just sit there," she said to the remnants of the Major's men. "Today's a good day to die, get up off your sorry arses and follow me!"

Begrudgingly they stood and fell in, as she moved towards the tunnel. The intricately-carved wooden podium that had borne the painted Penal crest lay on one side, as if discarded. She pushed it away as they passed, then stepped into the brilliantly lit rabbit hole that lay open before them, leading downwards into the depths of the hill. Taking a deep breath, Selena followed Braxis and the portable shield, her feet making sploshing sounds in the gore as she led her troops down the tunnel at swift trot.

They were almost at the end when there were several deafening bangs and the tunnel filled with flying blades. They ricocheted from the shield with a reverberating *doommmmm*, followed by what sounded like falling glass.

"Quick," she shouted as the shield unit in Braxis' arm burst into flames and fell sparking to the floor. "Run!" She charged down the tunnel screaming at the top of her voice, those behind her following suit. As they neared the end, the sounds of battle could be heard—the *crump* of a grenade, the cough of shotguns, shrieks from beam weapons and the screams and cries of injured and dying.

They exploded from the tunnel into daylight and dived into what cover they could. As per her orders, her men held their fire.

"This is Commander Selena Dillon! All sides cease fire!" Selena shouted.

In response, a large group of Manta swung ponderously towards them. Huge and imposing, the arachnid come insect-like creatures raised their weapons and rushed them.

"Stop!" Selena shouted, rising to her feet and putting out her hand palm first in an attempt to prevent further bloodshed.

Braxis body-tackled her, knocking her clean off her feet; as the space she'd just vacated filled with projectiles and a horrible, red hissing beam that melted the rock behind her.

"Fuck this," Selena said. "Fire, take 'em down!"

The machine gun in her arms jerked and hammered at the enemy, while those besides her joined in, their combined fire knocking their enemy from their feet. Desperately she looked around. Here too, the pod-mounted defence guns had been destroyed. The barrier that sealed this tunnel's exit was gone too, cast aside like a child's toy. The air was filled with the bitter scent of weapon discharge;

while the lush, ankle-deep grass around them was blood soaked. Pieces of combatants and discarded weapons littered the landscape, along with the dead from both sides.

The massive trees ahead of them stretched far overhead, shielding all below from the sun with their generous arms, spread wide as if they were either greeting the sun or looking down in dismay.

Bullets tore at the side of the tunnel directly behind where Selena now lay and zinged inside.

"Sorry…" came a human voice over the battlefield.

"Prat!" came the reply from one of her troops.

The Manta charged again and were beaten backwards by the rain of fire, dancing death jigs as the slugs shattered their carapaces. Soldiers fell around her, jerking, writhing and screaming in pain. Their cries and choking coughs from blood-filled throats were ignored, as their comrades knelt, took aim and returned fire.

Grabbing a tracking grenade from her belt, Selena lobbed it towards them. The inertial guidance took over and the weapon, along with others, shot towards the Manta and exploded in their midst. The shrapnel scythed through them, and the explosion tossed the monstrous creatures aside like children's toys. Smoke from the detonations added to the haze of battle, while the screams of the dead and dying tore at their hearts.

"I can't stand up," someone said. "Why can't I stand up?"

"Because you've been shot, you twat," Braxis replied.

The Manta were caught in a crossfire and were being obliterated. Then Selena saw a familiar sight: one of the bugs had a long gore-dripping slash down one side of its face. Quickly she adjusted her hand-held to loud-speaker, and when she spoke, her voice cut through the din of battle.

"This is Commander Selena Dillon of the Penal Corps. All sides cease fire. Cease fire, I say! Skar, I can see you. You know me, we have to stop this before it's too late." To her amazement, the gunfire fell silent. The huge Manta stopped and stood swaying, many with huge chunks missing from them. Both sides eyed the enemy, the Manta slavering as if anticipating the taste of human flesh.

A lone Manta detached from its kin and strode towards her, tossing its weapons aside. The creature was at least nine feet tall, and had leather-like webbing across its chest that was festooned with weapons and insignia. Huge claw-like feet crushed the wounded as it made its way through the throng. That gaping wound from an old slash across its face dribbled horribly, and a change of wind brought the stench of decay from the wound. Of the six vermillion eyes that marched in pairs up towards the creature's forehead she noted that now, besides the top two mechanical ones, a third from the middle row had also been replaced.

"Hello Skar," she said. For once Selena was relieved to see it…him…whatever, despite the fact the Manta strode towards her as if intent on tearing her to shreds. It paused suddenly, and a large glowing orange orb appeared over its shoulder and began to swirl.

"Selena Dillon, you betrayed us!" A long, wheezy breath. "You destroyed our ships! My people are gone, dead. We are all that remain."

"For what it's worth," she replied, laying down her weapons and standing in turn, hands held up and wide. "I knew nothing of what happened. One of our people went mad with grief and acted alone. He has been punished. The Sken will bear witness."

Its breath whistling, as if in great pain, Skar regarded her, clenching and unclenching those long talons. "You expect us to believe?"

"It's true. As I said, ask the Sken. The one responsible for that act has been punished by death. Many of your kin have acted similarly in the past, and suffered the consequences. War is a terrible thing—it twists the mind."

"We will speak to the Sken, but for now let us go free of harm."

"I fully intend to."

From the corner of her eye Selena saw an officer she didn't know stamping his way towards her from the human defences. It was a colonel. She held up one hand, palm towards him. "Stand fast, Sir. I have command here, Admiral Van Pluy's orders."

"I've seen no such orders," her fox-faced senior snapped.

"Contact him, and he'll confirm what I say." She prayed he couldn't get through, or that the admiral would give her a chance. "In the meantime, Sir, I ask that you stay back." Dropping her hand, she turned to face Skar. "Let there be no more fighting, there should be peace between us. We wish to help. Where are you going?"

"You must know I cannot tell you," Skar replied.

"In that case my soldiers and I will escort you as far as we can, to ensure your safety. I ask that you trust me on this, I pledge my life."

"We trusted you once before and look what happened!" Skar appeared to grow in stature.

"We can debate this all day and get nowhere," She said, stepping forward and speaking quietly, so that only he could hear. "We obliterated Mantis and, in turn, you destroyed the Earth. Our races need to move on and work together, no matter how we feel about each other. We are as bad as each other, but the Lenars trust me and I'm asking that you do too."

The orb swirled silently for a few moments, then the other Manta slowly lowered their weapons.

"Very well," Skar said. "We will comply."

"All forces, lower your weapons!" Selena said, her voice magnified through the hand-held. She walked over and stood besides Skar, and gestured for the waiting colonel to approach.

"Dillon." Fox face's lip curled as he joined them.

"Colonel," she said cheerfully, noticing how the cropped reddish hair complemented his exceptionally pointed nose. She bit back a snort. "Sir, I ask that you bear with me. I'm following orders from the Admiralty and have full authority here. As I've said, if you check with Admiral Van Pluy, I'm sure he'll confirm it." She waited as he stalked away a few paces and spoke quietly into his hand-held. He looked like he'd swallowed a spider as he made his way back.

"Yes, Admiral Van Pluy confirms what you've said," the colonel spat. "So, what are your intentions?"

"Firstly, could you ask your men to move aside and allow this column through?"

He harrumphed, gave her a look of pure poison, and gave the order.

"Lead on," she said to Skar.

"So, you do intend coming with us?" Skar replied.

"Indeed; like I said, we'll escort you to safety. If anyone attacks you, they attack us both."

"I'm coming as well," the colonel interrupted. "Along with fifty of my men."

"With respect Sir, that's not going to happen. I cannot stop you personally, but I can your men."

"Really," he sneered, "and how exactly do you intend to do that?"

"As I see it, Colonel, your troops are a threat to the success of my mission, the survival of my men and our allies. I'll shoot them myself, if I have to. This conversation is being recorded and is being broadcast live, incidentally. Now, there'll be just my team; and you, if you insist."

Reddening, the Colonel began to bluster. "You'll pay for this, Commander!"

"Oh, I very much doubt it, Sir. Now, if we can proceed?"

\*\*\*

How Skar found his way through the forests, over the rivers and steaming swamps Selena had no idea. She had requisitioned Six skimmers from Eden's defenders, and they rode silently besides the tall aliens. During their journey, some of the injured Manta simply sat down and died. When she asked Skar about this, and offered to help by getting them aboard the skimmers, he told her that they were a drain on his resources and had been released from the hive mind. Without that guidance, they simply sat down and waited to die. Selena pondered the question for a moment and broached the subject again later.

"Tell me, what is the hive mind?"

"Ah, an inquisitive human. Who controls who, you ask?" he replied in sibilant tones. "We have what you may call leaders, kings. They control all."

"Which makes you?"

Skar swung his great head towards her, mechanical eyes whirring as they swivelled to look at her. "The last king."

"Now, why doesn't that surprise me... So, where are your queens?"

The orange orb above his shoulder swirled for a time. "We have no queens, only maidens."

"And they are?"

"Dead."

"What, all of them?" Selena was shocked and sounded it, even to herself.

Behind her in the skimmers Selena heard several subdued "Yay!"'s'

"Silence!" she snapped. "Or I'll see to it that the next person to make such a comment receives another ten years added to their sentence." A sullen silence answered her, but Kes slapped her on the shoulder for reassurance.

With the skimmer floating over the grassland they were traversing, she said, "If all your maidens are dead, who's going to create your eggs?"

There was a slight pause, and then the orb glowed slightly brighter. "We will see."

"Don't tell me, you have a hive somewhere – one with eggs."

The creature's long strides didn't falter but Scar's head swivelled to face her. "You are astute. We haven't been there in eons, but it is hoped that maidens will be hatched from the eggs that remain. It is a very old, abandoned nest. Now that you have these details, what will you do with them?"

"Nothing," Selena said, glancing sideways at the Colonel, warning him with her eyes to remain silent.

***

By dawn on the third day, they reached an uncharted Rabbit Hole that appeared from the bole of a huge tree. Selena and the others dismounted the skimmers, and watched as lines of Manta marched two abreast into the luminescence of the tube without stopping. At the very last moment, Skar paused before stepping into the tunnel, and turned to face her.

"Our races have both made mistakes. Neither are without blame. Should we meet again, let us hope that it is with more understanding and that there will be a long and lasting peace between us," he said.

It was one of the longest speeches she'd heard Skar make. "Indeed," she replied. "We wish you well, and hope that the maidens you need will be born."

"Racial memory says the eggs were stashed as an emergency measure, before the nest was abandoned. Their exact location is hazy, it's been so long that we will need to search. And even if we do find them, most will not hatch. If that happens, and there are no maidens, we are lost."

The gold and silver flecks amidst Skar's green-black chitin glittered in the light from the setting sun and they took a moment to watch it together. It was a telling moment, as Selena wondered if that setting sun reflected either or both of their race's futures. She also wondered whether the Sken, or even humanity itself, would forgive them for what had happened.

"Look," she said quietly, glancing behind to make sure the colonel was out of earshot. "I don't trust that fellow. Is there any way you can destroy the tunnel behind you?"

From amidst the trapping on its criss-crossed belts, Skar produced a milky foot-long egg-shaped object and showed it to Selena.

"Already thought of that, huh?" she replied, eying the strange object. "Just one other thing. The Sken, *do* they watch us?"

Skar didn't answer but instead turned that huge, ponderous maw towards the trees. Selena followed his gaze and thought she saw, just for a moment, the fluttering of wings amidst the foliage.

"They watch all of us," Skar said finally, and without another word marched into the Rabbit Hole after the others.

Selena found herself staring after the Manta, as they vanished in the downward curving tunnel. She noticed that the colonel had come up behind her and was now standing close by.

"You were talking. What did it say?"

A rueful smile twitched at Selena's lips. "Oh, that we shouldn't really hang around."

"And why is that?"

"The tunnel's going to blow any time now."

"What? You … you fool!" the colonel gasped, and raced towards the nearest skimmer, with Selena jogging behind him.

Selena sounded an immediate evac', as they both boarded the same craft. Braxis was driving, while Kes watched both Selena and the colonel carefully, as the other skimmers raced ahead.

They were a few miles away when the detonation came. The ground shook, the trees danced and scattered leaves. A muffled rumble sounded for a few moments before fading away and then, once again, all was still.

A sneer on his face the colonel jabbed a finger towards Selena. "You knew! We could have stopped them!"

"Don't point, Colonel, it's rude. The last time anyone did that, I accidentally snapped their finger. Why would we need to?" she asked. "They were our allies and we had no right to do that. Besides, they've gone now. Everyone's safe, and surely that's all that matters."

"My report will be on the admiral's desk as soon as we get back. We'll see what he has to say about this," he grated.

Kes raised a quizzical eye towards Selena and slipped his knife silently from its scabbard, but she shook her head. Killing the colonel wouldn't help. What would be, would be. That particular Rabbit Hole was gone and they'd know it had been sabotaged, but there were others. A senior officer who'd accompanied their team, and who had mysteriously gone missing, would only complicate matters.

They dropped the colonel off at base camp and re-entered the Rabbit Hole back to Loreen by foot. When arrived, they were faced with anxious guards and a sombre Admiral Van Pluy.

He shook Selena's hand. "Glad you made it back, Commander. Any later and you'd have missed the view."

The puzzled veterans left the cave and walked into the clearing in front of its entrance. Soldiers stood there, staring upwards, and when Selena raised her eyes, it was to see a fleet of Sken cellular ships sailing majestically past.

"Nowhere near as many as before," Van Pluy said, as the last of the swirling multi-coloured bubbles vanished into the darkness.

"No," Selena agreed. "and some of those ships don't look quite right. Seems to me that in the long run, everyone lost."

# Chapter Eleven

As the *Vampyre* approached the city lights of Capulet, glittering like jewels in the nightscape, Shadow seemed unsettled.

"What is it?" she asked.

*"My people, I can't sense them. Something is wrong."*

Her bond was strong with Shadow, and she could sense his emotions. He somehow spoke through them, and it was an odd but bizarrely natural way to communicate; one that Selena had never come across outside of his race.

His concern grew as they landed. Rage. Selena felt a blinding fury grow within him, but before she could ask him about it Shadow bounded down the gangway as it was still extending from the ship. He leapt the last few feet and disappeared quickly through the crowds. She called after him, both verbally and emotionally, but he didn't answer. Then she saw Jas making her way towards them, her face pale.

Shore-side Jas threw her arms around Selena, then whispered, "I must talk to you privately, it's urgent!"

"Jas, what's going on? Do you know why Shadow's so upset?"

"We can't speak out here. Let's go inside the ship, where it's safe. I need to tell everyone." In the wardroom, she told them quickly, "The Lenars have been killed, all of them from what I can tell—except Shadow, that is. It was a bomb, and nobody's admitted responsibility. Some people, including Colonel Delmar, are saying it's the Forerunners. It would have got Queen Miranda too, but she was late for the meeting."

"A bomb? It can't have been the ForeRunners, they're all dead," Selena said softly, "so who... Ah, you say the Queen was late?"

"Yes," Jas confirmed. "She got held up at the last moment and handed the package over to that scientist fellow, Cox."

"What package?" Selena asked.

"The cure for the Lenar illness. The Manta did it, Selena, after all of this time! They handed it over before they left. Everyone was so excited that the Queen was going to present it to the Lenars in person, in gratitude for all they'd done. But somebody tampered with the package and the Lenars, Cox and the Search Teams were all killed in the explosion—luckily for her, she'd been held up."

Sorrow filled Selena and she swallowed hastily. "But the Queen survived, how very convenient."

"The Lenars," Jessica said in a stricken voice, "they're dead?"

"Yup, all except for Shadow. I saw him running off through the crowds. Poor soul, I bet he can't believe it. His people, killed right at the end of a war that had nothing to do with them." There was a slight pause, and then Jas asked, "Where's Singh?"

Selena's team fell silent, as Jas repeated the question.

"He didn't make it," Selena replied. The team said nothing. Avoiding her gaze, they stood and made for the door, as Selena said, "Guys, go get some rest; I'll see you in the morrow. Jas, why don't you go home and knock us up some lunch? I need to see Colonel Delmar. I'll be home after that, we can talk then."

*** 

Delmar was waiting when Selena knocked on her door. "Ah, Dillon. I wondered how long it would take you to get here. Take a seat."

"I came as soon as I heard about the Lenars. A bomb, I'm told, planted by the ForeRunners. How did you come by that information?" She ignored the invitation to sit.

"It's the only obvious explanation."

"That's rubbish, we both know that the Sken exterminated them. They could detect the ForeRunners anywhere, and they did a damn good job of getting rid of them, so please, no bullshit, Ma'am."

"That's the official line, Commander. End of story."

Selena slammed both hands onto the colonel's wooden desk, making loose items jump. "Bullshit! The Queen's mysteriously called away at the very last moment. Don't tell me you believe that crap?"

Two anxious-looking guards popped their heads into the office, Delmar waved them away.

"It doesn't matter what I believe, what's happened is in the past. We have to move on, and the Alliance of Worlds needs both the Queen and this planet to do so. Let it go, Selena."

"Like hell I will, she can't get away with this! You have to do something."

Delmar pursed her lips and slowly shook her head. "Like what, exactly? She rules this world! There isn't much I can do except stage a coup and I'm not going to do that. I'm sorry, but you've been told what the official line is. Several worlds are already threatening to leave the A.O.W. We're firefighting, Selena, and trying to save what we can."

"Politics," Selena replied, angry and frustrated, "they never end." Simmering, she sat in the chair Delmar offered.

"Well, now that the enemy's been defeated I've recommended you be released from service. You've done more than your fair share, and voluntarily served past your sentence. The powers that be feel that now would be a good time for you to retire."

Selena clenched her teeth. "What you mean is, you want me out of the way too. I'm a threat."

"That's not the case." Delmar's lips pressed together. "Look, you're a hero, something the Penal Corps haven't had before. It's damned embarrassing to have a convicted criminal in the limelight. Let's face it, this force is made up of the worst of the worst, those who've been sentenced for horrendous crimes. We can't have someone serving in a penal unit, when people everywhere worship the ground they walk on."

Opening a drawer in her desk, Delmar pulled out a cream-coloured bottle and two glasses. She poured them both a measure and pushed one of the glasses towards Selena. "Belarian Milk Brandy, try it."

"I can arrange for you to be released on any world you wish, but as you know, our regulations state you can't be released here on Capulet. Besides, we both know it would be a grave mistake for you to remain here. This Queen of yours doesn't forgive easily."

Selena frowned. "No choice, huh? Very well, I'll tender my resignation to Admiral Van Pluy. No doubt it will be activated on my return to Loreen."

Delmar studied her for a moment, then said, "Maybe sooner. Look, off the record, pressure is being brought to get rid of you, and I expect you can guess who the main culprit is. Personally, I hate to see you go. You're a damned good soldier." She swallowed her drink, watched Selena do the same, and held out her hand.

Selena shook it. "I'm not gone yet, Colonel. I've a few things to do first. There's Jas to sort out, of course."

"That's fine. As it happens, the *Magellan* will be here the day after tomorrow and I've already asked them to drop you off at Loreen. I understand from Jas that the locals there have built you a residence. It looks quite beautiful in the image she showed me. She was quite enthusiastic about it."

"Was she?" Selena said with a frown. "Her coming with me isn't part of the plan, or anything we've discussed."

"Well, I suggest that now might be a good time to do so. I'll arrange for the *Magellan* to pick you up from the forest outside the city, so the Queen won't see it and suspect anything. With luck, you'll be gone long before she knows anything about it."

\*\*\*

Selena ordered her unit to gather in the dining room of the *Vampyre,* where they'd be assured of privacy. The stared at Selena in astonishment, as she told them she'd been advised to resign and intended doing so. It was Kes who broke the silence.

"Have you given up your quest for revenge? This isn't like you at all."

Selena shrugged. "With Aunt May gone, the Queen and the Admiral are the only so-called relatives I have left. There's been so much death that I think it's time to draw a line and let everyone live in peace, to try and come to grips with all that's happened. Franks and Amanda are waiting for me on Loreen. They could do with a friend, what with Hope going missing. I quite fancy the fish farm there now."

Jessica snorted. "A fish farm, you? Don't make me laugh."

"Everything's different now," Selena replied. "The Sken have gone back to wherever they came from; the ForeRunners have been … erased, and the Manta are all but finished. As for the Lenars, well, enough said about them. There's an old saying—'It's time to give peace a chance' —and I guess that's unlikely to happen with me hanging around."

"What about Jas?" Jessica asked.

"I've spoken to the orphanage and they're happy to take her. I guess that's the best place for her, she'll be with her friends. She'd grown quite attached to Singh, and hasn't forgiven me for what I did."

"Have you actually spoken to Jas about any of this?" Kes inquired.

"Not yet. I'm on my way home now, but thought I'd let you guys in on what's happening first. I know the genocide of the Lenars is on all of our minds but, like the colonel says, there's nothing anyone can do. The Queen's won. The Alliance needs her, and the population of Capulet on their side."

"Jas deserves better," Jessica said. "She cares for you a lot."

"I'm doing what I can."

Kes studied her, his eyes narrow and shrewd. "Anything you're not telling us?"

Selena looked at him, her face blank. "Like what, exactly?"

\*\*\*

Sweat trickled down Selena's face from the damp, musky warmth of the forest. Brilliant sunlight streamed into the clearing, in which she sat on the rough bark on the bole of a fallen tree. Like many others, it had been placed there in years past as a crudely crafted seat.

On all sides trees, bushes and bramble strained towards the clear, light-blue sky. There was the promise of summer in the buds pushing their way up through the fallen leaves.

Swirling the loam with her feet, she breathed in the earthy aroma, knowing without doubt that she'd miss all of this when she finally left this world for the last time. Clouds of insects droned and myriad multi-coloured birds swooped, feasting upon them before alighting on the branches around her, from where they sang in chorus.

Others hopped and rummaged, tossing aside pieces of bark and undergrowth to snatch at unlucky prey. Selena was glad man had brought them to this world, if only to try and control these damn midges. She waved a hand to dispel them, drinking in the scenery.

The others would be here before too long, she realised. She'd walked the wet city streets for the last time last night, watching the rain dribble down the outside of the poorer quarters windows like tears cast by the planet itself, perhaps if in sorrow at the loss of the Lenars. The city could have turned on their impeller fields, to deflect the rain, and she was glad that they realised the importance of the downpour cleansing the city, as if it were washing away blood and bad memory.

Memories came of playing hop-scotch as a child. One square, two squares, one square, two—a game passed down through generations. In her mind, she could hear her mother calling to her through the dusty, busy streets of her memory for them both to go to the games arena with Aunt May. Then suddenly Mother was climbing up atop a monument, looking down into Selena's eyes before falling...

"I hear you're leaving. Not even going to say goodbye?"

The words broke her reverie. She raised her head to see Queen Miranda walking towards her in a snowy trouser suit, hand weapon belted at her waist. A dozen or so guards, weapons at the ready, accompanied her.

"So much safer for the both of us if I wasn't here, don't you think?" Selena replied, watching as the monarch's guards fanned out and covered her with their assault rifles. "You had to be here and have the last word, huh?"

Miranda snorted. "You didn't think I'd let you just walk away, did you?" She slapped at the side of her neck, lips curling distastefully as she looked at the palm of her hand. "Damned midges! You can see why I don't come out here this time of the year."

"Yeah. Well, I guess it's a lot safer than it used to be. What with the Lenars all dead, thanks to you."

"Me?" the monarch's eye widened in feigned shock. "I don't know what you mean, they were killed by a bomb planted by the ForeRunners. A tragedy, I know." She sighed theatrically and shook her head, closing her eyes and briefly fanning her face with the back of one hand. She opened her eyes again and studied Selena, a half-smile curling one side of her mouth. "Oh, do excuse the guards, won't you? One has to be so careful these days."

Selena said nothing.

Still watching her, Miranda said carefully, "Your friend Baron tried to kill me. Did you know that?"

"I heard, but he was no friend of mine. It was you who put him in touch with me, remember?"

The queen's coal-black eyes continued to watch her, as she carefully weighed up every word Selena spoke. "He was a revolutionary, just like you."

"Like I *used to be*. I no longer have any dealings with them."

"So you say."

Selena laughed and said, "For what it's worth, I have no intention of killing you. Even though I know you murdered Aunt May, and I still hold you responsible for the death of my parents—not to mention the Lenars."

"Aunt May, hmmm. Well, I did warn you what would happen if you returned after our last little discussion. As for your parents, we've been over this so many times it's become boring. Do you honestly expect me to believe you're not going to try to kill me, after all that's happened?"

"That's what I said, and my word is my bond."

Miranda studied her. "Swear on your family."

"What family? Oh, very well. I so swear. You'll also note, I hope, that I came here unarmed."

"Yes indeed, I had you scanned. You *are* full of surprises, aren't you? Very well, let's walk," Miranda gestured with one hand for her guards to remain where they were, and tapped her holstered weapon, saying, "Don't try anything stupid, now will you. Damn!" She slapped again at her neck.

"I've given you my word." Selena fell in besides the monarch and, as they walked, she asked, "So, what are your intentions now? Apart from ensuring my demise, no doubt."

"To rebuild the destroyed cities and make this world prosper, of course. Like you said, everything has changed. The universe is a far more dangerous place than it used to be, and humanity can't afford to be seen as weak or divided anymore. What's left of us needs to come together, and I'll do what I can to ensure this happens. Of course, the only problem I have left … is you."

"I thought you might think that the case," Selena replied, coolly. "Colonel Delmar will no doubt have told you that I'm leaving the service, retiring back on Loreen. It's a one-way trip. I have no intention of coming back, or planning revenge. I have far too many bad memories of this world."

"Well, you know I can't take that risk," Miranda said, glancing back towards her guards several hundred yards away. She froze, eyes widening, shock evident on her face. Seeing them all laying on the ground, she said, "What the..."

"A little trick I learned from you, dear Stepmother. You'll recall that when my team and I tried to assassinate you all those years back, an airborne agent knocked us all out. I'm not affected because I took the antidote before you turned up, and what you thought was an insect bite a few moments ago was actually a frozen slither from a sniper rifle containing the antidote. Fired from someone I employed some time ago for just such an eventuality. Don't worry, it will have dissolved without trace and cause you no harm. You see, I wanted you conscious."

The Queen snatched at her pistol but never made it. With a roar, Shadow leapt from the shade of a nearby tree, his jaws crunching into her forearm. Miranda screamed as his teeth severed tendons and crushed bone. Collapsing to the ground she clutched at her ruined arm, and crawled away backwards from the Lenar, her face filled with terror. Shadow circled her, his eyes intent. "You swore on your family!" she shrieked.

"Indeed, and I intend to keep my word. I said that I wouldn't hurt you and I haven't, but Shadow here has a somewhat severe and personal grudge to settle. You killed his people with that bomb, remember? Unfortunately, for you that is, you didn't get all of them, no matter what you were led to believe. Shadow was with me at the time, and a mere handful of his kin hadn't attended the meeting— because, oddly, they didn't trust you. But, yes, they are the last of the Lenars."

"I told you, that bomb was planted by the Forerunners. I never tried to kill them!"

"Oh Miranda, do give me some credit," Selena said. "I know it was you. Poor Cox. You tricked him into carrying that bomb, telling him it was the cure from the Manta for the illness that was killing the Lenars. How lucky for you that something came up at the last minute, so that you weren't there when the bomb exploded. But you forgot about the listening posts that Jenks had set up. It was easy to check where the signal to detonate the bomb came from, your palace. That's attempted genocide in anybody's book."

"Just so you know," Miranda snarled. "It *was* the cure, alongside the bomb. It's now aerated and will immunise any of them that are living. A splendid irony, don't you think?"

"So, you admit it."

"If I must." Miranda's pain-filled smile only enhanced her rodent-like features.

"There's something seriously wrong with you, Miranda."

"Why, thank you."

Just then a slim, dark-haired elvish figure walked out of the trees. A sniper rifle was gripped in her right hand, the barrel resting across her left. The Queen's eyes widened. "You," she gasped.

Selena frowned. "You two know each other?"

"Oh yes," the Queen gasped, clasping her injured arm as Jessica put down the rifle and picked up the Queen's side arm from where it had fallen. Miranda smiled as Jessica slowly turned the weapon towards Selena's face. Her right sleeve was semi-rolled up, displaying the tattoos on her arm. "By the way your friend, Lieutenant Roberts here, actually works for me."

"What?" Selena gasped. Stunned, she stared at Jessica, unable to take it in. Shadow continued circling the Queen, ignoring the assassin completely.

"I'm afraid so, Selena. I've been working for Queen Miranda for some time now," Jessica said. Then, with a faint smile, she pulled the trigger.

Selena was thrown backwards as the bullet tore through the top of her left shoulder, exiting from her back with a spray of blood as she fell.

Jessica slowly strolled over to Selena and looked down into her eyes. She smiled. "The Queen paid me to shoot you, not kill you." She held out a hand and helped Selena to her feet.

"What? You idiot, you've misunderstood. Shoot her!" Miranda snarled.

"I already have… My apologies, Selena. The Queen obviously researched our entire team. She found out about my past, even down to my assassin code name, *Charlotte*, and hired me to 'shoot' you, which is kind of ironic considering you wanted me here anyway.

"I knew she'd have this place staked out and that being here would be difficult, so naturally I accepted her offer. In doing so, I had to carry out her orders to shoot you— it's the assassin code, and I cannot break it. If I did, they would come for me. Besides, she pays well and I was sure you wouldn't mind me earning a little extra cash." Jessica rolled the Queen's pistol over in her hand and passed it to Selena. "I've fulfilled my contract with the Queen, and also my promise to you. No hard feelings, I hope."

Selena took the weapon in her good hand, trying to ignore the pain in her shoulder. "None at all, and thanks … I think." She studied the weapon, then dropped it and pressed her palm against her bloody shoulder. "I came here unarmed, and I intend leaving that way."

"No problem." Jessica looked all around and pursed her lips. "I'd say it looks as though the Queen tried to commit homicide, and that Shadow here came to your rescue."

"Ahh, I take it that Shadow knew what you were planning, and that you wouldn't kill me. Which is why he didn't have to protect me from you."

"We have quite an understanding, the Lenars and I. They're empathic, remember? They're wonderful creatures and I still can't believe this bitch killed most of them."

Together they looked at Miranda who for once remained quiet, her coal-black eyes darting from Jessica to Selena and then to Shadow. "You can't do this," she said, "I'm the Queen, you can't just kill me." She got to her knees and shuffled forwards, sidling towards the pistol while raising her good arm in a vain attempt to distract them as she spoke.

"Like I said earlier, I don't intend to," Selena replied. "But if anything were to happen to you, then of course I'm next in line to the throne. I'd have to change my plans and remain here after all. Let's just hope nothing does happen… Goodbye, your *Majesty*."

"Selena—"

With a roar, the *Magellan* dropped from the sky, hovered briefly and settled into the far side of the clearing.

A gangway lowered with a slight hum and caressed the grass, a door in the side of the ship opening noiselessly. Jessica at her side, Selena paused at the gangway and looked back to see that the queen had snatched up the side arm.

"Hah!" Miranda barked. "You're so damned stupid, I can't believe I once wished that you'd been my real daughter." Then she gave a loud, sickening scream of agony.

The hand holding the weapon was no longer there. Instead, the stump of her arm pumped blood across the grass. Shrieking, Queen Miranda fell to her knees and stared at the ruins of both arms—and then in disbelief towards Shadow, who now stood growling above her. What was left of her hand, pistol still gripped, dangled from his jaws. Then, with a crunch of bone, her limb was thrown aside.

"You're so predictable, Miranda," Selena said. Together the two friends turned their backs on the queen and strolled up the gangway. Selena stopped suddenly at the hatch and looked back towards Shadow, who gazed at her expectantly. "Dinner," she said, with a half-smile.

They bore witness as the queen's disbelieving, agonised screams turned silent.

"Shadow," Selena said, "you'd better disappear. Once I'm established as Monarch I'll keep my word and pardon you. I'll also make an official apology on behalf of humanity to all Lenars. In the meantime, go, boy. Run, be safe."

Selena and Jessica watched as the silken black creature, jaws dripping with blood, padded into the undergrowth. The two of them entered the *Magellan* and the hatch shut behind them.

***

Instead of leaving Capulet as Colonel Delmar had planned, the ship dropped them back at the space port. Delmar's jaw gapped open when Selena walked into her office, alone.

"Commander, what are you doing here? You're supposed to be on the *Magellan*."

When Selena told her what had happened, that the Queen had been waiting for her in the forest apparently knowing of her plans to leave the world for good, Delmar didn't say anything for a moment. Then, "Are you sure she's dead?"

"Oh, most definitely," Selena replied. "It's dangerous to disturb a Lenar when it's feeding and, of course, I was unarmed. I have witnesses and bee video evidence of what happened, which proves that I walked away and left her unharmed. It was only when she tried to kill me that Shadow leapt into action."

"Where's the Queen's body now?"

"Oh, there's a bit here, a bit there, a bit missing. You know how it is."

Delmar's complexion turned ashen. "What about Shadow?"

"He's gone. Doesn't trust the authorities anymore and, come to that, nor do I. Do you mind if I sit?" Without waiting for an answer, she dropped herself into the colonel's chair and visibly relaxed. "Talking about trust, I know it was you who passed on the information about Jessica being an assassin to the queen. If you recall, when we were looking for that child-killer, I told you we didn't need to look at my team, as I was happy with them. I've no doubt that, being the suspicious person you are, you checked them out anyway. And that's when Jess flagged up."

Delmar's lips quivered for a moment, as if she was stuck for what to say. "I had to warn the Queen, in case you hired Jessica to kill her. It was my duty."

Selena chucked, in spite of herself. "Well, for your information the Queen employed Jessica to take me out instead. In one way, you were right. I *had* hired Jess, but only to immunise her against the agent I used to disable her bodyguards, so that she and I could talk in peace. Unfortunately, things got a little out of hand, if you excuse the pun. Luckily Jess stayed loyal to me.

"Oh, and just so you know, you'll find that the recorders in this room are no longer functioning, so there won't be any evidence of what's being said here."

"Why do I get the feeling you've played me?"

"If you like to put it that way." Selena felt herself grinning, despite all good intent. "No offence intended Colonel, but let's keep it sweet, shall we? After all, I'm sure you realise that you wouldn't want me as an enemy."

Face graying even further, Delmar swallowed and said, "Look, I really don't understand what's going on here."

"Of course you don't, so let me explain. When the Queen met me in the forest, she had the satellite feeds blocked, so they wouldn't record any evidence that she'd killed me. What she didn't know was that I suspected you'd tip her off as to where I'd be. Consequently, I'd hidden surveillance bees in the trees and of course they recorded everything that happened. If you check them, you'll be able to hear the Queen telling her guards to remain behind. As for the rest, well, feel free to watch it for yourself.

"Jessica never let on that the Queen had hired her. As for Shadow, how he restrained himself after she murdered his people I'll never know. He never took any action until I myself was under threat; you have to admire him for that. Tell me, is that coffee that I can smell?"

"My apologies," Delmar said, almost wincing. "Would you like a cup?"

Selena gave her a smile. "Colonel, I can see that the penny has finally dropped and you've realised that I'm next in line to the throne. But it's a bit late to be nice now, isn't it. However, as you've said before, the past is the past. As for Shadow, he protected me and I will ensure that he and what's left of his race are pardoned and remain free here on Capulet. After all, this is their home as much as ours. If they die naturally, so be it. But there will be no hand raised against them by anyone. After all, we both know who's watching. Don't we."

Delmar blew slowly through puffed up cheeks, finished pouring Selena's drink and placed it before her before sitting again. "So, what now ... are you going to assume the throne?"

"As much as I dislike the idea, I've really no choice. If I don't, then someone of her inner circle will, and that could lead to all kinds of trouble. So yes, I'll take the crown—with you and the admiral behind me of course. I take it that I *will* have your full support?"

Delmar's ashen complexion flushed slightly as she realised that she was off the hook. "Yes, of course. It'll be both my duty and my pleasure."

Selena took a sip of the coffee, noting that it was better than the normal crap and gave the colonel a cheery smile. "Excellent. In return, I'll forget about any past indiscretions, and ensure that the admiral's aware that I want you to stay on here. In the meantime, I'd like two hundred penal troops, including my own unit, to replace the former royal bodyguard, and I'd be grateful if you would see to that immediately." Putting down her cup, she stood up and dusted off her already immaculate uniform. "Good day, Colonel. Many thanks for the coffee."

Delmar stood and offered her hand, which Selena shook before turning and leaving her office with a triumphant grin.

As the news spread, congratulations and demands for audiences flowed, from local authorities and promotion companies right down to individual citizens. Selena denied them all, until she'd met with the Privy Council who declared her Queen two days later. Once that was done, she ordered the arrest of her stepmother's cronies. They would remain in the city prisons, where she'd once resided herself, until full investigations into their past abuses had been completed. Then they'd face whatever punishment was forthcoming. With a sense of deep satisfaction, she ordered that the cases be investigated by off-world judges, as her own had been.

The next day the coronation was held in the City's cathedral, after which she stood in front of the waiting cameras. As the cheers slowly died down, Selena raised her right hand. Behind her stood Jessica, Kes, Braxis and Kotes —all armed, ready, and watching the crowd. Five hundred uniformed troopers stood amidst the audience. Just them being there spoke volumes to any dissenters.

"Citizens," Selena began. "As Queen of Capulet I'm here to assure you that things are to change for the better. Many of the former Queen's cohorts have been dismissed, are in prison, or have fled. Any citizens with grievances about the previous administration are to report them to the appropriate authorities. You have my word that all cases will be fully investigated and dealt with accordingly.

"This morning I was also released from Penal servitude, with my full time served. Consequently, I no longer hold a commission. By my invitation, the Penal

Corps will remain on this world and they have replaced the royal bodyguard, many of whom are themselves under investigation. I can assure you that justice will be done and peace will reign here on Capulet."

More cheers. Hats were thrown, a profusion of multi-colored fireworks went off and streamers floated up and down, despite the air currents.

Selena raised one hand and slowly the crowd quietened. "The Lenars have been pardoned and I have brought a law into place that protects them. These are the last of the Lenars! It is every citizen's responsibility to protect and help them survive the coming years."

The roars from the crowd showed the people's approval and after a few more words, Selena turned and entered the waiting transport, her friends and team-mates following behind in other vehicles.

***

The next two years were peaceful and passed quickly. For once there was little piracy, and no wars or conflicts of any kind. Much to Selena's surprise only one world left the A.O.W., and that re-joined at their next change of government. Peace ruled mankind's empire, and it grew once again. But neither the Manta nor the Sken made themselves known.

*Could it be*, Selena often wondered as she sat in the royal gardens gazing up at Romeo and Juliette, as they forever chased each other through the heavens, *that we've finally achieved the peace we craved? Yes, the Federation of Man has fallen and the ForeRunners destroyed. Even the Manta no longer stalk the stars as they once had.* The citizens of Capulet no longer feared their government. What else was there left to do?

Selena's words echoed strongly in the council of the Alliance of World. Its motto became "To ensure peace, prepare for war." For they knew that somewhere, out in the deep depths of space, there was a good chance that the Manta remained, and who knew what other dark denizens might lurk out there?

Two years after claiming the throne, Selena abdicated and handed the crown over to her uncle, Admiral Van Pluy. That night, she strode up the steps of the *Magellan* for the final time. While millions watched her, the crowds remained strangely silent, even as she turned to wave before disappearing into the depths of the ship.

# Chapter Twelve

"Mother, I've got something to tell you."

"Don't bother," Selena replied, leaning back in her chair on the patio. "I know. You got thrown out of college again, didn't you Jas?"

"It wasn't my fault!"

"It never is. Let me guess, they didn't like your eyes." Selena's now bright blue eyes looked upon her daughter's completely black ones in despair. "I told you that getting them done like mine used to be wasn't a good idea."

Jas stiffened. "I'm seventeen now. I'm not a child, I can make my own decisions. Besides, someone has to look after you, and that person is me. I won't have anyone bad mouth you, and I won't take any crap either. We're alone now, you and I. Apart from a few, your old unit is back on Capulet until the end of their service."

"They have to finish their sentences, no matter what they've done for mankind," Selena said.

"We have few friends here, only Franks and Amanda and they've become distant because of Hope's disappearance. You said it would be easier on Loreen, but it's not. People here hate me."

Exasperated, Selena said carefully, "The people here don't hate you, Jas. They're *scared* of you, of me. It *is* easier here, and much safer than … out there. Give these people a chance, they'll learn to like you and will soon realise that you're not the person you make yourself out to be. But above all, behave. Remember, the people of Loreen built this house for us, out of the wood from this forest. It was a labour of love, of thanks for what we did and for our loss. As for friends, Kes and Jessica will be here before long. Their house is already built, as you know and in six months their sentences will be over. The wedding will be talked about for years. You, a bridesmaid. Who'd believe it?"

"It wasn't built for *us*," Jas snapped, her hair now in dreadlocks down to her shoulders. "It was built for you and Bryn. For what you did in crushing those rebels all those years ago."

"It was made for us to become a family, and that's what you and I are. I've adopted you, remember?" Selena could still feel the excitement of telling her. She could hear Jas's squeals of delight, feel how she'd flung herself into her arms. "I may not be your real mother, Jas, but I wish I was. Remember, I love you, and so would Bryn have. Come here." She enfolded Jas into her arms, and kissed her daughter on the forehead.

Selena held Jas a long time, comforting her. Finally she said, "Both of our childhoods were torn apart, and we both lost our mothers. Aunt May looked after me, and I'll look after you. As for college, don't worry. I've already spoken to the principle, she rang me. They understand how hard it is. That we are what we are. I'd like you to get your eyes reverted, become a normal child and have friends."

"But I have to protect you!" Jas said.

"Oh, I don't think you do. I can look after myself."

Jas's coal-like eyes glittered. "Oh, I know that. But there might still be Forerunner spies out there, somewhere, and they'll want you dead."

Despite herself, Selena grinned. "We both know that the ForeRunners are gone. All of them. The Sken told us so; they destroyed entire worlds to eradicate the last of them."

A low rumble rose from the darkness and a dark shape entered the veranda and stood beside them.

"Shadow," Selena said softly. Both she and Jas both leant down to run their fingers through his fur, as they sat together looking out over their fish farm and the glittering stars. "I already have guardians, as you can see."

"One Lenar isn't enough," Jas responded. "The world's a dangerous place and even they can be overcome. This is a log cabin, not a fortress."

"There's a small pride of Lenars here on Loreen now, as you well know. Now, get yourself off to bed. Enough arguing, Jas. Back to college for you tomorrow. They daren't refuse you, there'd be an uprising."

"There's one more thing," Jas said timidly. "I know you said not to, but I showed those troublemakers my knives. I told them that if they bothered me again I'd carve my name into their foreheads."

"You're too like me, Jas. But relax, there's no threat. We're safe. If you carry knives, others will too and you'll make yourself a target. Leave them here in future or you'll end up in the Penal Corps too. Now get to bed."

Grumbling, Jas disappeared into the building and Selena turned to face the lake that perfectly reflected the glittering starlight. She sat back in her rocking chair and sighed in relief at being able to relax at last. Shadow laid down beside her and she stroked his short fur lazily. She listened to her daughter stropping noisily to her room across the polished wooden floor, and hid a smile. Her eyes roamed, watching the treetops and branches swaying gently against the backdrop of the heavens. The wind whispered its dark secrets amidst the boles and she waited for a few minutes more, until she was sure that Jas had turned out the light.

"You can come out now," she said at length. "I know you're there."

Silence.

"It's no good hiding, I can feel your presence through Shadow."

A light burst into life and fluttered across to sit on the arm of the chair, its many tentacles with black-tipped eyes writhing like snakes. The transparent seahorse-like creature swivelled its many eyes towards her, and she could almost sense its displeasure at being discovered.

"When you said you were leaving, I knew that a few of you would remain," Selena said. "So, what happens now?"

"Nothing." The Sken's words fluttered through her mind. "The Manta, as you call them, have gone their own way. For the time being, there's just you Humans and the Lenars."

Selena stared thoughtfully and found she was chewing her lips. "In those final battles with the ForeRunners, some of your ships were blasted back through time. Is that how you were able to watch us all these years, through the crews of those ships?"

"We never made contact with those vessels, and they remain lost to us. We do understand the concept of time travel, however, and other ships have visited briefly. But the past cannot be altered. If we tried, we would not be here to do so in the future, and so what has happened—and will happen—remains. Time is a complicated thing."

"I'm sure," Selena said, with a snort.

"As for the future, that depends on many variables. All we can see is what may be, and that chops and changes with unfolding events."

Selena eyed the Sken. "So, you *have* been into the future. Will we war with the Manta again? If so, it's likely one of us will be completely destroyed. I'm surprised you didn't kill humanity off, to be honest."

The Sken did a lap around the porch, before alighting once again on the armrest.

"We considered it. What saved humanity was your compassion, and I mean *yours* personally. You, Selena Dillon, reached out to the Lenars and cared for them, and they in turn for you.

"For you to show mercy to the Manta at the end, when you could so have easily destroyed them, unthinkable! You, who had more reason than most to hate them. The one you call Skar has taught them well since they left, but they fear humanity and what you may become. They recollect the wars so, like I said, the future depends on a great many things."

Selena found herself chewing her lip again. "What of my friends' daughter, Hope? It was you who repaired her, wasn't it, not the Cetra. I don't understand why you would do that."

"It was our race who created the Caretakers, not the Cetra. They were built to serve all intelligent species, but eventually our enemy corrupted them. In turn, we used their methods to turn their own robotic fleet against themselves in the final battles, and we helped the girl because she is one like you."

"What's that supposed to mean?" Selena asked, frustrated. "Will you let her return? Her parents are worried, and I'd like to be able to give them some good news." Selena felt something from the Sken, but was unsure what it was. Humour, respect, warmth, sympathy?

"The girl was broken, we fixed her. She is not like other humans now. By mending her, she became ours, and she knew it. As for the answer to your question … maybe."

"At least that will give her parents a chance. I can tell them she's alive and all right, that you didn't kill her as a ForeRunner agent. In the meantime, guess I should warn humanity that the Manta will come again."

A flutter in her mind said, "Again, maybe."

"That your favourite word, is it?"

"Many of your former colleagues were dismayed that you let the last of the Manta go," the Sken said, in her mind. "And yet you still dream of war."

"Those are called nightmares."

"Ghosts and monsters haunt the corridors of your mind, Selena Dillon. We know, we've seen them. Other humans will say this meeting is just one of those dreams. They no longer trust you, for you also gave up your crown and left them when they needed you."

"They didn't need me, they just thought they did." Selena blew through her lips, making a loud rasping sound. "I never wanted to be queen. But it was a job that needed doing and so I did it, and then I left Capulet in good hands. Someone once said 'Those who seek power don't have it.' I, for one, never wanted it."

"Ah the crux of the matter." The Jelly glowed brighter. "That's because you're a cornerstone. Few such beings are born with such power. What you do affects many, even without you realising it. The other such rests with us, the girl. There is only space for one at a time. Have you any idea what you've done?"

Selena's eyes drifted back to the trees, ignoring the small creature by her right hand. "No, do tell."

"Your path led to the destruction of one race, the demise of two, and the survival of your own. We spared humanity because of your compassion. To many, you're a saviour and to others a monster. Yet you also killed someone you held dear in an attempt to save your entire race. We Sken commend you."

"His name was Singh." Selena's lip hurt and she realised she'd now badly bitten it. "He did what he thought was right, although that doesn't mean I agreed with him. Aren't you a little bit afraid that given the chance to destroy your race, I will?"

"Maybe. That's a part of why we love you. For you do what must be done, no matter what. By your own standards, you're a dark angel. What you do determines the future."

"I hope and pray that's not the case, but I guess if we do badly, then you'll destroy us?"

"We could try. But by then it may be too late, even for us; and, given the circumstances, we may no longer be here. Our people still sicken… Meanwhile we will continue to watch. Maybe in time we will return, but until then what happens is down to you. Now, it is time for me to go."

A black globe rolled down a tree trunk and across the grass towards them. Small black beads raced across the lawn and merged with it. Swelling, the craft rose into the air and absorbed the Sken as it flew towards it, before the small vessel turned away and disappeared amidst the trees.

War with the Manta, maybe even the Sken. Both were possible futures, Selena realised. Did the Sken speak the truth, that what she did shaped the future? She shivered. It was getting cold out here on the porch.

In the wardrobe of her room lay her immaculate black uniform. Maybe she should go and put it on.

Just to keep warm.

End

# About Mark Iles

Mark's short stories have been published in *Back Brain Recluse, Dream, New Moon, Haunts, Kalkion, Screaming Dreams*, and the anthologies *Write to Fight, Escape Velocity, Auguries* and *Monk Punk*. With over forty years' experience in the martial arts and a 9th Degree Black Belt in Taekwondo, he's written features for the magazines *Combat, Taekwondo & Korean Martial Arts, Fighters, Junk, Martial Arts Illustrated, profwritingacademy.com and calmzone.net*. He also runs a writer's group for the British Science Fiction Association, along with *The Scribe* for Veterans with the help of The Royal British Legion.

His first full length work *'Kwak's Competition Taekwondo'*, was published in Hong Kong, while he was based there with the Royal Navy for three years in 1985. His debut novel *'A Pride of Lions'*, Book I in *The Darkening Stars,* was published by Solstice in September 2013. Book II, *'The Cull of Lions'*, was published a year later. *'Roar of Lions'* is the third book in the series.

Solstice have also published four novellas: *'A Connoisseur of the Bizarre', 'Sally Jane', 'Nightshade'* and *'Santa Claws is Coming'* – along with the short story compilation *'Falling From Grace & Others'*.

## Social Media Links

Website: http://www.markiles.co.uk

Amazon Author Page: http://www.amazon.co.uk/Mark-Iles/e/B004YZBP3I

Solstice Publishing:

http://solsticepublishing.com/search.php?search_query=mark+iles&x=0&y=0

Twitter: http://www.twitter.com/welcometoearth

## Acknowledgements

Magali Frechette: https://twitter.com/stormowl7

My special thanks to the following Beta Readers: Annette Sindall, Peter Wilhelmsen, and Jason Kurt Easter. Also to The British Science Fiction Association 'Orbiter 7' writing group members, who critiqued this book through its many stages: David Allan, Shellie Hurst, Dunstan Power, Alana Farrell, Rosie Oliver, Shellie Hurst.

Mark Rutley for portrait image:

http://www.markrutleyphotography.co.uk/

To Charlotte, a promise kept.

# If you enjoyed this story, check out these other Solstice Publishing books by Mark Iles:

## Novels

### A Pride of Lions

When Selena Dillon is caught in an assassination attempt on her planets ruler, she finds herself sentenced to 25 years servitude in mankind's most feared military force, the Penal Regiments. Much to her surprise she enjoys the harsh military life and is quickly selected for officer training.

But something's wrong, worlds are falling silent. There's no cry for help and no warning, just a sudden eerie silence. When a flotilla of ships is despatched to investigate, they exit hyperspace to find themselves facing a massive alien armada. Outnumbered and outgunned the flotilla fight a rearguard action, allowing one of their number to slip away and warn mankind.

As worlds fall in battle, and man's fleets are decimated, Selena is selected to lead a team of the Penal Regiments most battle-hardened veterans, in a last ditch attempt to destroy the aliens' home world. If she fails then mankind is doomed. But little does Selena know what fate has in store for her, that one of her crew is a psychopathic killer and a second the husband of one of his victims.

Can she hold her team together, get them to their target and succeed in the attack? Selena knows that if she fails then there will be nothing at all left to go home to.

https://www.amazon.co.uk/Pride-Lions-Darkening-Stars/dp/149425445X/

## The Cull of Lions

Selena Dillon and her team return to Loreen after their attack on the Manta homeworld, only to find the myriad worlds of Mankind once again plunged into war. As the Penal Regiments are betrayed by the Federation of Man, and fighting spills throughout the galaxy, the dreaded Manta raise their heads once again.

Selena soon finds herself trying to track down her friends' daughter, Hope, from the rabbit holes of Loreen, and then fights to free her home planet from alien invaders.

While a general amnesty means previous sins are forgiven, the Queen has not forgotten Selena's attempt on her life. Selena soon finds herself torn between obeying orders to protect the monarch, and her ravening thirst for revenge. But strange forces are stirring amidst the stars and Mankind finds itself with surprising new allies, while a terrifying enemy that's manipulated events from behind the scenes finally reveals itself for the very first time.

https://www.amazon.co.uk/Cull-Lions-Darkening-Stars/dp/162526089X/

## Novellas

### A Connoisseur of the Bizarre

A carful of police officers' swerves in the rain to avoid a shadowy figure. Detective Chets Owen and his two companions immediately recognise the local lunatic, O'Neal, but they're shocked to see a gun in his hand. Then O'Neal mentions that he knows where a missing child is.

Does he, or doesn't he - and is O'Neal really who he seems?

https://www.amazon.co.uk/Connoisseur-Bizarre-Mark-Iles-ebook/dp/B00HQOP54O/

## Sally Jane

When Jim Anderson is asked to boat-sit the Sally Jane, an aged canal boat moored on the side of the river Thames, he thinks he's found the idyllic writing retreat. New friends, the rush of water past the port holes, and manic duck chatter only adds to this perfect scene. But then perfection depends on exactly who, or what, you share that little piece of heaven with.

https://www.amazon.co.uk/Sally-Jane-Mark-Iles-ebook/dp/B00HQOOZ40/

## Nightshade

Bob Roberts, second in command of the starship Argonaut becomes concerned when members of the crew are brutally murdered. Then the ship's doctor points something out, that all the victims are drained of blood. When explosions force their space-born vessel to land for repairs on their destination, the planet Nightshade, their sighs of relief turn to screams of terror. For Nightshade is so very aptly named.

https://www.amazon.co.uk/Nightshade-Mark-Iles-ebook/dp/B00HQOP1BQ/

## Santa Claws is Coming

Six-year-old Clare is beside herself with excitement. It's Christmas Eve and she's expecting Santa to bring her lots of presents. But she doesn't take into account mankind's war on the planet of Halloween, or its inhabitant's evil intent.

https://www.amazon.co.uk/Santa-Claws-Coming-Mark-Iles-ebook/dp/B00HQOP0D0/

## Falling From Grace & Others

Here you'll find tales of the supernatural, betrayal and murder; the mistakes that lead to the fall of empires and the constant tug of war that haunts mankind. There's a blend of science fiction, fantasy and horror - from a modern-day detective facing a serial killer, to a future utopia filled with disloyalty. Lovers of romance will find a little something for them too, but within these bright sparks of hope shades of darkness lurk.

https://www.amazon.co.uk/Falling-Grace-Others-Mark-Iles-ebook/dp/B00OYV3CHE/